GO
AWAY
BIRDS

GO AWAY BIRDS

Michelle Edwards

modjaji books

Published in 2021 by Modjaji Books
Cape Town, South Africa
www.modjajibooks.co.za

Edited by Emily Buchanan
Cover text and artwork by Jesse Breytenbach
Book layout by Andy Thesen
Set in Berling

Printed and bound by Digital Action, Cape Town
ISBN print: 978-1-928433-05-7
ISBN ebook: 978-1-928433-06-4

For my phoenix family

Mpumalanga
26 December 2016

I emerge, blinking, into the snare of heat and flat white morning sunshine outside the Kruger Mpumalanga International Airport. There is a man waving to me in the parking lot.

He ambles up to me, comes into focus, his face seamed by deep grooves. He points out his dented silver sedan in the taxi bay.

"I've been the only taxi here all morning. Everyone else probably has a babalas after Christmas yesterday." He reaches out for my backpack and narrows his eyes in the direction of my thighs, which are barely covered by my dress.

"No more bags?" he asks.

I shake my head.

He eyes me suspiciously before flinging the backpack into the boot.

"Where'd you fly from?"

"Cape Town."

"Holiday here?"

"No."

"Family?"

I nod.

He clearly thinks I'm some kind of drifter, but I don't feel like I'm inhabiting my body and can't work myself up to caring what I look like. I ask him to get me to The Pines. He's never heard of it, but I tell him it's near Hazyview and that seems good enough.

"I'll take you to White River and you direct me from there," he says. The grubby laminated card hanging from the rearview mirror says his name's Siya.

As we're leaving the parking lot, I ask Siya if he's got a maps app on his phone, worried that I'll forget the way. It's been how many years – eight, nine? – since my last visit, when I came for Lola's wake, and only stayed two days.

"Nah, no map because my bloody data keeps disappearing off my phone. Bloody rip-off," he says, clicking his tongue and hitting play on the tape-deck.

Despite the gospel music blaring out of the single functioning speaker in the back, I fall asleep against the dubious headrest. I have to check the sides of my mouth for drool when Siya stops the car at the robot on the intersection heading into White River.

We've come up what I still think of as the back road, which used to be a rutted red dirt track until the airport was built. To our right are the deep blue, palm-fringed pools of the Hibiscus Hotel, the first place I ever got drunk (fifteenth birthday party, not mine; Old Brown Sherry, also not mine; puke in the driveway, mine, apparently). Ahead of us stretches White River's main road, the single street that qualified as "town", before the malls rose up out of the dust.

Memories flood in, all tastes and textures.

Deeply sweet melted ice lollies in thick plastic moulds shaped like teddy bears from the home industry shop, holes chewed through the top so we could suck the cold-drink out.

The scratchy end of Andile's sleeve wiping away the luminous green stain around my mouth before we went home so Heather wouldn't know we'd bought them.

The shiny red booths of the Greasy Spoon diner sticking to the backs of my thighs in summer, runny eggs dotted with oil on cold crunchy toast on Saturday mornings while Lola and Heather were doing the grocery shopping.

On the right-hand corner of the intersection is the antique shop, with the same faded sign it's had since I was in primary school.

A sudden image of Lola superimposes itself over the darkened shop doorway. With copper bracelets slinking down her forearms, she's carrying a footstool lined with pine-green velvet, part of the mahogany lounge suite in our sitting room. My mother peddled the stool, or, more likely, bartered it, without telling Lola, and she's gone in to retrieve it.

"Bloody Roger charged me asking price, so Heather owes me thirty per cent on top of the value of this damn thing, which is so much that I don't want to tell you!" she says and slams the canopy of the bakkie closed. I'm straddling the gearbox in the cabin, wedged in tight with Andile. We exchange bemused side-eyes because we both know Lola will never see any money from Heather, who doesn't believe in it.

The light turns green, and Lola is gone.

"Turn right here," I tell Siya. We glide past new fast food restaurants and a shiny second-hand car dealership. "Stay on this road, it's the R40. We'll go straight past The Pines if we stick to it."

My voice comes out strangled. Siya looks up at my reflection in the rearview mirror.

"Everything okay?" he asks.

A woman alone, in a crumpled, tiny dress at 10 in the morning, no luggage, but clearly plenty of baggage, face swollen from crying: of course he's concerned. But kindness from a stranger is not something I can deal with, frankly, so I avoid his eyes and turn my face to the window.

Outside, the world is dense and lush and thriving, the rolling hills of pines and the leaves of the mopane trees a saturated, luxurious green in contrast to the drought-bleached lawns of the Cape Town I left a few hours ago. As we weave through the man-made forests marching neatly away on either side of the road, I roll down the window an inch, drawing in the familiar fresh-scrubbed air that smells like home.

Maybe this won't be so hard, I think. Maybe this wasn't the worst decision I've made since agreeing to get married. Maybe coming back to The Pines is what I needed, instead of the only thing left for me to do after leaving everything I have to my name thousands of kilometres away at the cusp of the continent. "Feel free to tone down the drama," says Heather's voice in my head.

We pass the dam on the left, and the small wooden strut with the erf number 143-143 on a white metal sheet jumps out at me, almost obscured by the long grass on the roadside.

"Here!"

Siya brakes too hard and takes the right turn with a screech of tyres as his car scrapes on the gravel entrance before it creaks to a halt at the gate.

I slowly push my door open and step out of the car. Immediately my white sneakers are coated in The Pines's relentless fine red dust. It crosses my mind that if I moved back here I'd have to give up all my white clothing. It's a distressing thought. I remember my school uniform ankle socks, which always turned a smudged rust colour before the end of the first term, and how I had to keep wearing them until Heather had the budget for new ones.

We used to have a simple farm gate that swung open when you lifted a warped metal clasp as long as my forearm. Now there's a proper gate, a serious one, wrought iron, and an intercom buzzer, with the words

MAIN HOUSE: THE PINES *typed out on a slip of paper next to the top button. The first thing I think is, when did Heather get a computer? And a printer?*

There's new electric fencing stretching along the boundary on either side of the gate, where before there was a crude chain-link fence with barbed wire along the top.

When Andile and I were growing up, Heather would never have wanted to draw this much attention to The Pines. Until we were six years old, she would have done whatever she could to hide it from the road.

I was hoping to get to the house before she or Andile realised I was here, so they wouldn't have a chance to turn me away. It takes me a few seconds to gather myself before holding in the button.

"Hello?" *My mother's voice.*

"Heather, it's me."

A beat.

"It's Skye. Um, Roo."

"Roo? Are you alright?"

"Yes!"

She doesn't answer.

"Can you let me in?"

There's a fumbling sound and the gate splits in two in the middle, drawing itself open graciously.

The road is deeply rutted, a sign of recent rains. It hasn't been graded in a while. As Siya and I bump along, with the long shadows of the pines beating a light-and-dark staccato into the car, he says, "I drive the R40 every day but never noticed that fancy gate. This your family's place?"

"My mother's."

"No father?"

"Nope."

"But it's not safe here for a woman alone."

"Oh, no. My mother's never alone."

5

We inch down the hairpin bend, where the old gum trees almost touch overhead. During the big rains at the beginning of 2000, this section of road was flooded for five weeks at the end of the school holidays. We were stuck on the farm, and my mother and Lola were so busy with their guests that they hardly noticed that Andile and I missed whole weeks of the first term.

We spent our days sleeping until noon, then sharing a single joint in the ancient avocado plantation, far from the house and the cottages, reading Catch-22 *out loud to each other and laughing into the sky, cradled in the two hammocks stretched between the biggest trees. We were 15, living on gifted time, and the days stretched on and on.*

That was the last holiday Andile spent at The Pines. He got the private school scholarship that year and spent most of his holidays with mates after that, usually on the coast somewhere. He'd bring me back little knickknacks: a leather necklace from the Durban aquarium with a dolphin on it, a magnet from Sodwana Bay. I kept them all in an old Ricoffy tin on the top shelf of my cupboard. I resented his freedom but couldn't bear to throw the stuff away.

We're passing the avocado trees, tightly packed together, gnarled branches intertwining, probably planted in the early 1900s by the workers who lived here when The Pines was still a functioning timber plantation. The avocados are all West Indies, with knobbly skin and waxy flesh, barely edible compared to the supermarket-perfect avocados grown on the neighbouring farms.

And in an instant, we're heading down the tree-lined gravel drive, straight out of a colonial farmer's gin-and-tonic dreams – my grandfather's dreams, in fact – crunching up to an A-frame, slate-roofed farmhouse, the house where Andile and I grew up, thick-walled and wrapped around with a smooth, cool-floored veranda.

In the wide, high doorway of the kitchen, half in shadow, half in sun, stands my mother.

"My god," I think, as Siya pulls up alongside the house. She's cut her hair.

Part 1

Misty Cliffs

One

Cam was usually unflappable, except when he thought I was going to make him late for something. Right now, he was one hundred per cent flappable, hopping around our bedroom in his Tamboerskloof flat on one foot, looking for his missing shoe.

"I can't believe you scheduled this interview for today!" he said, crouching to look under the bed.

"*I* didn't schedule it – they could *only* do it today if they're going to make the March print run."

"But you knew we were going down to The Cottage later."

"They've already done all the pics. It's a quick chat with Talia, it won't take very long."

He straightened up and exhaled through puffed-out cheeks.

"We're going to have to rush to get all the food for Christmas when you're done," he said.

I checked myself in the mirror to see if the hairdresser had taken too much off the day before. I wanted to look like an adult for the interview, a competent, confident professional, hoping that my comfortable shoes, unfussy clothes and asymmetric haircut were up for the job.

I had settled on olive-green skinny jeans, a white linen

shirt ("blouse", I supposed) and tan-coloured pumps. I was wearing both my white pearl stud earrings and my wedding band, all the jewellery I owned, and had done my make-up for the first time since our wedding six months ago.

I'd never been this side of a magazine interview. I'd left Mon Petit Chou before food had become fetishised, and 10 years since qualifying, this was the closest I'd come to foodie fame. I was probably the only woman chef and restaurateur in Cape Town who hadn't been profiled in *Fig & Brie*, the food magazine where I'd worked after leaving Mon Petit. I had to keep reminding myself that it didn't bother me that it had taken this long.

I closed the cupboard door and kicked Cam's shoe out from where it was wedged between the bed and my side table.

"I don't know why we have to be the ones doing all the groceries. It's not like there aren't any shops down there."

"Remember last Christmas? Old carrots and leftover hummus?"

Cam's family weren't exactly big on food. Once they arrived at The Cottage, they didn't leave, not even to go grocery shopping, until they went back to Johannesburg. It was a tradition, and that was something they *were* big on.

"We'll make it down there in time, I promise. Aren't you excited, though? This is going to be great for Bushy Bun."

"To be honest," Cam said, grabbing my hand and pulling me close for a hug, "I don't think we need the publicity. But I know it's a big deal for you." He kissed me on the forehead. "Are you packed?"

He knew I wasn't.

"I'll throw some stuff in my backpack. It'll take two seconds."

He raised an eyebrow, navy eyes gleaming, and flipped open the lid of his suitcase.

I admired him, absentmindedly, from across the room, his skinny-Clark-Kent almost comical handsomeness that I could only appreciate from a distance. Up close, he was all eyebrows and sparkly dark-blue eyes and prominent cheekbones and wavy hair that he kept a touch too long. He had one of those clean-cut, smooth faces that made people instantly like and trust him. It had certainly worked on me when we'd met 18 months ago.

As I left the flat, he was counting out pairs of underpants into his suitcase. He always took exactly the right number so he wouldn't have to do laundry while we were away. That was Cam: forward-thinking, efficient, infuriating. Maybe six months is the point when everyone starts getting annoyed with their husbands, I thought, as I walked down the stairs.

Talia, the deputy editor of *Fig & Brie*, had asked to meet me at the office. It had taken me three years to get a parking bay in the building, and when Cam had suggested that I leave to open our restaurant, the thought of losing it and forever being at the mercy of the dire lack of parking in the City Bowl had almost been enough to make me turn him down. Now I'd have to walk.

The office was maybe 500 metres from Cam's flat, but after the mugging I hated walking around town alone, always making sure to count things I passed to make myself seem alert: street lamps, parked cars, paving stones. I kept my tiny can of mace in my back pocket and never carried my wallet with me.

But on a Friday morning in the middle of December, with town buzzing on a holiday high, all the side streets and alleys I walked down were full of people. There was noise and movement everywhere: the constant construction on Buitengracht, the GP Jeeps tailgating up to the robots, man-bunned hipsters greeting each other outside the coffee bar on Kloof Nek, the South-Easter whipping around corners and bullying the art students by lifting their ungainly portfolio folders and tiny skirts.

When I got to Bree Street, I dared to pull my phone out my bag to check the time. I still had half an hour before the interview and decided to treat myself to a pain au chocolat from the craft bakery on the corner. I handed the hundred-rand note scrunched in the front pocket of my bag through the hatch, ordered two, and got way less change than I would have liked.

But then I sank my teeth through the flaky layers of powdered-sugar-dusted butter pastry and hit a hard chunk of dark chocolate with the smooth, delicate tang of minimum 70 per cent cocoa solids.

It tasted like rebellion, reminding me of all the pâte à choux I turned into beignets, eclairs and churros at chef school. I'd made a point of eating at least one of every batch I churned out, defying Heather with every crispy, puffy, sugary bite.

Along with money, desserts, pastries and confectionery were on the list of everyday things Heather didn't believe in. Case in point, the peppermint crisp tart I made in Standard 5 for Lola's birthday. I was shaving a chocolate bar into tiny careful whorls over the top when Heather came in from the garden. She pulled off her gloves and carried the tart straight out of the kitchen and up to the big rubbish bins outside. "Sugar is poison, Roo," she'd said when she'd come back empty-handed, and that was the last she'd say on the subject.

As I savoured the pastry on that sweet December morning, I was reminded how good it felt to give my animal body what it craved. I stood in the shadow of the bakery with the morning sun edging over the buildings across the street, licking sugar off my fingers.

I brushed crumbs off my shirt and started off again but stopped when I passed the entrance to Bushy Bun. I needed to check that things had been left in order the night before, that everything was straightened out and ready for the place to be abandoned for two weeks while we were at The Cottage. I'd planned on doing it on my way back from the interview, but I still had a few minutes to spare.

I reflexively leaned into the door with my shoulder as I unlocked it, pushing against the legacy of old wood swollen by long-ago Cape rains. The alarm started beeping and I dodged the tightly packed tables to get to the back office to key in the code.

I made my slow way through the darkened dining room, straightening the chairs of the four tables, pushing in each of the six bar stools at the window counter, checking serviettes in kitsch plastic holders, counting toothpicks in tiny ceramic pots, and lining up plastic-covered disposable chopsticks next to shiny black noodle bowls.

Having grown up with Heather, who was way ahead of her time when it came to adding single-use plastic to her list of Things Not To Believe In, I was uncomfortable with our "cutlery" at Bushy Bun. Cam insisted that the disposable utensils added to the authenticity, and he wanted Bushy Bun to look as if it had been transplanted whole from the working-class streets of Zhong-Li in Taiwan, where people ate most of their meals from street carts or mom-and-pop noodle shops: loud, echoing spaces with fluorescent lighting and plastic chairs, catering to families, businessmen, road workers and glamorously groomed teenagers with heaped dishes of fresh, hot, fast, simple food, designed for sharing.

When Cam and I had come back from our trip to Taiwan, I'd spent weeks perfecting the dishes that became the staples on the Bushy Bun menu, using traditional recipes that Cam translated from a popular Taiwanese recipe book, sometimes adding French elements I'd learned at Mon Petit.

Clear, delicately salty bone broths bobbing with plump shredded-pork dumplings. The softest pulled-beef bao, filled with steam and salt. Plump LM prawn tails on skewers, heavily dusted in chilli and MSG, night-market-style. Vegetarian chao mian with five different kinds of mushrooms and chewy, robust wheat noodles. I did a gourmet version of dan bing, Taiwan's famous breakfast takeaway, egg crepes layered with shavings of seared tuna, chives and homemade ricotta instead of the typical processed cheese and tinned tuna. Zhou, the Taiwanese cook we employed, contributed his beef noodle soup, heavy on the heat, our customers' perennial favourite.

I had left Bushy Bun the night before as soon as the last table cleared out at 10 o'clock, an after-work drinks crowd who wouldn't leave. We weren't licensed, which meant people could bring in their own drinks. It was only supposed to be one bottle of wine or three beers per person, but we didn't monitor it because, as Cam pointed out, the more people drank, the more they ate.

I'd left the scrub-down for the meticulous Zhou, but wanted to check on it before closing shop for the holiday. A single crumb left out would attract the monster rats of the City Bowl.

Cam and I were almost certainly the only restaurant owners in the city who took a holiday in December, at the height of tourist season, in the heart of Cape Town. We could only afford it because Bushy Bun had been so packed since we'd first launched. Our opening hours were notoriously erratic, too, so our clientele wouldn't expect us to stay open over Christmas. Cam had set it up this way because he wanted to be able to go travelling and to make space for Tie-Pay, his import-export business. It had seemed extremely risky to me the year before, going on my first Christmas holiday since graduating from chef school, but this year I'd decided to lean into it. To trust Cam's savvy, and his faith in Bushy Bun's popularity.

Zhou had ticked everything off on the cleaning roster, and there was a lingering smell of pine-fragranced cleaner in the galley kitchen. I'd long since banned ammonia-based products at Bushy Bun. I couldn't risk a flashback during a hectic shift.

The cold room was empty, with a meat delivery due in the second week of January, when we were going to reopen, and the pantry shelves were faultless, with spice jars lined up as if with a ruler and spirit level.

I set the alarm and locked the door behind me.

By the time I arrived at *Fig & Brie*, I was officially late. I signed in with Ashwin, the security guard who was the closest friend I'd made when I worked there, handed him the second pain au chocolat, and caught the lift up to the eighth floor.

≈

The *Fig & Brie* team, who also contributed to five other lifestyle titles, sprawled across three white melamine desks pushed together. I hadn't spent much time working up here – I'd had to be downstairs in the basement studio most of the day – but it was a nice spot, the best in the whole block, spacious and decorated with potted delicious monsters, the sun beaming in through the high windows, and a view of the cranes and container ships in the harbour.

"Well, if it isn't Missus Bushy Bun herself!" June, the impeccably groomed, plucked, smoothed and contoured Editor-in-Chief stood up as I walked in. I gave her a hug over her screen, and she gave me three of her pretentious cheek-kisses.

June had never liked any reminders that her food-stylist-slash-recipe-tester-slash-video-recipe-slave was, in fact, a chef, that I had four years' worth of shifts in the Mon Petit kitchen, that, if I hadn't walked out, I'd probably be chef de cuisine there by now.

Everyone knew June was an old friend of the CEO of the umbrella company that owned *Fig & Brie* and the other titles in the building. But she also knew everything there was to know about food trends, and if there was one thing you could say about her recipes it was that they were ambitious. Every video I'd made for *Fig & Brie*'s social media had been a challenge.

When I'd asked whether June thought ordinary people would have been able to make the recipes in their homes, considering that some of the ingredients, like the popping candy in her Explosive Cake Pops, cost as much as an entire week of groceries for most middle-class people, she'd said, "We're not supposed to be attainable, Skye, we're aspirational. If people want to learn how to make fucking blueberry flapjacks, they're following the wrong account."

"Skye, we are *so* proud of you," she said. "We've heard the most amazing things about Bushy Bun. I wish we could get in there! You can't review a place where you can never get a table!" She winked, but her fake-lashed eyes were steely.

I shrugged. "I do the food – Cam does all the concept stuff."

"And congrats on the wedding! Quite … sudden, wasn't it?"

Talia popped out of the conference room, thank god, and waved to me.

"Sorry, June, I'm late for Talia. I'll talk to Cam about putting a table aside for you."

"Oh, don't worry about it, I can hardly check out every hipster dive that opens up. Anyway. You're in good hands with Tally." She reached out her hand to squeeze mine and her pointed nails grazed my palm.

Talia was as bubbly as ever, talking non-stop while she made us coffee. She remembered at the last minute that I preferred tea and dunked a black tea bag in a mug of lukewarm water, sloshing in long-life milk before fishing the bag out.

I carried my pale drink into the conference room behind Talia and waited for her to get her notebook and pen out. She was the only writer on the team who used hard-copy notebooks. She bound them herself using leftover fabric from the colourful cotton ankle-sweeping skirts she made on her sewing machine. Today, like every day, her notebook and her skirt were an exact match.

The thought of putting so much effort into a notebook exhausted me. How many other women did feminine things like that – making their own clothes and, I don't know, crocheting things? Neither my mother nor Lola had ever done anything crafty. On the farm, everything had been a practical task to make sure we were fed and had clean clothes and bodies.

"Our plan for this story," Talia said, "is to post a teaser for the interview on the blog by lunchtime today because

Bushy Bun's become this kind of enigma, you know? It's probably the most Instagrammed spot in Cape Town but nobody knows who or what it's about? The sign outside the restaurant isn't really visible. Is that part of the plan?"

"The concept and the publicity ... or lack of it ... stuff like that is all Cam's thing."

"Cam's your husband now, right? How wild, that you guys eloped!"

"We didn't want any fuss. And we didn't elope. His parents were there."

"It's his dad who's funding the restaurant, right? Deacon Carlisle?"

"That's right. He invests in brands he thinks can be franchised down the line." I hadn't expected *funding* to come up. *Fig & Brie* didn't usually dig into the financials of restaurants they reviewed.

Talia nodded, scratched something out in her book, made a few notes.

"Okay. And you're the chef? The brains of the operation? You do all the cooking, right, and create the recipes?"

"Well, Cam lived in Taiwan, in Zhong-Li, a city in the north, for eight years, and when he came back, he started his business, Tie-Pay, importing Taiwanese ingredients. But what he'd always wanted to do was open a restaurant that offered Taiwanese street food."

"Have you ever been to Taiwan?"

"We went for a few weeks, about a year ago, after I left here, while I was developing the ideas and recipes." I described the burly fry cooks operating behind barbecues and hotplates outside every little restaurant on the treacherous, uneven pavements; how Cam wanted a street food restaurant here, right in the heart of hipster Cape Town, that subverted all the ideas of what a restaurant should be, with unpretentious menus, no décor, a tiny space and hot, fast, authentic good food.

Talia was listening to me, chin on hand, clicking the top of her pen.

"Have you eaten at Bushy Bun?" I asked.

She blinked and straightened. "You're only serving twelve people per night, and there are queues down the street from four p.m. to get in. You don't turn tables … and you're not always open. So, no."

"It's twenty-two pax, in fact. Next year we want to start doing lunchtime takeaways from the hatch, so hopefully you guys can get some of those. I want to know what a proper critic thinks of the food. At the moment I think most people are only going because it's so hard to get in."

Talia smiled. "That's Cape Town for you. Tell me about the name."

I started explaining about the cram school, or "busiban" in Mandarin, pronounced similarly to the name of the restaurant – except for the Mandarin tones, I added quickly, which are almost impossible for non-native speakers to get a handle on – where Cam used to teach in Taiwan, where kids would go in the evenings to study English, how he wanted the restaurant to teach South Africans about Taiwanese food.

"I've seen the food all over Insta. It's Chinese?"

"Well, technically, it's Hakka."

I did a quick run-down of the flavours – big, punchy, lots of salt – and mentioned our Sichuan-influenced dishes like gong bao ji ding, cubed chicken breasts with cashews and chilli. I told her about my favourite dish, the Hakka-style stir-fry, made with dried squid that's reconstituted, which Cam imports, and fatty streaks of pork belly. I described the fried tofu that was silky on the inside and crunchy on the outside, with a sticky dipping sauce.

I waited while Talia wrote, remembering Cam in the restaurant in Hua-Lian digging the cheek meat out of a whole fish topped with impossibly thin spirals of chilli and spring onion and served on a platter that took up most of the round table. He placed a sliver of the delicacy on my tongue with his chopsticks. The meat melted instantly. It was probably the most erotic moment of our relationship, of my life.

My favourite food from Taiwan couldn't be imported – sea snails the size of 10-cent coins with dark green whorled shells. Before we came back to Cape Town, Cam and I spent a weekend on the Penghu Islands, tiny spits of land off another tiny spit of land, where we scooped dripping handfuls of snails out of plastic buckets that an ancient woman sold in the courtyard of her home.

We walked around the crumbling ghost village, with its unbelievable views of white sand and turquoise sea, sucking the umami flesh out of the shells, and throwing them, empty, into the sea. I could still feel the warm little screws of muscle against the back of my tongue. My mouth filled with saliva.

"Who helps you in the kitchen? Do you have staff? You're not standing there cooking alone every night?"

Since when did *Fig & Brie* care about kitchen staff? I knew I wasn't supposed to talk too much about Zhou, but I trusted Talia, and needed to start wrapping things up.

"So, this can't get out, okay?"

Talia inhaled sharply and cocked her head. I'd always considered us to be friends, in a distant way. It hadn't occurred to me before that I didn't know anything about her.

"Well, because of visa issues, Taiwanese people struggle to stay here legally. The trip we took to Taiwan before we opened the restaurant was mostly to recruit the guy from Cam's favourite food stall. His name's Zhou, he's in his twenties, he worked as a fry cook on his family's food stall in Zhong-Li, and his English is decent. Cam offered him a job and a way to, I guess, see the world, and he came with us.

"Cam's trying to work something out so he can work here legally. I mostly supervise him, do the plating, the serving, test everything he makes. But, yeah, Bushy Bun without Zhou would be very difficult to pull off."

I didn't like how many notes Talia was taking.

"Where does he live? With you?"

"Oh, no. Cam's flat is tiny. There's a room above the restaurant that Zhou's renting."

"How much does it cost?"

I hesitated. "I don't know. Cam takes the rent out of Zhou's wages. That, and the cost of his flight over here."

"How much does he get paid?"

I chewed my lip. I had never asked. I saw Zhou nearly every day but didn't think about him much. He never spoke in the kitchen. He cooked, I tasted, I served, on repeat, night after night. He didn't seem particularly happy, I supposed, but did he seem … *oppressed*?

"Tally, he could be deported. Maybe you can say that we have cooks in the kitchen? Something vague?"

She waved her hand in a gesture that reminded me of June.

"I think I've got everything I need. One more thing – would you say the restaurant is yours? Or Cam's? It sounds like it was all Cam's idea, and you're not doing much of the actual cooking … I want to make sure I get it right."

I went hot.

"It's ours. We both own the business. I'm the one there every day. Well, almost every day. Whenever we're open."

Talia laughed.

She walked me to the lifts, hugged me, thanked me, and waved as the lift doors closed.

Two

As a welcome-home present when he'd moved back from Taiwan, Cam's dad had bought Cam, who didn't know how to drive, a Land Rover. A way to convince him to get his licence, Cam had explained, but when we started living together, we'd traded it in – with exactly 34 kilometres on the clock – and I'd chosen the hybrid I was currently manoeuvring down the steep driveway of Carlisle Cottage in Misty Cliffs.

Through Cam's open window, the sea was sparkly, a blinking, sequinned sheet tucked in at the horizon, with placid waves lapping in the foreground.

Cam took a deep breath, held the air in his lungs.

"This smell always reminds me of coming here from Joburg when we were little. Rory and I'd hang our heads out the window all the way down Chapman's, fight for the seat behind Dad so we'd get the sea view."

I parked under the carport next to Deacon's latest elephantine CO_2-emitter. Cam's good mood was impenetrable, despite our arriving three hours after we'd said we would. He hopped out of the car and opened the boot, started gathering the canvas grocery bags. I was about to heave one onto my shoulder when Cam's mother, Julia, came out the screen door, her two rescue greyhounds, Dusk and Dawn, slithering around her legs.

Julia was in her Cottage uniform of jeans, a polo shirt and those weird sneakers that probably cost a fortune and looked like they were made of mesh. Julia looked good in clothes. Any clothes. It was something about the way she carried her shoulders, rolled her hips. She looked impressive, even when she wasn't trying.

The first time I'd met her I'd put her innate elegance down to the twinkly string of diamonds round her neck and the couture she was draped in, but now I knew it was just Julia. After we'd got engaged, Cam had taken me up to Johannesburg to meet her and Deacon at their six-bedroom house in Craighall Park with huge jacaranda trees in full purple bloom. On the drive from the airport, he told me how devastated he'd been when his parents had "downsized" to this house from the place in Westcliff where he and his sister had grown up. I couldn't imagine a house so big that this one in Craighall was the smaller of the two.

When we'd arrived, Julia was about to leave for a fundraiser, wearing a floor-length, navy, off-the-shoulder dress with some kind of gauze thing going on in the skirt. She'd seemed so pleased to meet me and had Cam's same irresistible aura of good-naturedness. I fell for her as quickly as I'd fallen for him.

"Oh, love, you've had your hair cut shorter! You look so edgy!" She hugged me long and hard. Julia's own hair was completely grey, in a Diane Keaton bob, and her hazel eyes crinkled and glittered behind her glasses.

I knew that she talked to everyone the way she talked to me, that she made everyone feel special, which meant that no one was; but try telling that to my stupid, affection-starved heart, which hadn't known this kind of warmth since Lola had died.

She squeezed Cam tightly, linked arms with me and led me into the house, clicking her fingers for her dogs to follow her.

Moments later, we were in the chrome and wood kitchen, perched on the white leather bar stools of the breakfast nook, watching Julia open an unlabelled bottle of San Tropez rosé that she'd brought back from her stay in their timeshare apartment there.

"Where's Dad?" Cam asked, lifting his glass.

"He went for a walk on the beach. He's thinking of getting into that stand-up-paddle-boarding thing. There are a few guys doing it in the surf and he saw them out the window and went and asked them to give him lessons. I don't know. It's not for me, I'll tell you that much."

I circled round on my stool to look out the lounge windows. It was floor-to-ceiling glass, a complete 180-degree view of the sea. A door between the windows opened onto a small fynbos garden with stepping stones down to the sand.

The Cottage wasn't a cottage at all. It was a grand old three-storey house with Cape Cod cladding and a widow's walk, and it required two maintenance men for upkeep year-round. It had been in Deacon's family since he'd been a boy in the 60s, when Misty Cliffs hadn't yet become a "conservation village", before it had electricity, before it had a name, as he liked to tell me – it had been nothing more than a stretch of beach between Scarborough and Kommetjie with one or two lonely houses perched near the beach and on the mountainside.

Julia winked at me as she clinked her glass against mine, then Cam's. "To Christmas!" she said.

"Maybe this will be the year," Cam replied, and the wistfulness in his voice forced me off my chair. I started unpacking groceries in the kitchen.

He was talking about Rory – Aurora – his fragile artist twin sister who'd dropped off the face of the planet two years ago. He was hoping she'd finally come home.

"I found one of her ranges, did I tell you?" Julia said.

"At the auction in Saxonwold?"

"Yes! She must have done it recently, all the pieces since she disappeared are in much bolder colours. This one's glazed in a kind of lapis lazuli."

The only clues Cam, Julia and Deacon had about the state of Rory's mind while she was MIA were her ceramics, which she'd continued to produce, wherever she was, and which Julia had devoted pretty much all her time (when she wasn't horse riding or fundraising or travelling) to sourcing at auctions around the country.

"Is it an arty one? Or a homey one?"

"Homey. Let me find you a picture," Julia said, scrolling through her phone, looking over the top of her glasses.

The pieces Rory produced as feminist art were exhibited from New York to Barcelona to Beijing. There was one in a custom-built inset in the kitchen at The Cottage, a piece she'd titled "Tip Of The Iceberg". It was a glistening, bright red wishbone cradling an upside-down, aubergine-coloured heart. The colours were so dense and deep that the sculpture almost vibrated with life. The glossy card mounted in the inset explained that this was the structure of the human clitoris. Bullet points on the card listed five mind-blowing facts about the part of my body I'd always thought was no bigger than the nub between my labia. The only thing more surprising than the fact that most of my clitoris was *inside me* – why were we never taught this in sex ed? – was the idea of having this intimate piece of art in your kitchen.

When she wasn't feeling inspired to make statements about the patriarchy, Rory made crockery that she intended for home use and to which she didn't put her name. But she was so mysterious and such a big deal in these high end art circles that her sets of 16 bowls, each one infinitesimally smaller than the next, were snatched up by collectors and auctioned off for obscene amounts of money.

"How much?" Cam asked, when he saw the picture.

"Well, I splashed out a bit."

"So … like, fifty?"

"Seventy-five," Julia said. "But it's stunning, Cam. I brought you the smallest bowl to keep."

I closed the fridge door harder than I meant to. Seventy-five *thousand* for a set of bowls made by your own daughter, who couldn't be bothered to let you know if she was alive or dead?

"How do you know they're hers?"

Julia and Cam looked up sharply from the bright blue bowl Cam was holding in his palm, which was so small he could have closed his fingers over it. "I mean, what if they're a clever imitation? Would you be able to tell?"

Julia smiled sadly. "Rory always puts a little indentation on the base of each bowl. She measures it precisely so it's in the same place every single time. And besides, I know the stroke of her hand. I know how she straddles the wheel. She's the only person who can make a bowl look like this."

Cam took a deep pull on his wine, raising his eyebrows at me over the glass, a look that meant I'd said something wrong.

"Should we go unpack, love?" he asked.

"Yes, yes, you two go ahead. Your first married Christmas together! It's so exciting," Julia said, taking trays of lamb chops out of my hand and kissing my cheek softly.

"You're so pretty, Skye," she whispered, still with her sad smile, and turned to open the freezer, dismissing me. Her breath had the sweet-rotten smell of afternoon wine.

"Was I asking too many questions?" I asked as I followed Cam up the stairs to his room in the loft.

He stopped and turned on the landing, his face dark above me with the sun pouring in through the skylight. I couldn't see his eyebrows, which were always a dead giveaway.

"You were getting defensive. You always do when it's about Rory. We miss her. We're not going to stop talking about her. I know you don't get it because your family's not as close as mine."

"I'm not asking you to stop talking about her."

He turned without answering me and started climbing the narrow staircase to his bedroom in the loft. It was stuffy and cosy, the walls covered with Nirvana and Smashing Pumpkins posters from when Cam had been a boy.

"This is going to sound weird," he said, "but I have to ask. Are you *jealous* of her? You act like she's my ex or something. Like talking about her is some kind of taboo."

Well, obviously I was jealous, I wanted to say. He'd been right – my family wasn't close. Not anymore, not since Lola had died. My mother and I hadn't had contact for months. She wouldn't know if I disappeared.

I watched Cam force open the window next to the widow's walk, its delicate railing separating it from the rocks and sea below. A savoury lick of air curled into the loft.

29

"Here's the thing. Sometimes, with your family, I can't believe the way they talk about money. It makes me uncomfortable."

Cam's face relaxed. He folded me in his arms, dropped his head and kissed me on the tendon holding my shoulder and my neck together.

"I know, love. But now they're your family, too."

≈

The wind had picked up during the afternoon and hadn't died down after sunset. I sat on the widow's walk with my legs between the railings and my feet dangling over the edge, listening to the white noise of the waves churning the stones three storeys below, staring up at the moonless sky and its shards of stars. I felt the floor of the widow's walk shift beneath me.

I turned around, expecting to see Cam, surprised that he'd come up to bed so soon. He and Julia had been opening their third bottle when I'd come upstairs, in full wine-talk mode, repeating the same stories I'd heard countless times about when Cam and Rory were small and adorable and inseparable.

But it was Deacon, stooping to fit through the little door, kicking it shut behind him. He was carrying two flutes of pink bubbly.

"Thought you'd be up here," he said, smiling, reaching down to hand me a glass.

I took the glass and tilted it, looking for the tiny pearls swirling to the surface of the champagne in the hazy light from the window. It felt like a living thing I was holding, with its capsules of air forever spinning upwards. They never stopped moving, I thought, whether you were watching them or not.

"It's funny, I'd never come up here until you started visiting. It always seemed a bit, I don't know, morbid to me," Deacon said, taking a sip and leaning on the railing.

"I suppose it is. But I love old houses – the one I grew up in was only built in the seventies."

But it had been full of old things, furniture and appliances my grandparents had brought over from England, and which my mother occasionally tried to give away in exchange for food she couldn't grow.

I'd discovered my grandmother's black-and-gold hand-operated Singer sewing machine with a thread still dangling from the needle at the top of the cupboard in the dining room when I was about 10. It made me feel like I knew her. I kept it on the desk in my room, projecting onto it all my pre-teen fantasies about a white-haired kindly old woman who'd find me delightful and who'd defend me to my mother by saying things like, "Don't be so hard on her, she's a good girl" .

"Well, this house was built in the thirties," Deacon was saying. "By a rich British guy, a merchant with a shipping company. He built it for his wife. She had bad lungs, or a bad heart, I can't remember which, and couldn't stay in England, so he shipped her out to Africa. I'm sure she spent a fair bit of time up here. He never came back for her, apparently."

The image of the woman sitting up here, listening to the sea alone on the desolate, wild Cape Peninsula brought on a wave of sudden sadness.

"My father always joked that it wasn't technically a widow's walk, that we should start calling it the first wife's walk instead, but I think 'widow' is much more romantic. The word itself, in this context. You know what I mean," Deacon said.

I looked up at him. He was 10 years younger than Julia, in his late 50s, but looked as if he was maybe in his 40s. You'd never guess he'd spent his whole career working for a tobacco giant before he'd retired.

"You want to join me on my run tomorrow?"

"I might – though I had some wine earlier, and after this I might not be feeling so hot," I said, lifting my glass.

"Best thing for it. Fizzy vitamin, run, sea swim, coffee, in that order."

"I'm not sure I believe you. I'm more of an evening runner. Plus, I don't drink coffee."

He chuckled. "Well, I'll be leaving at about seven, so come down if you feel like it. It won't be a long one, I did a half today so could do with a short leg stretcher."

"Wouldn't Julia go with you?"

"Skye, I've been with Julia for thirty-five years and have never once seen her running. She sometimes makes plans with her school friends to go to a Pilates class, but I don't think she's ever followed through."

"I think Cam's been to the gym twice since I've known him, both times to meet a buyer at the café."

Deacon shook his head. "I tried so hard with that boy. I had visions of us crossing the Comrades finish line together."

I took my first sip of bubbly, holding it against my tongue as long as I could before swallowing. It was cold, bone-dry.

"Speaking of that boy. I came up to toast the restaurant with you," Deacon said. "I see it's been doing phenomenally well."

"Oh! Yes, it's taken us both a bit by surprise."

He tilted his head – just like Cam, I thought – and clinked his glass against mine. "Not me. I've always known

Cam would do something like this. He's always loved food so much. And Asian things."

I laughed.

"Seriously, since he was little and we first went to Hong Kong, he was obsessed with the East. But as much as Bushy Bun's a natural fit for him, he wouldn't have been able to pull it off without you."

"Oh, I don't know."

"You need to start claiming some credit, Skye. I always tell the women I work with to stop being so modest. Own your talents! The food is all you."

"Zhou, too."

"Yes, well, let's not mention him. You're the chef." He drained his glass. "I must admit, last year, when Cam first told me what his new girlfriend did for a living, I thought it was almost too convenient. He'd been talking about opening a restaurant for a while and the next thing I hear, he's dating a chef."

I frowned. "Did he tell you I was working at a magazine at the time? Not as a chef?"

"Well, yes, and as soon as I met you I realised it wasn't a convenience thing. I wanted to say all this at the wedding, by the way, but Julia didn't think it was a good idea. Not proper. Father of the groom never speaks at a wedding, etcetera."

Deacon slid his back down the railing until he was sitting next to me, his legs stretched out along almost the entire length of the widow's walk behind my back.

"What I mean to say," he said, holding the stem of the flute with both hands, "is that you're obviously more than the chef who's made Cam's dream come true. I'm very happy for both of you and especially, well, maybe not especially, but also for my bottom line that the restaurant's doing so well. And it's mostly because of you – no matter how much Cam tries to claim credit for the queues round the block." He looked me in the eye. "If you'll excuse me, I'd better go to bed because, like you, I don't drink very much, and it appears that I may be drunk." He squeezed my shoulder before standing up.

He had reached the door before I spoke.

"Does he?" I asked. "Cam. Does he claim all the credit for the restaurant?"

Deacon paused, peering into the champagne flute as if inspecting it for any remaining bubbles.

"I'm sure he's trying to impress his mother and me. He wants so badly to do well, he always has, and I think with Rory, Cam feels he has to make up for something, so he's very keen for me to know how well the restaurant's doing. But I wanted to thank you. You could be doing anything, working anywhere, and instead you're using your talents for my son's whacky gamble of a restaurant."

I got to my feet. Would I get through a solid hour this holiday without a moment eclipsed by the family's longing for Rory?

"I was asking because something happened today that made me think I needed to be more involved."

Deacon put an arm round my shoulder as he opened the tiny door. Cam's family believed in touching. "I wouldn't worry about it. It's late, and we've got that run in the morning."

I laughed. "You've got that run. I've got a sleep-in."

"We'll see," he said, gesturing me inside, into the close comfort of Cam's room, where my husband himself was lying on the bed, face down, shoes still on and fully clothed.

"Enjoy," Deacon whispered with a laugh in his voice. "See you at seven!"

Three

I woke up with the gulls mewling and scrabbling on the roof above our heads. I couldn't remember the last time I'd woken up without an alarm.

Weak light framed the blinds round the window. I reached for my phone to check the time before remembering that it was in a basket in the pantry downstairs. Deacon's rule: at The Cottage, everyone lived unplugged. Since leaving *Fig & Brie* I'd become a lot less dependent on my phone, but I still didn't like being without it. I couldn't see what time it was, for one thing.

I tried to lift Cam's wrist to check his watch, but he had his arms clutched between his legs, in the fetal position. For a lanky guy, he slept very neatly, barely taking up half of the bed. His dark hair was mussed against his pillow, and his face, turned towards me, was totally still, so different to what he was like when he was awake, animated and chatty and all mobile eyebrows and scrunching nose.

I put my hand on his shoulder, stroking it through the warm cotton of Deacon's old 1994 Comrades Marathon shirt that Cam always slept in, hoping he'd wake up and pull me towards him. I resolved to be nicer, to be better, to be more loving, less resentful. He was so good-natured, so big-hearted, and I wanted to deserve him.

Cam took a deeper breath and turned onto his other side, away from me. I strained my ears for any movement from downstairs, but the old building with its thick walls kept the loft soundproof. All I could hear were the waves rolling in and rolling out and rolling in on the other side of the widow's walk door, and I realised that the wind had stopped.

I decided to go for a run after all. I moved around as quietly as I could, digging my shoes out of the bottom of my backpack, pulling a pair of Cam's socks out of his suitcase and sticking a bobby pin in my fringe so it wouldn't flop into my eyes.

I took the stairs slowly, trying to prevent them creaking, but found Julia and Deacon both sitting in the kitchen when I got down there. The clock above the sink showed quarter-past six. They were sitting in absolute silence, the metronome of the clock counting the seconds.

"You're early!" Deacon said when he looked up and saw me. He was wearing a crumpled polo shirt and *boxer shorts*. I did my best to keep my eyes level with his.

Julia was wearing a black silk nightgown embroidered with blooming hibiscus flowers. I felt as if I'd barged into their bedroom. Deacon was cupping the landline phone in both his hands like it was a baby or small animal.

"I thought I'd beat the wind," I replied, aiming for casual breeziness. They were both looking a little wild-eyed.

"Cool. See you later," Deacon said, unsteadily, and Julia stretched out her arms for a hug. She sniffed as she held me. If it hadn't been so early, I'd have put her crying down to too much wine.

But as soon as I left the house and made my way down to the beach through the succulent garden I forgot about Deacon and Julia. I couldn't think while

I was plodding. It was the only thing that had got me through the months after the mugging – the blind routine of getting into my kit and leaving the Mowbray house and concentrating on putting one foot in front of the other until I was finished.

The tide was going out, the sand soft under my feet, and my ankles and knees started protesting almost immediately. But by the time I'd got to the small path leading up to the road, I was numb to the creaking of my joints, and when I descended to Scarborough beach through the parking lot, I had the rhythm that would carry me all the way to the rocks at the end of the beach. I turned around and followed my own footsteps back, passing the gumboot-shod mussel hunters armed with screwdrivers, dodging the slimy ribbons of kelp along the waterline, and passing the same pair of oystercatchers I'd seen on my way up the beach, hooting and striding scarlet-legged away from me.

Three pied kingfishers hovered above the rock pools. Sandpipers scuttled along the wet sand, leaving looping ellipses of tiny footprints. Cormorants floated out by the backline, alternately diving and popping out, no two below the surface or above at the same time, as if they were practising an elaborate routine or were remote-controlled.

By the time I got back to The Cottage, the South-Easter was starting to swirl the tops of the dunes. With each step that took me closer to the door, a flame of dread flickered in my stomach.

The kitchen, living room and bar were empty when I stepped into the house, but I heard heavy footfalls on the stairs and Cam's whistling.

"Hey, you," he said when he saw me in the kitchen. "Do you have any idea how I got out of my clothes last night?" He was still wearing the Comrades shirt, with a pair of boardshorts.

"I had to help you get changed. You weren't super-cooperative."

"I blame the cognac." He opened the fridge door and pulled out the milk, slopping it into a glass and taking three deep gulps.

Cold milk was the answer to all of Cam's life's ills, including hangovers. Except insomnia, which called for warm milk, with a bit of honey in it. I used to think it was adorable, Cam's belief in this quaint nursery cure, until I realised that it was a symptom of how fiercely he clung to his childhood.

"You hate cognac," I said, scanning the pantry shelves for the eggs, thinking of throwing together a courgette and parmesan frittata, something I could put in the oven before I took a shower. "Where are the eggs?"

"Mother refuses to believe it. She says it's something I need to develop a taste for in my old age." Cam kissed the back of my head. "Have you checked the fridge?"

"No, because eggs don't go in the fridge."

He opened it and passed two eggs to me in each hand. "Why do fridge doors all come with those little holes for eggs, silly?"

I put the four eggs he'd given me into a nest of a tea towel and reached into the fridge for four more, gearing up to telling him about the weird vibe I'd got from Deacon and Julia in the kitchen earlier.

"Have you seen your folks this morning?" I asked, keeping my voice neutral, as I cracked the eggs into a metal mixing bowl. I'd started peeling the courgettes into ribbons before realising he wasn't in the kitchen anymore. I heard him shut the front door a moment later.

"Paper's come," he called out.

"You guys get the newspaper delivered here? By an actual physical human being?"

"We're not allowed phones. How else would we get the news?" He pulled the lifestyle section out of the centre of the newspaper and flipped through it, an intent expression on his face. A moment later, he slapped the supplement on the counter next to the chopping board.

"Look who made it into Mood for Food this week!"

Cam, in his faded jeans and favourite black V-neck jersey, the sleeves rolled up to his elbows, was leaning against the counter in the Bushy Bun kitchen, a lazy half-smile on his face, his eyebrows quirking together in an expression of bemused irony, looking as rakish as I'd ever seen him. Behind him were the shelves holding Zhou's colourful spices and pickles and relishes.

The headline scrolled across the spread read, "Bringing it home". I took in the bold-type blurb:

"Those on the Cape Town foodie scene know Cameron Carlisle as the entrepreneur behind the flourishing Tie-Pay brand of East Asian delicacies stocked at boutique food stores. Carlisle started the business at the tender age of 28, when he first returned to South Africa after spending a decade in Taiwan, learning the language and falling in love with the food.

"But these days, he's perhaps better known as the owner and founder of Bushy Bun, a tiny Taiwanese eatery of almost mythical proportions on Cape Town's bustling Bree Street. Carlisle's spot serves 22 people per night and doesn't take bookings. They have no alcohol licence and don't turn tables. It's impossible to know on any given night whether Bushy Bun is open, never mind whether or not you'll get a table. Despite, or perhaps because of, driving Cape Town foodies insane and defying all the rules of the hospitality industry, Carlisle's new business is wildly successful, a testament to his originality and, of course, the sheer gorgeousness and authenticity of the food."

I carefully put the peeler and the courgette on the chopping board and fought to keep my hands from clenching into fists. Cam was reading the article over my shoulder. I felt his warm breath on my ear and could tell that he was smiling as he read.

I shifted away and bent down to get the grater from the cabinet underneath the sink. The kitchen utensils were kept in mysterious places in the vast Cottage kitchen. I had found the silicone spatulas in the sideboard with the family silver.

"You didn't tell me you had an interview with the paper."

"Oh, it was months ago. I wanted to keep it a surprise. It'll be great for the business."

I straightened up. "Am I in it? Did you mention me at all?"

Cam's shoulders dropped, as did his smile. "I said my wife was the chef." He started measuring coffee beans into the brushed chrome Rancilio espresso machine Julia had brought back from Italy as a Christmas present "for the house" last year.

I put a slice of butter and a swirl of olive oil in a flawless non-stick copper pan that had probably never been used. Say what you wanted about the disorder of the Carlisles' kitchen, every utensil and piece of equipment was literally the best that money could buy. I started gently whisking the eggs, marvelling at how steady my hands were while a blood-pressure headache was starting to sneak up on me.

"Not my name?"

"Christ, Skye. No, I didn't mention your name, okay? It was a profile of me, as you can see. I got to punt Bushy Bun and Tie-Pay and they took some cute photos of me, and that's it. If you read it, you'd realise that."

He flicked the switch on the machine, and the grinding of the beans was too loud for me to respond to him. He wasn't looking at me anymore, having snatched up the supplement and hidden his face behind it to finish the story.

I carried on with the frittata, knowing that following each step methodically and precisely was as close to a meditative and calming experience as I was going to get. For a merciful few minutes, my mind was occupied with spreading parmesan cheese evenly on the meniscus of the beaten egg mixture and on the careful criss-crossing of paper-thin courgette ribbons in a lattice over the cheese.

As I put it in the oven, the Rancilio started its discreet beeping. As I put Cam's mug under the coffee machine tap, I heard Deacon's car pulling up alongside the house. Cam's jaw dropped, his eyebrows shot up and he whispered, "Holy shit." Then he sprang to the door.

The tiny flicker of dread I'd felt before erupted into a scorched-earth fire as I heard a desperate sound I didn't recognise – Cam gulping with sobs. I busied myself with rinsing the cutting board and peeler under the tap, turning the pressure right up so it drowned out Cam's voice. When I couldn't bear it anymore, I turned it off, took a deep breath and dried my hands.

Through the screen door, I saw Cam holding someone in his arms. She was tall for a woman, only about a head shorter than he was, and her pale, thin arms were loosely clutched around him, his head in her long, tumbling auburn hair. Cam's shoulders were shaking, but her arms were completely still.

Cam was still holding her when the sound of a child's squawk came from the car. He pulled away from the woman like she'd burned him. He held her at arm's length for what felt like a long time. I couldn't see her face.

It was Deacon who opened the back door of the car and gathered a child into his arms. I caught a glimpse of springy black hair and thin legs sticking out of a loose nappy. Cam wiped his eyes with the heels of his hands and grabbed the woman's wrist and practically dragged her to the screen door, and then they were inside and there was nowhere I could hide.

The photos I'd seen had prepared me for Aurora's sharp grey-green eyes under thick, dark brows, but not the bags underneath them. She had a cracked cold sore on her upper lip – Cam got those too, when he was stressed – and was dressed in a white cheesecloth thing that looked like a toga. She was so thin that her skin looked taut over her cheekbones. Her lean thighs curved gently into smooth, delicate knees, and her posture was statuesque, her shoulders thrown back. She was magnificent, and terrifying.

Rory's sea eyes travelled slowly down my body and up again, a reminder that I was still sweaty and in running clothes, that I'd left my shoes at the door and was wearing Cam's too-big socks.

Deacon and Julia pushed through the screen door behind Cam and Rory, but still Rory didn't move. I had no idea how long she and I stood assessing each other before Julia said, "Coffee, Cam?", and we blinked back into life.

I showed Julia the cups I'd lined up at the machine. Cam gave a watery smile and said, "Rory, this is Skye. She's, we're, we got …"

"I'm his wife," I said.

She didn't move. When she spoke, her voice sounded rusty.

"Seriously?"

Julia's laugh tinkled from the direction of the kitchen and she turned to wink at me, as if to say, "Isn't Rory hilarious?"

Rory turned to Cam. "I never pictured you with the tomboy type."

I hadn't been called a tomboy since I was about 15. I'd been called "down to earth", and "approachable", and described, once, by a sous chef who didn't think I was listening, as "kind-of hot if she grew her hair." (After the bang of his cleaver against the chopping board, he said, "Or some tits.")

But Rory clearly didn't do euphemisms. I did a mental inventory of what I looked like to her. Dark blonde hair, no highlights, "mousy", probably, shorn short on one side and in a longish bob on the other. A skew bobby pin keeping the long side off my face. Flushed cheeks, sweaty running gear and freckles.

She turned to Cam, "How did you two meet?"

"Oh no, you don't," Cam said, taking her by the elbow and steering her to the living room, where Deacon had settled the child in one of the yellow armchairs under a blue-striped blanket.

I took a closer look and noticed a ring of dried white granules around the little girl's mouth, yellow crusts in the corner of her eyes, and dirt under her long fingernails. Her big eyes moved from Cam to Rory and back as Cam dropped to one of the couches and pulled Rory down next to him.

"You first," he said to her. His eyes were still full of tears. I could sense the monumental effort it was taking him to keep them from spilling down his face.

Julia brought three cups of coffee on a tray with milk in a Wedgewood-blue jug and placed it on the coffee table. She joined Deacon in the kitchen. They stood holding each other.

I sat down on the arm of the other yellow armchair, not wanting to get too comfortable.

Rory eyed the tray. "Is there sugar for the coffee?"

"I'll go check," I said, heading for the kitchen.

"Do you want milk in yours, love?" Cam called to me from the living room. Mercifully, there was a nearly empty bag of white sugar in the pantry cupboard, and by some miracle the ants hadn't got to it.

"No thanks, I ..."

Before I finished, Cam was passing me a mug of black coffee. I took it wordlessly, passing him the little packet of sugar, trying to catch his eye.

"Two teaspoons, Rory?"

Rory took the packet from him and poured the entire contents into her mug. Her fingernails were jagged at the edges, with specks of dried blood. With jerky movements, she stirred and downed her coffee. She poured the rest of the milk from the jug into her empty mug and gave it to the little girl, who grabbed it with both hands and took a small sip.

I put my mug down on the tray, still full. Cam's gaze stuck on it for a moment too long, and when he looked up it was as if he was seeing me through wavy glass, like he could barely make out my outline.

"Oh. I forgot you don't do coffee. Sorry," he said, shaking his head. I reached for his hand, but he had turned to watch the girl drinking. "Whose is she?" he asked.

Rory looked at him askance. "Uh, mine? Obviously? I didn't kidnap her, for god's sake."

Cam blinked. "But yours and whose? How old is she? What's her name?"

"Mine and Mzwandile's, also obviously," she said.

Cam's eyebrows shot up. "Who?"

"Mzwandile Menzi? Known as Em-Zee. If you followed politics, you'd know him."

Deacon spoke up from the kitchen. "Em-Zee Menzi, as in, tipped for leader of the New Communists."

Rory sat perfectly still, perfectly upright, not turning to look at Deacon when she replied. "Yes. We've been mobilising the movement for the last two years."

"That's where you've been? The whole time you've been missing you've been *mobilising*?" Deacon strode down into the living room. "With the New fucking Communists?"

"Oh, good god, Dad, I haven't been fucking *missing*. I've been in these urban little backwaters, places like Alice and Peddie, helping Em-Zee gather momentum among the working class in the informal settlements, college campuses, places like that. No fixed address. No fucking *Wi-Fi*."

"Okay," Cam shot Deacon a "cool it" look. "It doesn't matter where you've been. You're here now. But you have to tell us about the baby."

Rory shrugged, and slumped against the back of the couch, and I got a flash of her as a rebellious teenager.

"There's not much to tell. I met Em-Zee at a rally two years ago, we got together, I got pregnant, he didn't want me to be away from him while he was touring, so I went with him. I had her while we were in the Eastern Cape, in Peddie, on the eighth of August last year. Three pushes and she was out. Her name's Maya, second name Cyan. Em-Zee and his family call her Mawande, so she pretty much answers to both." She looked at me. "His family's Xhosa."

She pronounced it the white way, the wrong way, without the click. She didn't know I'd grown up hearing isiXhosa and English intertwined so closely that when I started speaking, I used them interchangeably. Or that I'd lost it completely after leaving home.

"What's on her birth certificate?" Cam asked. "Is she Maya Carlisle?"

Again, Rory shrugged. "We left Peddie a few days after she was born so I don't know if she has one."

"So, she's, what, sixteen months old?" Julia was crouching next to Maya's chair, flat-out ignored by her granddaughter. "She looks a bit small for her age," she said.

"She doesn't like food," Rory replied.

"Did you bring any clothes for her?" Julia sounded timid and I didn't recognise her voice.

"No. She doesn't have any. She's got what she's wearing and some dresses that Em-Zee's makhulu sewed for her. They're awful things, really thick and uncomfortable, I was *more* than happy to leave them behind."

Deacon unfolded his arms and exhaled long and slow, like a much older man. "Well, I suppose we've got some shopping to do," he said.

Four pairs of eyes shot up at him. Deacon was evangelical about not going to the shops at all, ever, from The Cottage.

"Well?" he said. "The child needs clothes. Nappies. Shoes. And a bath."

Julia smiled at him, and reached out to touch Maya's cheek. The child drew away and dropped the mug.

Rory laughed, a high-pitched bark. "She's not used to white people. I'm the only one she's ever known!"

Cam lifted his head. "Do you smell burning?"

The frittata. "Shit!" I said, leaping up and grabbing oven gloves off the counter. I got the pan out amid a cloud of smoke. It had started blackening around the edges. "Anyone for slightly charred courgette frittata?"

"Lovely!" Julia said.

I took a wild guess that Rory didn't like food either, and I saw the remaining days of the holiday stretched out in front of me. I didn't think I'd make it to the other side of them without losing my mind or my cool, or both.

≈

While Julia ran a bath for Rory and Maya, I went shopping with Cam and Deacon. I let them walk out the door before me so I could covertly snatch my phone out of the basket in the pantry. I was hoping to go somewhere alone so I could check the *Fig & Brie* blog for the interview teaser.

If there had been anyone who knew the situation with Cam and Rory, I'd be dying to tell them about her dramatic return, but I realised, with a jolt, that there was nobody I could tell. Andile and my mother didn't know anything about Cam, other than that I'd married him in June and hadn't invited them.

"Did you know she was coming back?" Cam asked Deacon. They were sitting in the front seats of Deacon's car. I was starting to feel carsick in the back, swaying around the bends in the road.

"Not till this morning," Deacon replied. "She called us from a tickey box at the bus station in town at six."

The wind was back, white horses frothing in little waves out at sea at Soetwater. The surf was messy and opaque, the colour of the grey water Heather liked to water her flowers with.

"I can't believe it," Cam said, with wonder in his voice. "Part of me thought she was –"

"I know. I have to keep pinching myself," Deacon said, craning his neck to check for traffic at the intersection. Across the road, sad-looking camels were walking around a rocky field with small children on their backs.

"Why now?" I asked.

Cam turned to look at me, his eyebrows questioning.

"I mean, she doesn't seem all that happy," I said, meaning that she looked downright pissed off to be home.

Deacon caught my eye in the rearview mirror. "I keep forgetting you've not met Rory before. She's never been what I'd call a happy person."

"She doesn't really *do* happy," Cam said. "I think that's why her art's so incredible. She's always been kind of tortured. Like she's grappling with something deep down."

Depressed? I thought. Bipolar?

"Cyan. That means blue, right?" I asked, as we were getting out the car in the mall parking lot, which was disconcertingly full for nine in the morning.

"Oh my god! The new collection," said Cam. "It's this brilliant blue colour. She must have made it after Maya was born! Maya Cyan. She made it for her. Or maybe she did the collection before having Maya and named her after it."

Deacon grinned like he couldn't help himself. "Who knows. I'm just so glad she's home."

As we headed for the mall entrance, I thought about Rory glazing and firing her work while she was in the Transkei. Did she have a portable kiln? Where had she got the clay? What if she'd done that blue collection before she disappeared, and it had only been discovered or released recently?

But watching Deacon nudging Cam with his elbow as they walked ahead of me, I knew I could never share this kind of scepticism with them. I had to leave them to it, and work on unclenching my jaw.

They were so physically close, the Carlisles. They were nothing like Heather and me, who had never said the word "love" to each other, who didn't show affection or talk about feelings. That had been Lola's remit. She was the mother who cuddled, reassured and nurtured. A safe space. What did it feel like to be Cam, knowing you had not one but two safe spaces to lean into?

One of my earliest memories of Heather was of her slack-jawed expression when she caught me emptying her precious bottle of Anaïs Anaïs perfume, her single luxury in our simple life, down the toilet. Her mother had given it to her for her 21st birthday, she'd told me, and she only used it on special occasions. I was seven or eight, and filled with the exhilaration of knowing I would hurt her feelings, that I had some kind of power over her.

She'd been horrified, and, for once, completely speechless. She snatched the bottle from me, jerked me by my upper arm away from the toilet, and pushed me out of the bathroom before shutting the door behind me. From the other side, I heard a single strangled sob. It was the first time I'd witnessed a moment of weakness from her.

I stayed at the door, listening for more, wanting to knock and go in and beg her to forgive me. The sense of triumph had been replaced by a sour swirl of regret and shame in my stomach. By the time she came out, she had composed her face into her usual neutral, calm expression. We never spoke about it, but whenever I thought about our stilted, cold relationship, I thought of my small body poised outside her bathroom door, wanting to reach out to her, but finding myself frozen in place.

"I'll go to the pharmacy," I told them, catching up. "I'll

get nappies and baby wipes and a sippy cup. I'll meet you – where? Outside the supermarket?"

"How will you know what to get?" Cam asked. "What kind of nappies?"

"I'll figure it out," I said, thinking that Maya was about a size three, though for her age she should probably have been closer to a four. Sixteen months ago, in a different life – around the time Maya was born, in fact – I'd spent sleepless nights researching the cost of different nappy brands, adding up the impossible costs of raising a baby on my *Fig & Brie* salary by myself.

"She'll need a car seat, too," I called to Cam, who was moving to grab a supermarket trolley. "Go to the baby shop when you're done and ask them for one that works with a seatbelt."

An hour later, after hurrying through the pharmacy and settling on a bench outside the supermarket, I switched on my phone, navigated to the *Fig & Brie* blog, and discovered … nothing. They were still leading with a story on a DIY molecular gastronomy Christmas pudding. There was nothing new on the home page, and I hadn't received an email alert either.

They're probably running behind, I thought, short-staffed because of the holiday. I tried to check the media monitoring app to see if there'd been any media updates on Bushy Bun, before remembering I hadn't downloaded the app onto my phone. Cam and Deacon were heading towards me and it was too late to shove my phone in my bag before Deacon saw it.

"Sorry," I rushed to apologise.

Deacon laughed. "What do you mean? It's your phone!"

"Just don't use it when we get back to The Cottage," Cam said.

Deacon shrugged. "I made that rule ten years ago when you and Rory first started sitting with your noses in your phones instead of talking to Mom and me. It's not a big deal anymore."

I looked up at Cam. He wouldn't meet my eyes, and a muscle in his jaw jumped.

Making a big issue about the unplugged rule had been yet another way for him to try to stop time, I realised, to go back to the way things were before Rory had left.

I laced my fingers through his and tugged his hand, getting him to look down at me. "You okay?" I mouthed.

One of the corners of his mouth turned up, and he nodded. "Let's go get my niece – our niece – a car seat," he said.

Four

Rory slept for the rest of the day, and in the afternoon, Julia took Maya down to the beach. She came back with her about four minutes later. She was completely rigid in Julia's arms, arching backwards and screaming, big pearls of tears rolling down her face.

"It's probably the wind," Julia said, sitting Maya back down on the yellow chair, where she stopped crying immediately.

She was wearing a very fetching light blue T-shirt and a pink tulle skirt. This ensemble was probably the most practical and comfortable of the clothes Deacon and Cam had bought for her. She looked like a different child, a loved child, despite her sniffles and wet face. Julia had tied her hair in two defiantly jaunty bunches on either side of her head. For the first time, I noticed very light freckles across her nose, and there was something about the shape of her mouth, maybe the deep crease between her nose and her top lip, that was all Carlisle.

I was tucked up on the couch trying to read one of the crime novels stashed away in the bookcase in the corner of the lounge. Neither Deacon nor Julia had any idea how the books had ended up there; they didn't know they had a bookcase until I'd come to stay the year before, when I'd ploughed my way through all 12 of the yellowed, stiff-paged paperbacks.

Cam was lying on the couch next to me with his head resting on my crossed legs, flipping the bright blue bowl from hand to hand. After Julia left Maya on the chair, Cam sat up and flicked the cover of my book with his index finger. I looked over the top at him, aware of Maya's eyes on us.

"Should I go wake Rory up?" he asked.

"She looked shattered."

He lay back in my lap. "I've never noticed before how boring it is here when the wind's blowing. No TV. No internet. What did we used to do here the whole time?"

"We walked a lot last year, remember? We went for sundowners at the Bru Shack. We went musselling and made moulles frites and played board games. You sharpened all the knives in the kitchen on that whetstone you found on the beach." I had told him it wasn't a whetstone and that it wasn't a good idea, but he'd gone ahead anyway. I'd had to organise a professional knife-sharpening service to come in the following week.

"It's driving me nuts that I can't ask Rory where she's been. What she did the whole time she was away. Isn't this colour incredible?" He was holding the bowl up again, moving it so it caught the light.

It was iridescent, like a wet periwinkle shell; not quite one colour, with a smooth sheen to it.

Maya sneezed. Her nose was oozing grey mucous.

"How is it possible for one child to have so much snot?"

"Why don't you get her a tissue?" I suggested.

Cam wrinkled his nose but got up and disappeared into the guest loo off the side of the kitchen.

54

I had got used to Maya's unblinking eyes on me, and realised I was starting to warm to those ridiculous fluffy pigtails.

"I'm going to keep reading, if you don't mind," I said to her. "If you turn your head about thirty degrees to the left, you'll see there's quite a nice view outside. Seagulls, ships, etcetera."

"You know she can't understand you, right?"

Rory was standing behind me, silhouetted under the skylight, her hair like plumes of smoke around her shadowed face.

She came around to the front of the couch and flopped down next to me with her feet on the coffee table. She was wearing a cropped white vest and a pair of rumpled khaki shorts. There were deep spider-web cracks radiating out from the heels of her delicate, slender feet, and her toenails were long and yellow. How liberating it must be, I thought, to not care about what you looked like, not to be constantly grooming and modifying and keeping your body at bay. I was not a glamorous woman, not by a long shot, but there were little improvements I felt compelled to make, constantly: my eyebrows, my nails, my heels.

"So, Skye. Where are you from?" Rory turned her head to me slowly. Maya was reaching out to her and babbling, the first noise I'd heard her make other than crying, but Rory ignored her. I tried to keep my eyes off her fever blister, which was almost visibly throbbing.

"I grew up on a farm between White River and Hazyview. In Mpumalanga."

Rory's eyes didn't leave my face. "Any idea who owned your farm before your family? How they got their hands on it?"

I could feel a flush starting to creep up my chest, but was saved from replying by Cam emerging from the bathroom with a handful of tissues.

"You're awake!" he said, shoving the tissues at me and hugging Rory from behind.

I supposed I was going to have to take care of Maya's face and nose. I approached her slowly and managed to get two swipes in before she started full-blown howling. Rory made a big show of extricating herself from Cam and jerking Maya off the chair with more force than was strictly necessary.

"Where's Mom?" she asked, one arm around Maya and one hand on her other hip.

"I don't know. She tried to take Maya to the beach earlier, but it wasn't exactly a success."

"She might be upstairs with Dad. I'm going to check. I'm desperate for a walk, maybe I can leave Maya with Mom and we can go down to the Bru Shack, have a drink?" Rory started up the stairs.

"Did she say my dad was in their room?" Cam whispered to me. "I've never seen him taking a nap. He's never taken a sick day. I mean, he went back to work the day after the car accident when he broke his collarbone."

The sound of Rory knocking on a door upstairs and the murmur of Deacon and Julia's voices drifted down.

"I thought he was out kite-surfing," Cam said, sounding stricken.

"You know how it is – you wish for something for ages but when it finally happens, you don't know what to do with yourself." I closed the book, giving up, and slipped my feet into my sandals.

Rory came thudding back down the stairs, still holding Maya. "Mom wants to rest, she says. So we've got to take Maya with us. Unless you want to stay with her, Skye?"

Cam must have seen the look on my face because he said hurriedly, "Why don't we all go. I want you and Skye to get to know each other! I'm guessing Maya doesn't have a pram?"

From the way Rory was looking at me I could tell she wasn't particularly keen on getting to know me, either. But no way was I going to volunteer to play babysitter while she and Cam went out for beers.

"Yes, let's walk. It'll be fun," I said.

"Fun," Rory repeated flatly. She was opening the linen cupboard in the hallway, grabbing a bright orange beach towel. She leaned forward with Maya balancing on her back, koala-ing on, and deftly wrapped the towel around the baby. She tied it in a double-knot in front of her chest. Maya leaned her head between Rory's pointed shoulder blades and looked content for the first time all day.

"Oh," Cam said, taken aback, but pretending not to be. "Okay. I'll grab my wallet."

He moved like a shot upstairs and Rory said to me, "He'd better. When I'm not with Em-Zee I don't have any money."

"Didn't your dad …?" There'd been mention of Rory no longer using Deacon's credit card after she disappeared. I'd wondered how she'd been surviving. Her ceramics might sell for absurd sums of money, but still, it couldn't have been enough for her to live off for almost two years.

"Oh, come on, I won't touch his filthy money. Blood money, white monopoly capital, destroying the environment, killing people."

I didn't dare ask how living in her father's house without paying anything or contributing at all was different to literally taking money from him.

Cam jumped down the last three stairs and grabbed my hand. "Ready, everyone?" he asked as he reached to open the front door.

The sun was like cut glass and the wind flung stinging sand into my face. Cam grinned, Rory scowled, and I thought about how comforting it must feel to carry a baby, who loves you, tightly curled against your back.

≈

The rest of the days leading up to Christmas followed the same pattern. Rory slept till after lunch, Julia looked after Maya, Maya was ratty and on edge until Rory emerged, then the three of us – me, Cam and Rory, barefoot, with Maya strapped to her back – walked to the Bru Shack, the ramshackle beach bar that had been opening in season to serve cheap, warm beer to holiday-makers for the last 15 years.

Rory flirted with the bartender, a spotty surfer called Kestrel. Cam managed to down two full pints in the time it took me to get halfway through a single gin and tonic. Maya attracted coos and oohs and aahs from the sunburned middle-aged British swallows drinking and playing cards in the courtyard.

I cooked every night, ridiculous, complicated meals that took hours to prepare and that no one but Deacon ever thanked me for: Beef Wellington with homemade puff pastry; caponata lasagne with homemade pasta sheets; seafood paella with mussels I'd pried off the rocks that morning; Marcella Hazen's crispy-skinned roast chicken; sous-vide pork neck in homemade cornflour tacos; oxtail stew with dense cheddar dumplings. It was the kind of cooking I'd never enjoyed, traditional and meaty and enough to feed an army, with limited finesse and too much elbow grease.

But I had to do something to fill the hours between 6 p.m. and the sun going down at eight-thirty, while Julia, Rory and Cam lay sprawled on the couches facing the beach, drinking wine and braying about one or other occasion when Rory had said something completely inappropriate and Cam had tried to cover for her and Julia had been laughing so hard she nearly wet herself.

Deacon spent more and more time kite-surfing, taking advantage of the wind that didn't stop whipping around the house and rattling the windows. It made me feel tight-chested and claustrophobic. I imagined getting in the car and driving away to somewhere quiet, maybe in the mountains, where I could hole up in a cabin by myself and eat grapes and bits of cheese, read books and go hiking with only birds for company.

In the odd moments when Deacon was inside the house and sitting with his family, I'd catch a faraway look in his eye, a wistfulness I couldn't account for. He seemed bereft.

It was on what Cam liked to call Christmas Eve-Eve when Rory insisted on finding out how Cam and I had met. I had put a deep dish of salmon and mushroom tagliatelle with a cream sauce on the dining room table and had come back with a glass of water for myself. Deacon poured Viognier into the others' wine glasses. Rory took a gulp and narrowed her eyes across the table at me.

"I'm starting to think you guys got together in a really shameful way or something."

"Well, I don't know if you'd call it shameful, but let's say we both swiped left," Cam joked, dishing up. "Or right. You'd think it would be left, if you liked someone, wouldn't you?"

"I have no idea," I said.

Rory frowned. "What?"

"Tinder?" Cam said, passing the dish of food to Julia. "The sex app?"

"I think it's more of a dating app, isn't it?" I said.

"No, I think it's for sex," Julia said. Deacon raised his eyebrows at her, and we laughed.

"I don't know what you're talking about," Rory said in a flat tone, passing the dish directly to Deacon without dishing up. This was how it had been since she arrived; she didn't even pretend to eat. "I don't have a phone anymore. I'm not really sure what an app is."

"Never mind," Cam said. "A joke. No, Skye and I met through work."

"Your work?" Rory asked, tilting her empty wine glass in Deacon's direction so he could top her up.

"Sort-of both," Cam replied, using his fork to twirl his tagliatelle onto his spoon. He had lovely table manners; it was one of the first things I'd noticed and loved about him. It was like he'd been born knowing how to eat like a civilised person, unlike most people, including chefs and foodies. I may have grown up poor, but Heather was a stickler for table manners.

"It was when I worked for the magazine. Cam came in for an interview as one of the year's top independent suppliers," I said.

"I won, by the way," Cam said after he'd swallowed.

"What, a magazine award?" Rory asked.

"The mag releases lists of the top restaurants, delis, suppliers, small producers, stuff like that. Cam got the award for his business."

"You're kidding me," Rory said, leaning back and nibbling the remains of the nail on her index finger. "There's such a thing as an award for importing soy sauce? Who in god's name decided *that* was something the world needed?"

Cam deftly changed the subject. "I went to the magazine offices for a photo shoot and interview, and Skye was there to film a video of one of the recipes I'd featured in a mailer, you know, as a value-add thing for my clients. It was something wintery, I think?"

"Stuffed cabbage rolls," I replied. It had been one of the coldest winters on record in Cape Town, and I'd dreaded every take because it meant having to pull my gloves off in the draughty studio before starting filming.

"I asked her out for a coffee, and she said no. I asked her out for a drink a week later, and she said no. I asked her out to dinner, and she said no. I asked her to come with me to the Import-Export convention, which is always a total drag, and she said yes." Cam had already emptied his bowl. He smiled at Rory and squeezed my knee under the table.

"You know what they say," Rory said. "If at first you don't succeed, try and try again until you reach full-blown stalker mode."

"I thought he was joking!" I said. "I couldn't believe he was seriously asking me out." He was so handsome and successful, a proper grown-up, someone who could save me from my mundane life of work, running, cooking, work, running, ad infinitum, if I let him, and it seemed too miraculous to be true.

"We snuck out of the convention early and went to an all-night sushi place and stayed there talking and eating California rolls till three in the morning," Cam added.

"I think it's romantic," Julia said, poking her fork into her bowl. "The next thing we knew, Cam told us Skye was moving in with him."

"She was living in a terrible place, I could never stay over, it was a big old Victorian house in Mowbray that was full of students, practically a commune – people made noodles in the kettle!"

"A few months later they'd opened Bushy Bun together, and a month or so after that, they were engaged! And that's when we met Skye, and of course we've never looked back," Julia finished, grinning at me over her fork.

"Sweet," Rory said, a bitter edge to her voice. "You got married when?"

"Six months ago," Cam replied. "Exactly a year after we met. A winter wedding. It was beautiful. We had it at that boutique hotel in the North West where we used to stay after the polo. It was small, Mom and Dad and the two of us."

"That's all?" Rory seemed to perk up, having caught a whiff of something.

"We basically eloped," I said. "That's what I tell people."

Cam nodded. "Skye's not really close to her family. Well, it's just her mom at home, right, love?"

"Yep," I said.

"Lola, the lady who worked for you while you were growing up, she passed away, what, ten years ago?" Cam said. "Her son, what was his name again? The one your mom took in and raised? Where's he now?"

The smoked salmon ribbons turned slimy in my mouth, the sauce immediately a chalky slush. "Andile," I said, swallowing hard. "He's living in Durban."

This narrative, the son-of-our-domestic-worker spiel, was the easiest one for people like the Carlisles to understand. It'd been the story Andile and I'd had to tell the kids at school and anyone visiting the farm who didn't know us. Until we were six, when Mandela was released, and Heather and Lola told us we didn't have to pretend anymore. But the suburbs and farms of White River back then were – well, very white. And very small. Hardly anyone we knew had one white parent and one black parent, and absolutely nobody had two moms.

I had hinted to Cam that Lola had never been our domestic worker and had told him that she was quite a slob and had probably never cleaned anything in her life, but I'd held back from telling him the whole story. It was probably too late to tell him now.

"Your mother adopted your domestic worker's son? What about *her* feelings? Did he ever learn to speak his mother tongue? Did he ever learn about his own culture?" Rory's head was cocked to one side, her eyes hard and flat as stones.

"No, not really."

"Did he at least get to keep his surname?"

That, at least, I could tell the truth about. "Yes. Gcobane."

"I'll bet anything his mom's name wasn't really Lola. Her real name. Gcobane's a Xhosa name, right?"

"It was Nolitha. She'd been called Lola since she was a baby. Her mother used to work for a family in Port Alfred in the Eastern Cape and the first day she brought Lola to work on her back, they'd misheard her and thought she'd said the baby's name was Lolita. They ended up calling her Lola, and it stuck."

I was bracing myself for the lecture about the white-washing of African heritage and history, and how problematic the domestic work culture was in South Africa and the rest of the continent. I had grown up listening to Heather and Andile having these sorts of discussions over dinner, Lola and I rolling our eyes at each other when things got heavy, starting our own conversations about that season's produce and the new dishes we could make for the guests.

My ache for Lola travelled from my seized-up throat to the tips of my fingers and the surface of my scalp, through all my cells.

Cam butted in before Rory could respond, and I almost jumped with fright when he slammed his empty wine glass too hard on the table. "I've got one thing you'll love, Rory," he said. "About Skye's name."

"That's enough, you two," Deacon said, gathering up our bowls. "You're making Skye uncomfortable."

Julia stood up, too. "More wine? I've got a case of some easy-drinking red that I brought back from Bandol."

Cam took my hand. "Please can I tell Rory about your name? It's such a good story!"

"Fine," I said. I wished I had a glass of wine to pour down my throat and drown my anxiety. But Deacon knew not to offer me any with dinner. One gin and tonic a day was about my limit, and more alcohol than I'd had for a long time. Since before the mugging.

"Get this. Her real name is Karoo-Sky. As in, the sky of the Karoo. Her mom's a total hippie! She's called herself Skye with an 'e' since she was like, ten. Isn't that awesome? Karoo-Sky Moore."

"Karoo-Sky Carlisle?" Rory asked.

I nodded, tired in my bones.

"Personally, I think marriage is this really archaic tradition, but I guess at least you're sticking to the full patriarchal package. If you're not a feminist, there's no real issue with changing your surname, right?"

Julia appeared before I could say the first thing that had come to mind, that I was regretting more than changing my name at this point.

"Enough with the diatribe, Rory. The name thing is a very personal choice," Julia said, twisting the screw-cap off a bottle and smiling at me a little droopily.

"The personal is political, Mother," Rory replied, and passed her glass across.

"The thing is," I said, knowing it was pointless to argue, but unable to stop myself. "If I'd had my father's surname growing up, changing it to my husband's wouldn't really be an issue, would it? I'd be swapping one man's name for another. But Moore is my mother's surname, her father's I suppose, because she and *my* father were never married. So yes, I grappled with it. But it was a choice I made. And isn't that the most important thing about feminism? Women being free to choose?"

Rory smiled and swirled the blood-red wine in her glass under her nose. "I'm never getting married. I don't think I could fulfil my agency as a woman or an artist if I was contractually bound to a man."

"While we're talking about romance, why don't you tell us about Em-Zee," Cam said, scrambling to keep a handle on this downhill conversation. "Why didn't you bring your celeb bae with you? Did he not want to meet your family?"

For a few beats, the only sound was the tinkle of Deacon putting dishes in the scullery.

"What do you think, Cameron?" Rory asked. "Why do you think I'm here? Do you think things are all peachy between me and Em-Zee? They obviously fucking *aren't*."

She smashed her empty wine glass against the edge of the table, where it exploded. She pushed herself up off her chair and stormed towards the stairs, a blur of auburn hair, anger coming off her in waves.

Cam hurried to follow her.

Julia watched them go, drinking her wine in one swallow. She picked up the glass she'd poured for Cam before weaving her way to the kitchen. "I'll get a dustpan," she called over her shoulder.

I'd come to admire the way Julia could load the dishwasher and tidy the kitchen single-handedly while she was three sheets to the wind, but gathering up the scattered glass was surely beyond her. I started picking up the bigger pieces in my hands, but she clasped my wrists and helped me shake the jagged splinters into the dustpan.

"I don't want you getting hurt," she said, slowly sweeping up the glass. It didn't seem fair, I thought, watching her crouched over, that she was the one left to clean up.

As I turned away, it occurred to me that maybe it *was* fair. Andile and I were proof that nurture trumped nature every time. We were raised by our mothers without a father figure in sight, and the people we'd turned into were direct products of both of them, of Lola's embracing arms and Heather's spine of steel.

Rory had been nurtured her whole life by this warm, welcoming woman, and maybe if she'd been made to pick up the pieces, from the beginning, she'd be less of a mess as an adult.

≈

On my way up to bed, I found Deacon sitting outside Rory's bedroom, leaning against the wall, with his hands upturned in his lap, balancing an invisible and heavy weight.

He got up and followed me onto the widow's walk. Outside, it was cool, a thin veil of clouds covering the stars and a fingernail moon reclined halfway up the sky.

"How're you doing?" Deacon asked, leaning on the railing next to me.

"I'm fine! Wish the wind would stop, but, you know. Fine."

He nodded and looked out to sea. "I feel I should apologise for how Rory's talking to you. You know she's jealous, don't you? She could never stand any of Cam's girlfriends. She pulled a knife on one of them. Did he tell you?"

My head snapped in his direction.

"I guess not. He's not particularly proud of it. Rory said she was joking afterwards but it felt very real. It was while Cam was at varsity. He had this gorgeous girlfriend, really well turned out, and, you know, very expensive looking. I can't remember her name, she didn't last long, for obvious reasons. He brought her home to Joburg when Rory was staying with us. She was going through one of her bad patches at the time, had a leave of absence for a few months from art school."

I wondered if right now qualified as one of her bad patches.

"Over dinner one night, the girl asked Rory something she didn't like, or in a way she didn't like. I'm hazy on the details. But the next minute, Rory's leaning over the table with her steak knife up against the girl's throat and she's just glaring at her. The girl burst into tears and Rory carried on eating. The girl flew home the next day and we never heard about her again."

"Huh," I squeezed out. In a corner of my brain I was struggling with the image of Rory eating.

He carried on like he hadn't heard me. "What got to me the most about the whole thing was how pleased she seemed when the girl started crying. Like that's what she'd been aiming for. She's always been so difficult. I thought it was the artistic temperament, but, really, I'm so worried about her." He dragged the heels of his hands down his forehead and into his eye sockets, rubbing them hard. "She's not a stable person. I can see that. But Julia and Cam, it's like they don't see it. And she's got a daughter, for god's sake! This tiny child that doesn't seem – she doesn't seem normal to you, does she?" His eyes darted across my face, searching.

"I don't know much about kids," I said. He wanted me to say Maya seemed fine, but I couldn't. I'd never seen her walk. She'd never said any words. The only thing I'd seen her eat was jelly, she ate it by the tub, Julia making big jewel-coloured bowls of it in hues I'd forgotten existed, so bright they were almost fluorescent, and absolutely not the colour of anything that a tiny human should be eating.

"I don't know what's going to happen to them. Are they going to come back to Joburg with us? Are Julia and I going to end up raising the baby? What's to stop Rory leaving again? I'm sorry to dump all this on you, but I can't talk to Julia frankly about Rory – I haven't been able to for years. Decades. She never wanted to get Rory properly assessed, she didn't want her to be *labelled*, so she never got help."

He was so vulnerable and wide open and I hated this. I hoped he didn't start crying. "Please don't apologise for Rory. I'm used to snide comments and rude questions about my upbringing. I'm a big girl," I said, hoping we could pretend from tomorrow that everything was normal.

"You're really not, though, Skye," he said, and I could swear he contemplated ruffling my hair like you'd do to a small boy or a puppy. "And I *am* sorry for all the questions. You're a very private person. I don't want you to ever feel like you have to talk about anything you're not comfortable with. Not with us. We're family. We've got the rest of our lives to learn more about you."

The breeze picked up Deacon's shirt collar and lifted the top of his hair. I smiled at him, seriously considering leaving. These people were not my family. As we stood up there on the widow's walk, I got the chilling feeling that I was seeing things clearly for the first time since I'd agreed to marry Cam. What had I got myself into?

≈

I lay awake in the loft in the dark, waiting for Cam to come to bed. My heart was galloping along unevenly, like I'd drunk too much coffee and was waiting for something awful to happen. It seemed as if the universe was conspiring against me, that I wasn't allowed to be happy now that I'd expanded my life and my heart to include Cam and this complicated family, that this was my punishment for deviating from the small, manageable life I'd had before I'd met him.

In the last five years, since leaving the crushing pressure at Mon Petit, I'd given up so many vices: coffee, alcohol, chasing an ambitious career by working unhealthily long hours. I'd spent years aspiring to get through each day without giving in to despair and had found a rhythm I thought I could sustain, thinking that I had whittled my life down to something attainable and so reduced that it *had* to make me happy. But then I'd met Cam, and I'd lost the control over the life I'd spent so long trying to achieve.

By the time Cam shuffled into the room, I was feeling properly sorry for myself, wishing for once that I could drop my careful defences, that I could open up to him.

Instead, I lay barely breathing, watching the shadow of my husband undress, pulling his Comrades shirt over his head, and falling face-first on the bed.

I touched his face and he jerked away with a gasp.

"Fuck, Skye, I thought you were asleep."

"Sorry. I was waiting for you."

"Ah, I'm sorry, love, I can't. Too much wine. Rory wouldn't come out her room so Mom and I drank like the whole case."

"I wasn't waiting for *that*."

"Okay, good, maybe in the morning if you don't go running so bloody early." He pulled me close to him and rested his chin on the top of my head, and I knew in a breath's time he'd be asleep.

I lifted his arm off me and leaned over to switch on the bedside lamp. Cam looked up groggily.

"Why didn't you tell me about Rory trying to stab your girlfriend with a steak knife?" My voice came out high-pitched and hysterical.

Cam pushed his hair out of his face. "Did my dad tell you about that? It was meant to be a joke."

"You think putting a knife to someone's throat is funny?"

"Rory was pissed off with her, she didn't like the way she dressed or something. Or the way she spoke. Rory's got a temper, I won't lie, but she wasn't *actually* going to stab her."

"You realise how crazy this is? That you're talking about the time your sister almost stabbed your girlfriend?"

Cam groaned into his pillow. "It's not a big deal, it was so long ago, can we please go to sleep? She was in a bad place, she's much better now, much more normal."

I sat up and pulled the covers off him.

"She is not normal, Cam. She is a wreck. She scares me. You never stand up for me around her."

Cam sat up, his nostrils flaring. I'd never seen him angry before.

"Why can't you be *happy* for me? Why can't you see how much I needed to know that Rory was okay, how much I needed her to come back? You're making this all about you, and it isn't."

He got out of bed and started yanking his jeans back on. "You know, Skye, if you'd had something good happen to you, I'd be happy for you because I love you. It's like you're incapable of being happy."

When we'd first got together, Cam said that what made him fall in love with me was that I was real and not full of bullshit like all the other women he knew, with their flattering selfies and filters and fakeness. He said I was so comfortable with myself, so calm and straightforward.

I needed to tell him about Lola, and about what happened after the mugging. I needed to tell him about keeping my life manageable and trying to get through it one day at a time.

"I'm trying to be happy."

"I'm sorry it's so hard for you. But I'm not going to let you make me unhappy too, not when my twin's come back from the dead and I've found out I've got a little niece and my restaurant's the most popular place in Cape Town and it's two days till Christmas." He pinched his nose to stop it from running. "I'm going to sleep downstairs."

I expected him to slam the door, but he pulled it shut softly behind him. I turned out the light and tried to time my breathing with the rolling of the waves, but when I eventually fell asleep, daylight was already seeping in around the blinds.

Five

I woke up a few hours later with gritty eyes and a pressure headache. Christmas Eve. I showered and dressed in the same crumpled denim top and white cotton shorts as the day before. I grabbed a banana and my phone on the way out the house. It was already 10 o'clock, and eerily quiet. There was not a breath of wind. I felt the concentrated warmth of the sun and heard the sounds of summer – the tinkling of an ice cream man's bicycle, muffled house music from the teenagers in the mansion next door, the roar of motorbikes on a breakfast run – distantly, as if there was a membrane between me and the rest of the world that I couldn't penetrate.

I drove to the mall, hoping to sit at the coffee shop and do some proper online digging to find out about the *Fig & Brie* story. I knew I could have done it at the house since Deacon had waived his unplugged policy, but, somehow, the idea of using my phone in the loft or on the couch or on the beach didn't feel right.

Plus, I thought, pulling into the mall parking lot, a discordant silent disco of brake lights and indicators and reverse lights, I needed to pick up pomegranate seeds for the gammon for Christmas lunch.

After eventually finding a parking spot at the gym across the street, I'd changed my mind: we'd have to do without the pomegranate garnish. The mall was a nightmare, full of strung-out young parents pushing trolley-loads of plastic toys, shrieking children in the snaking queues to Father Christmas, teenaged tourists mooching around in bikinis and sarongs and uneven sunburns, and those Dead Sea potions salespeople reaching a more desperate, aggressive pitch than usual.

I ducked into the packed coffee shop and managed to slide into a booth at a table at the window before anyone else could claim it. There wasn't a waiter anywhere to be seen. I got out my phone and switched it on, making a mental note to text my mother to wish her a happy Christmas.

My phone started vibrating with incoming messages that must have come in while it was turned off. It pinged again, and again, and again. Two middle-aged women at the table next to me turned at the buzzing, which I tried to stop by covering my phone with my hand, but still it vibrated endlessly against my palm. I muted the sound and gave the women an apologetic smile.

When it stopped vibrating in my lap after five solid minutes, I opened WhatsApp and saw the number 13 in the little green bubble next to an unknown contact. But the profile picture was achingly familiar – the world's widest, toothiest grin. My brother, Andile, who must have changed his number since the last time I'd contacted him.

Thirteen messages from Andile out of the blue could only mean bad news. My finger hovered over the messages before I lost my nerve and exited the app.

My home screen showed 207 Twitter notifications. As I stared at the icon of the blue bird, another came, and then another.

I managed the Bushy Bun Twitter account sporadically and didn't have my own, so the notifications could only be related to the restaurant. My heart sped up as I imagined a flurry of well wishes and compliments in the wake of Talia's interview. I decided to leave the good stuff for last and to go back to Andile's messages. The tweets could cheer me up after I discovered what fresh hell Andile had to tell me.

I ordered a chai latte from the harried waiter and clicked next to Andile's number in WhatsApp. There were 10 separate voice notes followed by three text messages. I read the texts first.

From three days ago: "Roo. I can see you haven't listened to your voice notes yet so I'm sending this to you as a text in the hopes it's more likely to get through to you. Where are you? Are you going home for Christmas? Heather's not coping so well. The Pines in trouble. Pls call."

From yesterday: "Me again. I'm home, flew in from DBN today. Heather won't admit it, but The Pines seems to be going bankrupt. Any chance you could come stay to help out? I'd have thought you needed somewhere to hide out during the shitstorm."

Shitstorm?

And from this morning: "Is this still your number? Phone me, Roo. Heather's in denial but the books look bad."

The waiter brought my drink, sloshing cinnamon-flecked milk onto the table as he set it down.

My breath came out in a relieved whoosh. Yes, this was a crisis, but it didn't have anything to do with me. Not directly, anyway. What could I do about The Pines's books? Andile had been overseeing them since Lola had died. Heather had mentioned it once or twice, but she hadn't said anything about money. She wouldn't, though, I thought, slurping the lukewarm, fragrant drink too quickly.

The guests' payments had always been done directly into the farm's bank account, on which, as I understood it, Andile had signing power. I wondered what could have gone wrong. Lola's business plan for what to do with the farm after 1990 had paid off, and the yuppies who stayed at The Pines paid handsomely for the privilege of taking an off-the-grid sabbatical on a scenic "working farm" in the middle of nowhere. They had bankrolled tuition and the upkeep of the farm for the last 20-something years. Unless Heather had been swindled, or given the money away.

"Anything else for you?" The waiter quivered at my elbow. There was a queue of people waiting for tables. I peered round the waiter and saw a stressed-out barista behind the espresso machine, multiple orders stuck on slips of paper on the wall behind his head.

"Uh, a coffee, please."

"What kind?"

"Um, an espresso?"

"Single or double?"

"I don't care!"

"Sorry?"

"A double, make it a double."

He blinked very fast and turned on his heel, leaving me to Andile's voice notes. I held the phone up horizontally so the speaker was right next to my ear, and hit the play button on the first one, sent on 17 December, which was the day Rory had arrived, and the last time I'd checked my phone.

"Hey, Roo. Long time. Listen, don't be freaked out by this, but I have a Google Alert set up for your name so that I don't miss any major news about you because you're so hopeless at keeping in touch. So, this morning for the first time in like a year, since you started your restaurant, I got a few notifications and went to check it out. It seems that your name is linked to this article on some online gossip site called DFI? Down, Far and Impersonal, apparently? Looks like it's Cape Town-based? Google it."

I pulled the phone away from my ear to frown at it, and realised that it had automatically jumped to playing the next voice note, sent a few minutes later. I shoved the bottom of the phone back against the bones of my ear.

"It occurs to me that this might not be your number anymore, I'm not getting two ticks, here. And you don't have a profile picture or anything."

The next one: "Roo, in case you don't see the article, it's about something you said at an interview with *Fig & Brie?*" I felt my throat constrict. "And that's been picked up by the gossip site. I did a bit of digging and I see they're in the same stable. Before you started your restaurant, you used to work at *Fig & Brie*, right? Again, don't freak out, I'm not stalking you, I swear. Anyway, I assume you would know what they put out there because that's where you used to work, but I checked Twitter and there's been no response from the restaurant account, so I thought maybe you had no idea? The fact that I've still not had any blue ticks makes me think you still have no idea? Okay. Well, call me when you get this, please. Or at least message me."

18 December, three of them:

"It's getting bad, Roo. I hope you see this soon or you'll have a total PR nightmare on your hands. I don't know much about this stuff, but it seems to me the nightmare's unfolding as we speak. Well, as I speak. Everyone's talking about it on Twitter, and there's an incriminating hashtag that's trending, and that Taiwanese vlogger Cindy has a video up about it and it's getting so many hits."

He'd always talked like this, a mile a minute, words pouring out of him like warm honey, but his cosily familiar voice couldn't soften the blow of words like "PR nightmare" and "incriminating hashtag" and "vlogger". What the fuck was happening?

A more sombre tone in the next few. "Roo. Look Cindy up on YouTube. Look for her video that has the most hits. That's the one about your place. Go check out her tweets. You should also read that DFI piece but I'd stay away from the comments, which I think is a good rule in life, generally."

"If what they're saying is true and it might not be because this is Down, Far and Impersonal we're talking about, not worth the paper or, uh, the screen it's printed on, but if it is true, your restaurant is in some serious shit."

19 December, two:

"If you need a PR agency, give me a shout – I can hook you up with someone I know."

"Okay, this is getting ridiculous. I thought I'd give you a heads-up but I have absolutely no clue where you are or if you'll ever get these. If you leave this any longer it's going to explode. You want to know what people are saying? The words 'modern-day slavery' are being thrown around."

20 December:

"Roo! I just read that someone's spray-painted the hashtag SlaveryMustFall all over the shop-front of your place."

The final one:

"I don't know what to say. I hope you're okay. Take care of this. I've got some other shit I'm dealing with, but I hope you can sort this out somehow. Alright. Bye."

The sides of my mouth filled with saliva. I was about to throw up. The waiter delivered my double espresso and

I left a hundred-rand note on the table, walking out while he was scrabbling in his apron for change.

I made it to the bathroom in time to slam into a stall ahead of a woman who'd been waiting, and promptly emptied the milky contents of my stomach into the toilet bowl while she bashed on the door and yelled, "There was a queue, you know!"

I sat on the closed toilet seat, pushed the home button on my phone, opened my browser and started searching. I couldn't bear to open the Twitter app.

Half an hour later, I had to coach myself to breathe when I eventually got the nerve to leave the toilet stall, attracting curious looks from the women in the queue. I pressed the lever on the silver soap dispenser with the heel of my shaking hand. A dribble of neon-pink goo eked out. I wet my fingers and pressed them against my eyes, my heart thudding in my chest and my stomach roiling. My armpits prickled as I started perspiring.

Zhou. This was all about Zhou.

I had to get back to The Cottage. I had to do some kind of damage control. I had to ask Cam what to say on Twitter. He'd been running his own business for years. He'd know what to do about this.

I left everything as it was, all the hateful tweets and the vindictive, violent, vitriolic comments on Cindy's YouTube channel that reeked of mob mentality. My god, Cam was going to be so angry, angrier than I was with myself. I was tempted to punch a wall or physically hurt myself some other way, and probably would have if I wasn't in a public place.

And Deacon. He was already so anxious, and now he was going to have to deal with this. It hurt to think about disappointing him.

I bought a bottle of water at a kiosk outside the mall and drank half of it before starting the car. I wiped my hands on my shorts, willed them to stop shaking and forced myself to concentrate on the road. The last thing I needed was to be in an accident. Although, I thought fleetingly, if I was in a car wreck, they couldn't be angry with me, about anything, not about not supporting Cam and Rory's relationship, not about letting slip the secret that our whole restaurant was built on, not about opening a Bushy Bun Twitter account without properly monitoring it or having any kind of strategy to cope with bad PR.

I was still half-seriously contemplating the best place to run my car off the road when I saw a familiar figure trudging up the road to Misty Cliffs from Scarborough. She was holding something in her hands and her head was hanging low. I overshot The Cottage and did a U-turn in the middle of the road, pulling up alongside her and putting my hazards on.

Rory turned to look at me sullenly as I opened the passenger door.

"Need a lift back to The Cottage?"

She was wearing a completely see-through white maxi dress. I could see the faint outline of her nipples and that she wasn't wearing panties. She wasn't wearing shoes, either. But when she got in the car, the most startling thing was the yellow party-sized bag of potato chips she had clutched in one hand. She shut the door, sniffed, and shoved a handful of chips in her mouth. I stared at her as she crunched, flecks stuck on her lip. I imagined the sting of the salt on her fever blister and the raw red tips of her fingers where her nails used to be.

"I can't do this anymore," she said in a cracked voice. She offered the bag to me and I shook my head. Maybe this was how she'd been sustaining herself, I thought, with junk food shovelled in on the sly.

"I miss him so much." More chips, more crunching.

"Em-Zee?"

She nodded. "He sent us home, me and Maya. Someone in the opposition found out about where I came from, the money, and it's bad for his reputation. He's supposed to be a man of the people, of the poor, and here he is shacked up with his rich white artist girlfriend and their love child. So his advisors put us on a bus when we got to East London."

I exhaled. A GP Jeep, one of the obnoxious orange ones with black flames painted on the hood, hooted at me as a line of cars crawled past us in the opposite direction, so I started the engine and eased out into the road.

"Have you spoken to him?"

She shook her head. "I don't know where they are, but I think they'll be around Port Elizabeth tomorrow, there's a rally happening in Motherwell, I think I heard them talking about it." She wet her finger and stuck it into the bag, picking up crumbs and licking them off. "He was always annoyed with me that Maya couldn't talk. I said it was probably a bilingualism thing. She's still only little. Maybe I could teach her to say 'Daddy' before we see him again."

We pulled up under the carport and Rory rolled up the packet and lodged it into the space between her seat and the centre console. We caught each other's eye, and for the first time hers were clear instead of hard and opaque.

"What are you going to do?"

She straightened her shoulders and said, "I don't have a choice."

She got out the car and slammed the door, and I hoped that whatever she was planning to do would take attention away from the fact that I may or may not have destroyed the restaurant's reputation and my marriage in a single moment of spectacular ignorance.

≈

"Isn't it the most glorious day?" were the first words I heard when I followed Rory into the kitchen. Julia was stretched out on one of the sea-facing couches wearing an orange kimono and a wide-brimmed hat, with her dogs standing at attention next to her face. She was holding a tall fizzy drink with a yellow twirly plastic straw.

"Maya and I sat on the beach for ages watching Grandpa and Uncle Cam body boarding, didn't we, love?"

Cam had Maya on his hip, rocking her from side to side in the open doorway leading down to the beach. He was wearing board shorts and a rash vest that still looked wet, and I caught something close to adoration or at least curiosity on Maya's face as she watched him. But as soon as she saw Rory, she lunged, and Cam almost dropped her.

Cam caught sight of me and shot me a sheepish look. I remembered suddenly about our fight the night before. It felt like it had happened in a previous relationship, a different life.

Rory took Maya from Cam and held her aloft, examining her face.

"Did you sunscreen her, Mother?"

"Of course. We don't want her getting any more freckles. Don't get me wrong, Skye, yours are adorable," Julia said with slurred sibilants, "But I'd rather be safe than sorry with my darling grandbaby."

"Skye's freckles are about the most adorable thing in the world," Cam said, coming up to me and planting a kiss on the crown of my head. "Sorry about last night," he whispered in my ear, looping his arms around my neck from behind. When I tried to lean away from his damp clothes, he pulled me closer.

"Where were you, dear?" Julia asked Rory, who was in the kitchen dishing a jelly into a plastic cup.

"At the Bru Shack."

"Little early, isn't it?" Cam teased.

"Not for G and T, and not for me!" Julia said, merrily waving her glass in the air. "This one had cucumber in it too, which I ate, so I may as well be having a green smoothie. I'm toasting the weather. Thank god for a windless day."

"I need to talk to you," I said, turning around to face Cam. His eyes fixed on mine.

"Okay. I'm going upstairs to change, Mom," he called to Julia, who sloshed some liquid from her glass onto the rug in reply.

When we got to the loft, Cam started stripping and speaking in a long, fast string of words that I struggled to catch. I heard, "don't remember" and "must have been something completely idiotic" and "sorry if I hurt your feelings", and it briefly crossed my mind that this was the definition of a faux-pology and that if I hadn't checked my phone this morning I'd have plenty of reason to still be seething about the night before, but when he paused as he pulled a shirt on, I interjected.

"Andile sent me some WhatsApps."

Cam ran his hand through his hair, flicking tiny water droplets onto the floor between us. "Andile? That's weird. We were talking about him last night."

"He found some stuff about Bushy Bun on Twitter."

"Oh, yes?" He wrung the water out his rash vest through the open window and slung it over the hook on the back of the door.

I couldn't feel my hands. "It's bad."

"Did something happen? Wait, let me go get my phone." He was out the door before I could stop him.

I chased him down both flights of stairs but couldn't match his long-legged pace, almost tripping down the last two. I eventually caught up with him when he was already in the pantry switching his phone on. Rory and Julia looked up from the lounge. Maya was sitting on the floor and digging into her cup with a teaspoon. I tried to close the pantry door, but it had swollen open.

"What are you doing? That door hasn't been closed in years. If ever."

"I wanted some privacy. I have to tell you something that I didn't tell you before. At that interview with *Fig & Brie*, Zhou came up."

Cam watched me, completely still except for the jumping muscle in his jaw.

I swallowed. "But I asked Talia not to say anything about it because he might get deported."

"His getting deported is the least of our worries." He entered his password, which I noticed for the first time was my date of birth. He must really love me, I thought absently.

"Now it looks like instead of the interview going into *Fig & Brie*, Talia gave it to the DFI team."

"DF what?" Cam's lips were pulled tight against his teeth.

"Down, Far and Impersonal. That Cape Town gossip site that's in the same building. They got a bit carried away with the whole thing, the headline's awful, and totally not true, but from there it kind of escalated."

Cam breathed in slowly through his nose. "Send me what you have," he said. "I'm going to get my dad."

He left me in a swirl of sea-scented air in the window-less pantry. I used my fingerprint to wake my phone up and opened my browser.

I forwarded Cam everything. The link to the Down, Far and Impersonal article, "This will make you want to boycott your favourite Cape Town hotspot". The Twitter page with the tweets that included the hashtag "#BushyBunSlave", including the independent restaurant reviewer with more than 50 000 followers whose tweet said, "So tired of these trendy CPT restaurant owners who are so far up their own arses they'll do anything for queues out the door. #BushyBunSlave". Cindy's YouTube video where she filmed herself standing outside the darkened restaurant, speaking about this as yet another example of white people and Westerners using Asian bodies for their own personal gain, not giving credit where it's due, turning Asian food and lifestyles, often borne out of poverty and famine, into a novelty, and why has Zhou, the real chef, the real foodie, been totally overlooked, who knows what kind of conditions the poor man is living in, he was basically kidnapped from his home country to spend his days in a tiny restaurant kitchen making the food of his forefathers for zero credit and probably a pittance, it was high time that Asian people were allowed to create the meals they loved for an appreciative audience and were celebrated for it instead of being pawns in a couple of ambitious, greedy white people's plans for foodie fame and fortune.

The worst, the very worst part about all of this, was that I couldn't fault her on a single thing. How had I let this happen? I was raised by a pair of gay mothers in a biracial family. I wasn't the typical greedy white person she was talking about. But I was scared and stupid and so desperately grateful to be working in a kitchen again that I'd let this happen. To everyone else, I probably did look like that kind of white person. The ignorant kind. The type who snorted when people spoke about white privilege, who didn't believe in it, who thought race didn't matter.

I sank to sitting on the floor in the gloomy pantry. I sent Cam links to the news sites that had picked up on the story, with their loosely collated articles that rehashed what had been said on Twitter ("Cape Town foodie influencers react to accusations of modern-day slavery"). I was about to forward him the voice note from Andile about the graffiti on the restaurant windows when the silhouetted figures of Deacon and Cam appeared in the pantry doorway. I hit send.

I had to listen to Andile's messages again, watching Cam and Deacon's shadows as they heard them for the first time.

Cam swore and left. Deacon was leaning against the pantry doorway and I was stuck, not wanting to push past him, but feeling the mildewed walls and the laden shelves bearing down on me.

"Can I get you a top-up, Mother?" I heard Rory ask, followed by the scrabble of Dusk and Dawn's claws on the wooden floor, then a heavy thud from the direction of the lounge and an "Oof!" in Julia's voice.

Deacon and I peered out the doorway. Julia was sitting on the floor next to the couch, giving it an annoyed look as if it had thrown her off.

"Oh, for heaven's sake, Julia, go to bed," Deacon said. "Rory, help your mother up the stairs, please. Take some water with you."

Rory let Julia lean on her one step at a time. They were so different – wobbly, round Julia, with her skew hat and half-mast eyes, and Rory with her thick plumes of copper hair, an exquisite geometry of angles. I wondered if Julia had ever recognised any part of herself in Rory, a glimmer of something, the shape of her eyes, or her small ears, or the curve of her jaw. Surely that was something you'd seek out, as a mother, a sign that this girl came from you, incontrovertible evidence that, on some level, you were made of the same stuff. Heather and I looked nothing alike, either.

Maya started banging her cup on the glass coffee table, and Deacon went to her. I followed him slowly and watched him gently wipe the stickiness off her hands, talking to her in low tones.

"I'm sorry," I said.

"I know," he replied.

"What can I do?"

Deacon sighed. "We'll have to do some kind of damage control, but I don't think there's anything we can do between Christmas and New Year's. I'll wait till the beginning of January and bring a PR agency on board. We'll have to make a big gesture if we've got any hope of salvaging this. Pull Zhou in and set the story straight, say that he was never supposed to be a secret."

My whole body was numb. "Cam's pretty angry."

Deacon stood up, balling the dirty wet wipe in his fist. "You know, I don't mind about the business, if it doesn't ever pick up – and you should expect a boycott, at least initially. We'll take the hit and shut it down. But I feel for Cam."

I nodded, my eyes on Maya, who was wearing a navy tunic with twinned red cherries embroidered on it. She was patting Dusk or Dawn – I'd never known which was which – letting the dog lick her fingers, and she was smiling, a thousand-watt grin that should have been celebrated because it represented so many good, new things.

"Bushy Bun was his chance to make a name for himself. It was his own thing, his passion project, and because of a silly mistake it's on the line."

He didn't say *my* silly mistake. He didn't say because of me. But that's what he meant, and his eyes were like two windows with the blinds down.

It didn't matter what I did with or for the Carlisles. I would never be first priority for any of them. They'd all choose one another first – even if Rory was unhinged, Cam was a selfish man-child, Julia was a drunk and Deacon would shut you out as soon as you transgressed.

"There's nothing we can do about it right now. Except close the Twitter account, disable the website, take down the Facebook page. Can you manage that? I'm going to take Cam out for a stiff drink. Keep an eye on Maya while I'm gone, please."

The only sound after he left was the screen door of the kitchen banging against the door frame.

≈

Oh, how glorious it was to be able to completely relax. I'd forgotten how much I loved alcohol's quick and easy tranquillising properties. Since the mugging, I hadn't let myself go completely, didn't trust myself to loosen up or concede an inch of control. Look at me now, not in control at all and it was amazing.

I took the last swallow of my – counting the lemon wedges in my glass – fifth very generous gin and tonic and watched Maya sleeping on the kilim rug. Her red leather pumps were discarded next to her. She eschewed shoes. So did I, I decided, trying to take off my sandals.

The buckle was too finnicky to undo with one hand so I stopped and decided to take them off after I'd put my glass down.

Imagine instantly falling asleep wherever you were, like Maya was able to do. Imagine lying down on this couch watching the sea with a toddler – maybe not a toddler, she couldn't toddle yet, not even a crawler, just a sitter – next to you while you fell asleep in a bright, cool room that smelled of the ocean and sounded like holiday as if you didn't have anything to worry about except a vague nagging concern that you'd wake up with a headache but, hey! You could have more lovely gin and carry on. Then I didn't have to imagine any more because I fell into sleep like a rock sinking underwater.

Six

Twenty-four hours later it was Christmas Day and I was breaking egg whites into the bone broth for the consommé that had been bubbling away for three hours fewer than necessary and wondering if it would ever clarify, sweating my way through a relentless hangover.

My memories of the afternoon before were patchy, but one thing I remembered in sharp detail was Cam yelling Maya's name, jerking me awake and gesturing wildly out to the beach, Deacon running down to the sea. It turned out that Maya could crawl, after all, and if they'd come home five minutes later, she'd probably have drowned while I slept off the gin. I'd gone up to bed and hadn't woken up till the gulls came calling.

I was trying to make up for it by putting together something resembling a traditional Christmas lunch. I'd thrown on the one dress I'd stuffed into my backpack, a short red one I'd quite liked on the rack and which left me feeling semi-naked, but at least made it look like I was making an effort. Deacon and Cam were both on their phones on the couches, simultaneously streaming a cricket match from 1995 ("don't worry about the data, Cam, I'll buy us each a big bundle") and Julia was setting the dining room table with a determinedly cheery air. Rory still hadn't surfaced, and Maya was once again napping on the rug. The glass stacker doors down to the beach were closed. The sun coming in through the skylight in the kitchen was beating down on my head, and I could barely breathe in the salty, stuffy air.

"Cam, could you go tell Rory it's almost lunchtime?" Julia said, though the consommé would take at least another forty-five minutes, and the only thing I'd put in the oven so far was the gammon. "We want to do presents before we eat."

They'd appeared this morning as if by magic, under the tree in the corner of the lounge. I'd come down to start cooking before six, so Julia must have put them there late last night, as if this was a normal Christmas, as if there were kids in the house who were expecting Santa, instead of a house full of adults who were barely speaking and a developmentally delayed 16-month-old. The Carlisles took Christmas seriously.

On the farm, we'd never had gifts for Christmas, other than the things we'd made for each other. I hadn't realised until recently what a stereotypical hippie thing it was to do, to exchange homemade gifts of love. I thought the tomato chutneys (me) and the watercolours (Lola) and the short stories (Heather) and the inexpertly drawn cartoons (Andile) we'd given each other every year were another shameful quirk of my family.

This year, Cam and I had agreed not to do presents so we could save money for a trip to Japan in the winter, but I supposed that was probably off the cards at this stage. He'd bought vouchers for his parents and I hadn't thought of getting anything for Rory. Although she'd probably not want a gift bought with dirty money.

I tossed the eggshells into the bin and was about to plug in the hand blender to make mayonnaise with the egg yolks when Cam bolted down the stairs so fast he almost face-planted at the bottom.

"Rory's not there! She left a note!"

I went cold.

Julia and Deacon were at his side, both reaching for the sheet of notebook paper Cam was holding out. I couldn't move.

"What does it say, Julia? I can't see it!"

Deacon grabbed it out of Julia's hand and as he read it, Cam's eyes drifted to me, standing rooted in the kitchen with my foot on the pedal of the bin.

"She wants us to keep Maya," he said.

"Us?" The words weren't making sense, I couldn't put them together in my head in any order that would fit.

Deacon sat down heavily on a bar stool as if his knees had given way. "She says she's gone back to Em-Zee and that she wants you and Cam to take guardianship of Maya."

"Me and Cam?" I remembered her saying that she had no choice the previous day. This is what she meant?

"Yes, Skye! You and Cam!" Julia said. "She bloody came into our room while it was still dark this morning and left Maya with us so she could get some more sleep, but she must have left the bloody fucking house!"

Maya started stirring and the three of them stared at her like she'd risen from the dead.

Deacon snapped out of it first. "How can we find out where she's gone? She can't drive, it was dark, so she couldn't have walked anywhere. She doesn't have any money ... hang on." He picked his phone up off the couch and clicked on something. "I've got a credit card notification here from seven a.m. From Rory's card. From SAA."

"But how did she get to the airport?"

I knew. I'd probably known since I'd picked her up in the car yesterday morning. It was exactly what I would have had done. It occurred to me that Rory and I would have been great friends in a parallel universe.

"Kestrel. That bartender at the Bru Shack. She's been flirting with him non-stop, and she was there yesterday, and he's the only other person she's spoken to here. He must have picked her up. She's gone to Motherwell – near Port Elizabeth, that's where she said Em-Zee would be today," I said in a rush.

Deacon was dialling a number on his phone. While he held it to his ear, he said, "I'm going to get on the soonest flight to Port Elizabeth and bring her back."

Julia looked up at him and put her hand on his arm. She shook her head, and after a silent moment, he hung up the phone.

The sound of the consommé bubbling behind me made me turn away. I opened drawer after drawer looking for a clean dish towel to strain it with. When I turned back Deacon had his arm around Julia's shoulder, and they were watching Cam trying to put Maya's shoes on. She was offering neither resistance nor help and looked more subdued than usual.

"Now what?" I asked.

Deacon and Julia turned to face me, Deacon frowning, Julia with her arms folded. Cam stared up at me from the lounge floor like he was in a trance. I had my hands on my hips and an apron over my dress and a dish towel over my shoulder and a dripping ladle in my hand and an angry heat spreading up my throat.

"I don't know what you mean," Deacon said.

"Are we not going to go get her? What about Maya?"

"She was very clear in her note, Skye," Julia said softly. "She doesn't want Maya. She wants Em-Zee."

"She's not a fit mother to that child in any case," Deacon said. "Maya's clearly malnourished. She'd be better off with you and Cam."

I tried to catch Cam's eye, but he was watching Maya, who was crawling across the carpet to the closed glass doors, as if she wanted as badly as I did to escape. Cam's eyes were glazed over.

"I'm sorry, but you can't be considering this as an option. We can't take over as her parents! It's not lawful, for one thing."

"Rory didn't know if Maya had a birth certificate, for starters. Look, no one's talking about this as a permanent solution. When Rory comes to her senses, she'll be begging for Maya back. It's an interim measure. Julia and I will help with any costs." Deacon was using his boardroom voice.

"But what if she's gone for years again? After raising her child, we'll have to give her back? There's no possible way this is going to work!"

Julia moved fast. She was standing nose to nose with me in an instant, her brown-gold eyes alight, yesterday's gin on her breath. "This isn't about you. It's about that little girl, who's done nothing wrong and deserves a chance to have a normal life. Of course this isn't ideal, but welcome to real life, welcome to life in the same family as Aurora Carlisle. You can't pick and choose what you take from us, you take the good with the bad, you take the restaurant and the support and the help with – well, with Rory. It's not our fault you sabotaged the business. It's not our fault Rory can't look after Maya. I'm sorry, but this isn't something you can say no to."

I tried again to find Cam's eyes, but he was still staring, transfixed, at Maya. I put down the ladle, took the dish towel off my shoulder, untied my apron strings and straightened my dress. I switched the stove off, switched the oven off, and walked up the stairs.

I don't know what anyone else did that day, but I do know that when I left the next morning, after a night spent under a duvet on the widow's walk, watching the moon rise and the stars blink awake and the darkest navy velvet giving way to a soft pink haze, carrying my backpack and the only shoes I could find in the pre-dawn gloom, there were no presents under the tree, the gammon was still in the oven, and Rory's note, torn out of a spiral-bound A4 notebook, had been left on the bar counter.

I tried to read it but couldn't see it properly. I reached up to my face and felt wetness on my cheeks. I blamed the all-nighter and the woefully shrunken, rubbery ball of gammon in the roasting dish in the oven, the rebuke of a pig snuffling around on the ground, feeling the sun beating on its skin, and now there wasn't that pig anymore, all because of the gammon that nobody would eat.

I held Rory's note, traced my fingers over the surface of it, saw that it was real and that the day before really had happened. It was two lines long. That's all it took if you were Rory – two lines.

I pulled my sneakers onto my bare feet. If she could walk out, with no money of her own, no car, no reason and no qualms, then I could, too.

The gulls watched me leave from the pitch of the roof above the loft. One of them flew into the air as I opened the door of the hybrid, and when I stopped at the top of the driveway before pulling out into the road, it hung, as if suspended by invisible strings, right outside my window. I waited for it to look at me, but it was gone in one fluid movement, returning in the direction of the sea.

Part 2

The Pines

One

I step out of the car once Siya has ground to a halt. Heather doesn't move from the back door. Her arms are crossed against her chest, and her pixie cut highlights her sharp cheekbones and deep eye sockets. Or maybe she's got thinner. In nine years, anything's possible.

"Your hair!" I call out as I try to open the boot of the Corolla. Siya is gesturing to me from inside the car, but I can't find the button or whatever it is I'm supposed to push.

"You're here!" she replies, smiling, crossing the space between us until we're next to each other. I have an urge to reach out to touch her, to squeeze her hand or her shoulder, maybe even to hug her, but we haven't been physically affectionate with each other for years, for decades. She used to hold me on her lap when we watched TV together when I was small, and that was it. I keep my hands at my sides.

Siya uses his key to open the boot and passes me the backpack. I dig my wallet out of the bottom of it, my fingers brushing against my phone, which has been switched off since I took off in Cape Town. I expected at least a text from Cam before the plane took off, but I had nothing, and I'm not about to switch it on now.

"Four-fifty, please," Siya says, and I count out notes. I drew a few thousand at the airport, and was tempted to clear out my account. Cam knows my internet banking details because he sometimes uses my salary from the restaurant to pay for his music and video streaming subscriptions, not wanting to charge them to the business account. I'm hoping that since money isn't something he thinks much about, getting his hands on mine won't occur to him.

"Why don't you offer him some of our honey or our kombucha instead, Roo?" In the hot white sunlight, I see that Heather's definitely thinner, more lined around her lips and eyes, but as ram-rod straight and tall as ever. Her hair, her only vanity, is still the shiny brown of macadamia shells.

"It's fine, Heather. I've got the money."

She looks straight at me in that unnerving, unflinching, intimate way that used to make me squirm. "You know how I feel about it. You could have called me or Andile to come pick you up."

"How do I get out the gate?" Siya asks, retreating.

"There's a keypad on the pole before you get to it, on the right-hand side of the road. The code's written on it."

"Wow, Heather," I say, "Leaving the code right where anyone can see it. That's safe."

"If the criminals want to come steal from me, I don't want to keep them locked on the property once they're done."

Siya pulls a business card out of his pocket, and hands it to me.

Siyabonga Khumalo. Driver to the stars.

"I drove Charlize to Singita once," he says. "Nice lady."

We watch him leave, lurching and crunching over the gravel. I listen to the go-away-birds rattling around in the branches of one of the trees above our heads. Their Afrikaans name's better. Kwêvoël, a word I forgot I knew, their distinctive rasping call right there in the name. Does what it says on the tin, as Heather would say.

She's listening too. She's good at appropriate silences. After all the talk and the noise and the drama at Misty Cliffs I feel almost clean inside, standing in the dappled shade. I'm surrounded by silence so thick that it's a presence, as if the trees have absorbed all ambient noise and left only the bright notes of birdsong.

"Andile's taken the guests on a game drive. It's too hot for any of the bushbuck to be out, but they might spot the hippo in the dam. Let's go inside where it's cooler. You can tell me what you think of my latest batch of kombucha."

"A game drive?" I raise my eyebrow at Heather's back as she leads me in the back door.

"Oh, you know. We've got some duiker, the bushbuck are doing well, there's a caracal that does the rounds. And there's a whole family of hippos. No walking around in the dark. The bull's a nasty one. I've lost track of the number of his babies he's killed."

When we enter the cool, dim kitchen, I catch a glimpse of the living room through the high open archway. Every stick of furniture is gone and the living room is an empty, echoing space with blocks of sunlight falling onto the exposed parquet flooring. The only thing that's left is the mahogany footstool that I remembered Lola retrieving from the antiques shop.

Heather follows my gaze, pouring opaque yellow liquid from a glass jar into two brown glass tumblers, older than I am and as familiar to me as the faint tang of the lukewarm rainwater that we used to gulp out of them, filtered twice before it came out of the tap, but never completely clear.

"I had to get rid of the furniture. It was all leather, you know. Disgusting. I left that footstool. Lola was so angry with me for trying to barter it to Roger. I couldn't bear to let go of it. She was magnificent when she was angry."

I take the cold glass from my mother, moisture already beading on the outer surface. I should be shocked about the furniture, or at least annoyed. My grandparents' stuff is as much my (ageing, probably completely useless) legacy as hers. What are we supposed to sit on? But I'm distracted by the look on her face when she says Lola's name.

"Helloooooo!" A woman's voice calls out from the side of the house and a blonde head pops in through the kitchen door.

"Oh, it's Diana – I totally forgot about the eggs. You're a honey," Heather says to the blonde woman, who is wearing a pair of filthy dungarees and red Hunter boots. She's standing in the kitchen with a basket over her arm and gawking at me.

"Skye! Ohmigod, you're home! It's Diana, Diana de Villiers, but Diana Murphy, it used to be. From school? I thought we'd never see you again! You're looking very sexy for eleven o'clock in the morning!" She's coming in for a hug, so I stand up stiffly. I have absolutely no memory of Diana, my fatigued brain tripping over itself to think of something to say.

"I don't think she remembers you, Di," Heather says, taking the basket off Diana's arm and moving small, mottled brown eggs onto a tea towel on the counter.

"Of course she does!" Diana turns to me. "Of course you do! They used to call me Bellow. Mister Crawford used to pull you, me and Leah into his lounge at hostel and feed us microwave popcorn and sweet champagne and try to talk to us about our sexual awakenings!"

Suddenly I remember the scent of artificial butter and the soft fizz of warm sparkling wine in my mouth, Leah and Diana loud and fearless, barely able to contain their laughter.

"We ate all the chocolate decorations off his Christmas tree that one time while he was in the kitchen," I say.

"Yes! He was such a creep, that dude. I mean, he never touched us, I think he was too scared, but how do guys like him become housemasters of a girls' hostel?"

"You never told me about that, Roo," Heather hands Diana back her basket and places a glass jar of amber into it. "Here's your honey, honey."

"What've we got today? Macadamia? Avocado blossom? Liam's convinced he can tell the difference."

"This is avo blossom, so you've got yourselves to thank for it," Heather replies.

"Your mom and I have a deal – I bring her eggs for her guests from our little Bantam hens every few days, and she pays me in honey. She tried to push that kombucha stuff on me," Diana gestures to my glass, which I've left untouched on the table, "but I said not a chance, lady."

"Thanks for these, Di. Malcolm will be so pleased."

"Oh good, well, you know, it's all about old Malcs round here! I saw the bakkie come down past the lake. I hope Andile's under the limit."

Heather flicks Diana's arm with her finger. "You're terrible, you know." She turns to fill me in. "Diana had Andile over to her farm for Christmas dinner last night – we didn't do anything here, the guests I've got are not exactly that way inclined, and I wasn't expecting him to be home for Christmas in any case, he showed up a few days ago out of nowhere, same as you. And he ended up at Diana's place and she and Jacques had him up till three a.m doing god-knows-what."

Diana laughs, a familiar cackle, and says, "We may or may not have ended up skinny dipping in the dam."

Diana must have married Jacques de Villiers, whose family owned Coucal Farm, a commercial avocado plantation next to The Pines that was bought out by a big agricultural corporation when we were in school. The parents retired in the States, leaving the manager and their eldest son, Jacques, in charge when we weren't much older than 18.

My memories of Jacques are of a sun-bleached, staunch Afrikaans boy who used to come around to ask Andile to play cricket with him and his little brothers. I always tagged along. They taught me how to score, which came in very handy in getting out of tennis and swimming in high school. Andile would interrupt their games to yell at me about wides and no-balls and why it was one and not the other, while Jacques and his brothers fidgeted impatiently. Andile was the only wicket keeper they had, so they put up with it.

"Hopefully your dam doesn't have any hippos," I say.

"Oh no, we swim in the little one next to the house. No hippos. Anyway, I'd better get going – Boxing Day's the one day of the year Jacques allows himself to sleep in, the bloody idiot, so the kids are basically unsupervised."

Diana pulls me in for another hug. "You should come around! Jacques would love to see you. If he remembers you. He's the worst, a total moron, really, he's lucky he's built like an Adonis, otherwise I'd have left him long ago. Left him with all the little rugrats, except Liam. I like Liam."

"How's Fallan's eczema doing?" Heather interjects. "The honey should help."

"What, put it on her skin?"

"No, feed it to her. It's full of natural antihistamines, it's made from local pollen."

"I'm sorry to say we caved and went to the dermatologist in Nelspruit a few days ago. She's on a very low-dose cortisone cream, it seems like it's the only thing that helps."

"You know what I think of that, don't you," Heather says, and it's not a question. I remember her arched-brow disapproval, but it seems lighter, less condescending – maybe because it's not directed at me.

"Yes, yes," Diana winks at me, reminding me of Julia, and I get a sharp pang in my solar plexus, my body remembering where I've just been.

"How long are you here for, Skye?"

Diana's outside and shielding her eyes from the sun, waiting for me to answer.

I shrug. "I don't know."

"Well, we'll have a braai on the weekend, a little welcome-home shindig. I'll invite some of the guys from school, lots of us are still living here, if you can believe it. Say hi to old Malcs for me, Heather!"

"Who's Malcs?" I ask Heather, once Diana's striding down the drive.

"One of the guests," she replies. "Malcolm. You'll meet him in a bit. Drink your kombucha and tell me what you're doing here."

≈

Half an hour later, I've managed to sip about half of my drink, which, to my surprise, doesn't taste as much like liquidised sauerkraut as I thought it would, and told Heather as much as I can bear to: that I said too much in an interview about the restaurant, which blew up on social media. Her reaction was as expected: "But you can't set any store by that, Roo, it's not real, it's people hiding behind their computers saying awful things. I'm sure it'll blow over soon." That Cam's nightmare of a sister appeared out of nowhere and left again: "What are her ceramics like? Would she be interested in exhibiting at the next Lowveld Art Fair, do you think? I've helped Patsy Doyle with organising it the last few years, and if this Aurora is so well known … you know, we haven't had any potters that I can think of, it seems like a bit of an under-appreciated art form, doesn't it?". That Cam and his parents had expectations that I didn't think I could meet: "You didn't discuss it with them? They're your family too, you could have given them the benefit of the doubt and at least tried to talk about it. You are *going* to talk to them about it, aren't you?". But I don't say anything about Maya, because it's too ludicrous. I don't want her to know how messy everything got at the end.

The grandfather clock in the corner of the kitchen, still running like, well, clockwork, chimes the half hour. It's the sound that punctuated my childhood. Heather looks up, frowning.

"Where *are* they? Megs will need to start on lunch soon. She's the one doing the cooking for this lot."

Heather's guests have to contribute to the running of the farm and the household, like a kibbutz, but with a constantly revolving set of residents who pay for the privilege. I remember Andile's texts for the first time today. If Heather has guests on the farm, what's the issue with money?

"I need to go change my clothes before everyone comes back."

"Yes, please do. That dress doesn't look very comfortable. I've been thinking about turning your room into a

103

meditation space but haven't got around to it, so it's more or less how you left it."

The cool, dark passage could do with skylights in the roof, especially with most of the doors closed. Past the family bathroom on the right, still with the 70s avocado-green bath and fittings, past the other entrance to the dusty living room on the left, past Andile's room on the right, with the door closed, past the library on the left, also with the door closed, and then I'm outside my door on the right of the passage, with Heather and Lola's – Heather's – room straight ahead and the little back veranda that leads off it. Instead of going into my room, I duck into Heather's. It's sparse, with only a bed and a dressing table, and her old sage-coloured cotton nightgown hanging off the back of the en-suite bathroom door. I step out onto the little veranda, screened in from the mosquitoes and the flies.

This was where we ate all our family meals when I was growing up, where we sat on the squashy couches and read back issues of *Mad* (me and Andile), the *New Yorker* (Heather) and *National Geographic* (Lola) from the charity bookshop on Sunday afternoons; where Andile and I studied for our exams before he got the scholarship; where we watched the weaver birds building their nests in the Ilala palm trees at the bottom of the lawn every year.

The two cycads in pots are still on the veranda, looking only slightly bigger than I remember them. This is where Heather tried to tell Andile and me about how babies were made when we were about five, using the cycads as examples of species that needed a male and a female to create smaller versions of themselves. She called them "the dinosaurs of the plant world".

During our bath that night, Lola had more success, using the full, correct anatomical words for our private parts ("No 'fanny' or 'willy' nonsense, we call them by their real names. There's power in their real names.") She told us that this thing called sex wasn't always about love, that anybody could love anybody else, no matter what their private parts looked like, that sex was how the two of us were made, but that she and Heather were both of our parents even though they didn't make us together, and that was the first time I realised that Andile and I must have had fathers.

The back veranda was the part of the house where we really lived, the part we made our own. The living room had been too formal, and I think it probably reminded Heather too much of her parents; the front veranda was too hot most of the year, and not private enough; and the kitchen was always populated by guests. When I think of home, it's this hemmed-in little space I think about. Standing there looking out at the lush grass and the fever trees and the tall, spindly, palm tree trunks, with the minor-key hum of cicadas everywhere, I feel like I'm 17 again, like my whole life is about to unroll in front of me.

"You got my texts! You could have replied to me, you shit!"

Andile, my big, toothy brother, is scooping me up in his arms and squeezing the breath out of me.

"I can't believe you're here. What are you wearing?" he says, setting me down.

"A red serviette that I fashioned into a dress. God, Andile, you stink."

"Do I?" He sniffs under his arms.

"You reek of booze."

He pulls a face and shifts his weight. "I've got pretty major memory loss from last night. Diana is bad news, man, she always was, but I thought having four kids would have calmed her down."

"Four?"

"She's Catholic, Jacques's Afrikaans, it's a dangerous combo."

We stare at each other, grinning. I am suddenly so happy.

"I need to change my clothes, and eat. Heather mentioned lunch and I'm starving."

"You don't want to do that, trust me. Come to my cottage. I always stay in Fever Tree when I'm here. I can't stay in the house. I haven't been out here once. Didn't want to have to walk through their room, not after my mom," he says, looking over his shoulder. "But seriously, get dressed and sneak out the front and come to mine. I've got some hot dogs I smuggled in yesterday. Megs's food is the worst, like, the *actual* worst food I've ever tasted."

"You had me at hot dogs."

When he's gone, I take a deep breath of warm air. All my tiredness has evaporated at the thought of eating forbidden food in secret with my brother while we hide from Heather, like old times.

She was right, my room is exactly how I remember it, a single-bed mattress sagging on an iron four-poster frame, with a faded blue duvet cover, too many pillows and a pink bed frill. I can't remember the last time I saw one of those. On the little desk with a matching pine chair is the Singer. I wipe the dust off it in hurried strokes using the fabric of my dress after I've taken it off. I never want to wear the thing again.

I pull my denim shorts out my backpack, shove my feet into my sneakers and check my wardrobe for a shirt. My white school golf shirt is hanging up, and it smells like the dried lavender potpourri sachet that Heather has tied on the hanger. I pull it over my head and marvel at how roomy and comfortable it is, wondering if our shirts were always two sizes too big on us or if I've shrunk. I hear voices in the kitchen and plan my escape through the living room, but as soon as I open my door, the voices in the kitchen fall silent.

A posh British man's voice says, "Heather, is there someone in the house? Ought we be worried?"

There's no chance of escaping out the front door now. I enter the kitchen reluctantly to find a stooped, white-haired man leaning against the counter next to Heather, who's washing dishes. A mousy-haired woman of indeterminate age is struggling to get the flame on the gas stove to catch. There's a woman with braids in a top knot and wide-framed hipster glasses crocheting at the table. Straight lines of tattooed text run down her arms. A guy with a bandanna tied round his head is picking his nails. They're all looking at me, mildly surprised, and none of them is the mid-life-crisis yuppie I was expecting.

Heather turns towards us and dries her hands on the dish towel she's slung over her shoulder.

"Karoo-Sky, or Roo, as we call her, or Skye, as she calls herself – this is everyone. The group of writers currently on retreat at The Pines. How long have you guys been here? Two weeks?"

"That's right. Ten left," says the woman at the stove. She's wearing hiking boots and a long linen skirt. "I'm Megs," she says, waving. "I don't suppose you can get the stove to work for me, can you? Heather's tried to show me a dozen times and I can't get it right."

I take the box of matches from her, light one, and hold the knob on the stove down, waiting for the third click before I touch the flame to the plate.

"Writers, you said?"

"I'm Tshidi, and that's Sullivan, not his real name," says the woman at the table, pointing to the bandanna guy with her crochet hook. Something chimes at the back of my mind, and as she lifts her eyes to meet mine, I get an instant hit of ammonia, a dazzling olfactory memory that leaves me dizzy. My palms are immediately damp, and my breath comes in short bursts.

"You mean it's not my *given* name," the guy says, but it's like he's talking from far away.

I can't take my eyes off Tshidi. She was in the *Fig & Brie* bathroom, which reeked of the ammonia the cleaners used, two weeks after the mugging. She was the one who took my phone out of my shaking hands and scrolled down to find the emergency number of my gynae. Her hair was different, but her wide-set eyes are those that met mine in the mirror that day. Does she recognise me?

Megs takes a break from measuring an ominous quantity of brown lentils from the 10-kilo bag on the counter to say in my direction, "You're looking pale. Do you need to sit down?" She pulls a chair out from the table for me and as I shakily lower myself into it, Tshidi snaps her fingers in my direction.

"I know you," she says.

"*Fig & Brie*," I say.

"Well, I was on the travel mag at the time. One floor below *Fig & Brie*. The day we met, our bathroom was out of order."

"You two know each other? From work?" Heather's voice is as close as it comes to sounding excited.

"We'd seen each other around," I say quickly, turning my head toward Heather but keeping Tshidi in my line of sight through the corner of my eyes.

"We ran into each other in the bathroom once. Before I got the book deal. I left not long after. That mag-hag vibe wasn't for me."

"That's why I never saw you again." I'd gone looking for her after I'd recovered, wanting to thank her for her help. But she was nowhere to be found.

I rub my hands against my shorts to dry them and practise the slow, deep breaths the counsellor taught me after the mugging to make my heart stop thudding so painfully.

"Only one more person to introduce you to, Roo," Heather says, touching the old man on the shoulder. "This is Malcolm." She smiles at him fondly and turns around to carry on with the dishes. Malcolm absently strokes her bum through her slacks, and I can't take my eye off the veins sticking out on the back of his hand, the skin mottled like Diana's eggs.

Heather swats his hand away with the dish cloth, and says, "I'm busy, you," in a tone of voice I haven't heard since Lola was alive.

He shuffles towards me.

In his deep aristocratic voice, he says, "I suppose we're going to be roommates." He claps me on the shoulder. "Right! Who's having eggs? I need the shells."

"I'll put them in the lentil soup," Megs offers.

"Roommates?"

Heather flicks the water off her fingers and picks up a small plastic bucket, filling it with water from the sink. "Malcolm is living in the house. When Andile came home, he needed his cottage back, so Malcolm moved in here."

"In Andile's room?"

Heather frowns at me. "No. He's in my room, with me."

"They're an Item," Megs says, smiling. "They only got together a couple of days ago, but we all saw it coming."

"He's the most wonderful poet, Roo," Heather says. "I think we should have a reading tonight, what do you guys think? I'm dying to see how you're coming along."

Megs starts breaking the eggs into the pot the lentils are cooking in. The water hasn't come to the boil. The lentils will still be hard as stones. She hands the shells one by one to Malcolm, who starts crushing them with the pestle directly onto the counter.

"What do you do with the eggshells?" I'm almost afraid to ask.

"I put them in my homemade oatcakes," Malcolm says, grinding the pestle in a way that looks lewder than it should. "It's all I eat. How do you think I manage to stay this young and virile?"

I laugh shakily, and sneak a glance at Tshidi. She's watching me too.

"Let's go for a walk to catch up," she says to me. "I'd love to hear all the office gossip."

"Lunch is soon! Don't go too far," Megs calls out.

As I follow Tshidi outside, I say under my breath, "There's no way lunch will be ready anytime soon."

She barks out a laugh and slaps a hand against her mouth. "Megs's cooking. Honestly. It's amazing how little time it takes to completely fuck up a meal."

We walk to the end of the driveway, not speaking, and it should be tense between us, but isn't. It's hard to reconcile this relaxed version of Tshidi with the aloof, immaculately dressed woman I remember from the bathroom on what was one of the three worst days of my life.

I don't know how to start this conversation, and am relieved when she eventually says, quietly, "I wondered how you were doing after I left the mag. Was it all – the baby …?"

I thought my tear ducts were completely dehydrated after the kind of morning I'd had, but, what do you know, I find myself blinking hard to keep more tears from squeezing out of my eyes. That little bean, the miraculous accident, gone.

Tshidi pulls me towards her in a tight, sudden squeeze and I take a shuddering breath. Her sympathy feels like it's going to end me.

"I'm so sorry. I didn't know your name so couldn't ask anyone about you. Or if anyone knew anything."

"No one knew. You were the only one."

"Your mom?"

"Oh, god, no."

She gives me a small smile. "She won't find out about it from me. I know about keeping things from mothers. What do you think my mom thinks I'm doing right now? She doesn't know I quit my job fifteen months ago to write dystopian novels full time. I'm waiting till I'm a success before I tell her."

"You're not a success yet?"

It's Tshidi's turn to shrug, as we make our way back up to the kitchen. "I mean, my royalties were okay. My first book sold pretty well overseas, it got a second print run, which was just, wow. Made it onto a couple of longlists and whatever. But my mom won't think I'm a success till my books can bankroll me completely and take us on a holiday to Greece and/or Bali. So no, I'm not there yet."

I stop and look up into the boughs of the nearest teak tree. There's a rustling of heavy-bodied birds near the top and the distinctive "kweeeeeeh" of the go-away-birds. I point when I've spotted them.

"They're my favourite. I love their black eyes."

Tshidi's gaze follows the direction of my arm. "They're like paw-paw pips. The eyes. So round and shiny."

"They're very gleamy," I agree, as we watch the birds hop around, full of bluster and self-importance and noise. By the time we walk through the back door, I'm 70 per cent confident that tears aren't imminent.

After fixating for a moment on the sight of Heather's fingers stroking Malcolm's arm where it lies around her waist, I reverse back out the door. I make my way to Andile's cottage, wishing I could scrub the image of Heather fondling Malcolm's mottled skin from my brain.

Two

"I'm way out of my depth with this Malcolm thing," I tell Andile a few minutes later, as I watch him squirting tomato sauce and neon-yellow mustard out of little takeaway sachets onto four hotdogs lined up on the kitchenette counter of Fever Tree Cottage. He hands a plate to me and I start salivating. This must be the first time in my life that I haven't eaten in over 24 hours.

"Same. It's why I've been disappearing to Coucal Farm so often." Andile slots half a hotdog into his mouth in one bite.

My first bite is an assault of nostalgia, tasting of humid Saturday mornings at the Lowveld Show, the viennas soothing and salty, the sauces light and sweet. I'm fully aware that this isn't food – it's junk scraped from the slaughter-house floor and loaded up with sugar and preservatives – but my body welcomes the immediate artificial hit.

"But it's not just Malcolm," I say, swallowing a soft lump of bread. The yellow of the mustard has stained the tips of my fingers. "It's everything. Why are there writers here? And why do you think the farm's going bankrupt?"

Andile makes quick work of the second hotdog but takes his time before he replies. "Because Heather, as far as I can tell, has not had any income for the last three months."

"You mean these writers aren't paying to stay?"

He shakes his head, and drops his plate in the sink on top of a pile of dishes in varying states of crustiness. "I asked her about it. She said, 'They pay me with their words', and that's when I got worried."

My stomach coils itself tightly into a knot. We called it "shongololo belly" when we were growing up. I couldn't eat breakfast for the whole of the first week when Andile went away to private school. Lola hugged me every morning and whispered "Shongololo belly?" in my ear and put my oats aside for the worm farm without chiding me for wasting food.

I hand Andile my plate and he finishes the hotdog-and-a-half that I can't manage.

"But where did she find them? They're staying here *for free?*"

"I don't know, but if she doesn't start getting some income soon, there's going to be big trouble. You think that new fence is cheap to maintain? And private security? Kolobe Moru doesn't take payment in kind, obviously."

"What does that mean? Kolobe Moru?"

"Bush pig in Sotho. They're the hard-core security company Heather's been using for years. If you see some dudes jumping out of the back of a black double-cab with full riot kit on, that's them."

"What about Themba's guys?"

Andile is peering into the little gas-powered bar fridge under the counter, but closes it and turns around empty-handed. When he looks at me, there's something new in his expression, something like irritation or disbelief.

"Roo, Themba's guys haven't been on the farm in about ten years."

I think back to Lola's wake but my memory from that time is hazy, shrouded in a mist like the pine-scented blue steam that rises out of the treetops here during heatwaves.

"That long?"

Themba was one of Heather and Lola's MK contacts from the 80s, when the farm was a halfway house for activists on their way to Swaziland and Mozambique. Shortly after Lola arrived, he sent three of his comrades from the militarised wing of the ANC to keep burglars and trespassers off the farm. They wore overalls and caps so they'd pass as farm workers. Andile and I didn't know who they were or why they were there. They lived in the guards' cottage up at the gate, and we hardly ever saw them.

Once, on our way to school, we must have been in Grade 1 or 2 because I was wearing the scratchy tunic that was part of the convent's summer uniform, the tallest guy, the bald one, was changing his shirt in the cottage and had left the door open. I caught a glimpse of automatic rifles leaning against the wall inside the cottage, which usually had its curtains drawn. They were the kind of guns I'd seen on the walls of the Post Office, where various weapons – landmines, hand grenades, AK-47s – were displayed to tell us what "the terrorists" were going to do if we let them win.

The three men left soon after 1994 to join the Defence Force, but they came back the following summer, and until I left home they were a regular feature patrolling the borders of the farm. We never learned their names, and I'd taken their presence for granted.

"They're all ancient. Themba died, and they stopped coming. Security's been the farm's biggest expense. Heather's been lucky, but if we stop paying Kolobe, she's going to have to sleep with a gun under her pillow or something."

Heather and Lola never had guns, unlike probably every other farm-owner in the area. Our mothers objected to guns: we weren't at war anymore, the states of emergency were over, it was peacetime, we'd won.

Andile sits down on the plastic chair across from me and rubs the back of his neck. "See if you can talk to her about it. Find out what her plan is, where she found these people, if there's any way she can charge them for the stay retrospectively."

"You think she'll tell me?"

"You have to try. It's why you came, isn't it? To help?"

I avoid his eyes. "Yes, in a way. Also to avoid 'the shitstorm', as you called it."

"Oh, geez. I'd almost forgotten. What happened with that?" There's a furry layer of concern over his voice.

"Well, for one thing, I'm pretty sure the business is doomed."

"It'll blow over. Surely."

"It might, but either way I'm pretty sure my relationship with Cam – my husband, my business partner – is over anyway."

Andile's eyes don't leave my face. "Are you serious?"

I sigh. "We had a fight. A few fights. I realise I might have rushed into things with him." I shift in my seat. I need to change the subject. I can't think about Cam. "What about you? Are *you* seeing anyone?"

"Yes. Well, I don't know if it's official or anything. She's also a Politics post-doc. Virika. Her parents are pretty devout, though, and probably wouldn't peg a heathen like me as the best match for their daughter."

"Photographic evidence, please."

He digs his phone out his pocket and scrolls down a couple of times. He's wearing a rugby shirt in the photo, his arm around a girl with a perfect bob and a long yellow-gold bracelet snaking up her lower arm. They're both holding cocktails on a deck with the beach in the background.

"*She's* obviously not super-devout," I point at the drink in her hand.

He puts his phone back in his pocket. "She's Hindu. Beer, yes, beef, no. I wanted to invite her, but can you imagine? 'Here, Virika, classiest person I've ever met in my life, meet my other mother Heather and her creepy boyfriend – nope, I didn't know she liked men either – and the bunch of weird strangers who are currently living with her for free. Here's my sister, Roo, who hasn't slept in about three days and is dressed like a tramp and has run away from the husband I've never met. What do you mean you don't think we're long-term compatible?'"

He's laughing, but it's hollow. If Lola was still alive, there'd be no question about Andile bringing his girlfriend home. Lola would make her feel so welcome, she'd never want to leave.

"Bugger off, now," he says to me, after another yawn so wide I can see the bits of bread stuck in his back teeth. "I need to sleep. See what you can find out about the writers, and we'll talk later. Let's go fishing this evening."

"Are there any bass still in the lake?"

"Nice big, fat ones since Heather's sworn off all animal products. Nobody's fished there for a decade. I'll bring two rods."

"You'll only need the one," I say. He knows fly-fishing is something I've never mastered, no matter how many times he tried to teach me. The worse I was, the less I wanted to try, whereas Andile would keep going, keep bowling a cricket ball against the side of the house, keep casting and reeling in and casting, until he got it right, until it was perfect. Maybe if I was more like him I'd still be in Misty Cliffs, with a foster daughter and a happy marriage and a salvageable business.

"Fine, but you're doing the gutting," he says, opening the cottage door and letting me out onto the red dirt path, where the midday sun feels like it's filling the whole sky.

≈

The house is quiet when I get back inside, with the hot, bitter smell of burnt garlic hanging in the kitchen. Sullivan is stacking my grandmother's china plates, beige flecked with brown, with bright orange geraniums in the centre. He's slotting them into the top left-hand cupboard, above the chopping board, exactly where they've always been kept.

"You're on tidy-up duty?"

He turns around. "Every day. I'm not much good with the other stuff."

"Couldn't you swap with Megs and take over the cooking?"

"I wish." He opens the cutlery drawer and starts throwing spoons and knives into the correct compartments with a practised hand. His fingertips are straight, not curved like most people's, and the smooth caramel skin of his arms is completely hairless. The motion is mesmerising and I realise I'm probably standing too close. There's a clean kind of heat coming off him.

He smiles at me and says, in a soft accent I recognise from working at *Fig & Brie*, where the team of designers were friends who had grown up in the Bo-Kaap, "I've never eaten this many dried pulses in my life. My mother would be shocked. I've never liked dal."

"Where are you from?"

118

He snorts. "Are you asking where my family's from? Originally?"

"No – I mean, where in South Africa."

He slides the cutlery drawer closed smoothly. It used to stick, every time. It's been oiled recently. I notice other signs of care: the wooden cupboard doors are gleaming, the cushions on the riempie chairs at the kitchen table are puffy-stuffed. Nothing's crumbling or lifting or worn or faded. No outward signs of poverty.

"White people always ask me where I'm from, but they mean, like, what are you. It's my eyes. They throw people off."

I look more closely at him. His irises are a light hazel, almost yellow. I study his face for a beat too long, noticing his dark hairline under his turquoise bandanna, his long, straight nose. He studies me back, and I feel my throat working.

"But you're from Cape Town, right?"

He nods, leaning against the counter with his arms folded. "When I'm not on book tour or on retreat, I stay with my mom. She sews my bandannas, bakes big batches of koesiesters for me at dawn. The whole thing. She knows I'm lapsed, that I don't practise our religion anymore. I'm a huge embarrassment to her, obviously, but she can't turn me away. I'm her only boy."

A corner of his mouth lifts and it occurs to me that I haven't thought about a man in this way since I met Cam.

I drag my eyes away from his face and try to gather my thoughts. "How'd you hear about The Pines?"

"From my agent. We're all with the same agent in Texas."

I blink twice, feeling like the conversation's got away from me. His proximity is scrambling my brain.

"You know, in America? The local fiction market's not really viable if you want to make a living. We sell mostly in the States."

"You were sent here, to The Pines, in the middle of nowhere, by an agent in Texas?"

"Her name's Adrienne Brown. She's a friend of Heather's from way back. We're the third group she's sent here. It seemed like too sweet a deal to turn down."

I pull out a chair at the table and sit down, waiting for him to join me, but he stays upright. He swats at a fly in front of his face.

"The insecticide is in that cupboard over there."

"We're not allowed to kill flies. It's one of Heather's conditions." He starts ticking things off on his fingers. "Don't kill insects – or anything, obviously. Only eat produce grown on the farm. Tend the land. No locked doors. No phones. No meat. No dairy. You know, her whole earth-friendly, sustainable thing."

"This is all new to me. I haven't been home in, well, in a while. Look – can you tell me about what's going on here? My mother hates talking about money and I don't think I'd get anything out of her."

Sullivan shrugs, his T-shirt shifting beautifully across his chest. "She hasn't said a word about our arrangement since we got here. I was expecting to have to sign something with her at least. All we've got is the contract we signed with Adrienne before we came."

"There's a contract? It's all official? Because I was chatting to Andile, he does the books for my mother, you know, and he's concerned about, well, payment? This used to be a farm-stay for rich retired people, a sabbatical for businessmen with stressful jobs, or people who needed to get away and, I don't know, hide for a bit. They paid for that, and you guys aren't … paying anything. Right?"

He turns around to let the dishwater out of the sink before I can stop him. Heather would have wanted it for the flowerbeds.

"It's a scholarship deal. Fairly typical of writers' retreats."

"You probably don't know this, but my mother's not in a position to be offering anything for free." I can feel my blood pulsing in my ears. Is this arrangement my mother's latest strategy in her cold war against capitalism, to give everything away until she's left with nothing?

"But she *is* getting paid. It's Adrienne's agency that gave us the scholarship."

"She's paying Heather for you to stay here? What's in it for her? For the agency?"

"We finish our manuscripts. Which means we honour our deals with our publishers. We don't have to pay back the advances, and our agents get to keep their cut, their ten per cent. Except they're paying Heather two per cent of it, so they get to keep eight per cent. Which is better than zero, which is what they'd get if we didn't come here. Before we arrived, we were all stuck."

It's hard for me to visualise numbers in my head at the best of times without seeing them in front of me, and with the heat and my shongololo belly and Sullivan so close, it's hopeless for me to try to understand what he's saying.

He can see I'm floundering. "What I'm saying is, you don't have to worry about Heather not getting paid. The agency's paid her upfront." He has a long dimple, or maybe a crease, in his left cheek when he smiles.

"What do you write?"

"Megs writes gruesome crime novels, Tshidi's carving out a niche for African feminist dystopian fiction, Malcolm does poetry and essays but is busy with his memoir. Stuff that does well overseas. Nothing you'll have heard of, we're not exactly winning prizes, but we do okay. I think Malcolm got one of his poems in the *New Yorker* once, in the eighties or something."

Heather must love that. I bet she has the exact copy in the library. She collected every single issue of the *New Yorker* from 1983 to 1994, their covers laminated and pages neatly punched and ring-bound.

"Does Heather choose who comes?"

"That, I have no idea. Maybe she likes our stuff? We've all been published before. I'm on a three-book deal, I think Tshidi's on her second, Malcolm's a household name if poetry's your thing, and who knows how many books Megs has written. I don't know who chooses us out of all the applications, or how, and haven't asked." He looks towards the door. "I need to get back to writing, so, if there's nothing else?"

"Last thing, I promise. Why Heather? Why here?"

He pats his pockets before stopping mid-air and clicking his tongue. "Fuck's sake. I keep forgetting we're not allowed to smoke. All I know is that Heather's a contact of Adrienne's, and this retreat was like the final push in getting us to finish our books. Adrienne's ruthless, so I'm surprised she's given up so much of her commission, I have to tell you. This is definitely an exceptional circumstance. Your mother seems to know a lot about literature, too. Did she work with Adrienne, maybe?"

"She studied English at university." She's never mentioned anyone called Adrienne, and she's never worked anywhere but at The Pines.

The clock clacks loudly behind me and the fly tries to kamikaze itself on the window above the sink.

"I've got to get back to work," Sullivan says. "I'm glad we got a chance to talk, Skye. I'm always interested in people who change their names."

Before he leaves, I ask him what kind of books he writes.

"Romance," he says, glancing at me over his shoulder before he steps out into the light. "Contemporary romance."

Three

I am cursing myself for wearing shorts to the lake. The mosquitoes whine on their descent to my ankles and calves, and there is a cloud of midges in front of my face. They're only interested in me for the moisture of my eyeballs, but their relentlessness feels personal.

I slap at my ankle and watch Andile languidly swish his fishing rod above his head once, twice, three times, before the line whirs quietly over the still water and the fly plops delicately onto the surface.

"Where are the hippos?"

"They hang out by the reeds on the other side. You worried?"

"I don't feel like being stampeded by an enormous wild animal who thinks it needs to trample me to mark its territory."

"Nah, they're pretty tame, these ones. Hand me a beer, will you? Grab one for yourself if you like."

I get up off the lid of the cooler box and draw two brown bottles out. I twist the lids off and wade through the high grass to the edge of the water. Andile's standing barefoot in the silt, with his khaki trousers rolled up his calves. I wonder if the beer will help ease the edge of my two-day hangover after my Christmas Eve gin binge. As much as I'm trying not to think about Misty Cliffs, my body remembers.

"What did Heather say?"

"I didn't see her. I was napping until about five minutes ago. I did speak to one of the writers about it." I relay Sullivan's story to him, and he snorts.

"He's wrong. There's been nothing coming into Heather's accounts. Zilch. Fok-all."

His line goes taut and he gives his bottle back to me, freeing up his hand to reel the fish in. I hate this part. The struggle, the fish taken completely unawares, its blind, mindless, desperate flailing that some ancient part of its DNA tells it will keep it alive.

I turn away and take a deep pull of the beer, icy and fizzy and bitter. Andile stuns the fish with a single dull thwack.

He straightens up and pretends to throw it at me, and I duck instinctively. It's bigger than the bass I remember, plump and pearly, a moment ago an undulating muscle in the cool, murky water, and now a limp, bloody-eyed corpse. Andile chuckles and slings it into the cooler box he's got at his feet. I give him his bottle back and he clinks it against mine. The beer catches the back of my throat as I swallow.

"Do you think Sullivan was lying?"

Andile groans. "I have no idea. I've started the conversation a million times with Heather since I've got here, and she keeps dodging it."

He casts his line again. He is the picture of skill, with the strong, smooth swirls of his arms, his hands wrapped comfortably around the rod. No hesitation, as if it's the most natural movement in the world.

"I'll try to talk to her, but only if you come with me to this reading tonight. I'm ninety-nine per cent sure the writers' stuff is going to be terrible and I want you to come so I'm not the only one trying not to laugh. Or cry."

"You'll talk to Heather afterwards?"

"Cross my heart."

He drains his beer. "Fine. Hopefully we can straighten this out and be out of here by the weekend."

"Di's throwing a party on Saturday," I remember out loud.

"By Monday then. I'd say Sunday but if the party's anything like last night, I won't be fit for travel the next day."

He's caught another one, and he leans back against the force of the fish on the line. "But right now," he says, gritting his teeth, "let's eat!"

Andile's brought charcoal, firelighters, tin foil, onions and lemons. I use his disconcertingly sharp pen knife to slit the two fish open and I empty them by the light of the spare headlamp he's brought, plopping the cool innards into a plastic bag. I rinse out the cavities using the jerrycan in the back of the bakkie, slice the onions and the lemons, fill the cavities, wrap the cold bodies in foil and tuck them in between the coals in the brick braai under the willow tree.

We eat the fish with our fingers, standing next to the fire as the sky gets darker and the frogs start trilling. The slivers of hot flesh we pick out from around the bones are soft and lemony, and I think of Cam using a chopstick to poke the cheeks out of the fish in Hua-Lian and giving them to me because he knew they'd make me happy. The simplicity of that knocks the wind out of me.

We lick our fingers and wipe them on the grass like we used to – the one thing Andile didn't bother bringing was serviettes – and wordlessly start packing up. The stars are out, and for the first time in nine years I remember how the Milky Way got its name.

"I'd forgotten how good the stars are here," Andile says, looking up.

He drives back to the main house with a bottle of beer in his left hand, and I change gears for him when I see his thigh move to press the clutch in with his left foot, a rhythm we learned when we were 16 and started sneaking off to the lake to drink.

"Do you remember those litchi alco-pop things we used to drink?"

He flicks his lights to bright. "I can still taste them."

"They'd probably be too sweet now."

"Essentially a three-forty-mil bottle of sugar."

"We were probably on a sugar high the whole time, not drunk at all."

"Except I'm fairly sure having a sugar high doesn't make people puke –"

"And swallow it!"

"And deny it."

"Did I?" The nights at the lake, straight out of a Springsteen song, with kids from school in their parents' bakkies, loaded with contraband six-packs, all blur together. "We're lucky none of us drowned."

He pulls up alongside the house. "That's a sobering thought."

The light's on in the living room, and the curtains are open. Heather sits cross-legged in front of the fireplace, with the writers in a circle around her. Their eyes are closed.

"Oh god, Roo. If I have to meditate with these weirdos, I might lose my cool for real."

I click my fingers in the direction of his beer and he hands it to me. It's warm and flat. Heather's eyes snap open in the living room, and meet mine over the writers' heads, across the empty floor, through the closed sash window, across the front veranda, through the open window of the bakkie, and I lower the beer bottle. For one second, two seconds, we look at each other, and then she beckons us in.

There are two empty cushions in the circle. I take the one between Sullivan and Tshidi, Andile lowers himself slowly into the space between Heather and Malcolm. I sit cross-legged; he tries to do the same, fails, and sits with his legs out in front of him, looking uncomfortable for possibly the first time in his life. The writers are holding stacks of loose-leaf paper.

"Let's start tonight with Malcolm," Heather says, gesturing to him with a cupped hand, like a yogi.

"Some background for our guests," Malcolm says, clearing his throat, "I'm experimenting with the Elizabethan sonnet form at the beginning of every chapter of my memoir. That's –"

"Three quatrains and a rhyming couplet," Andile finishes, looking as if he's caught himself unawares.

Heather smiles. She took it upon herself to educate Andile and me in classical literature instead of fairy tales. She read to us from the books she'd used at university: Shakespeare, and *The Faerie Queen*, and Milton, who was ruined for me when Heather told us he was blind and used his daughter as a scribe – "what was her name?" I asked once, and Heather had looked startled before replying, "I never learned her name" – and Keats, my favourite, the tragic hero.

When we were 10, Heather swapped out our school set-work readers with *Great Expectations*, sending us to school with her copy and a note to the teacher about our respective reading ages. We had recently moved from the convent to the government primary because schools were no longer segregated. Mrs Greville ("The Devil", we called her, though she was too timid to deserve it) didn't know what to do with us, so she put us in a reading group by ourselves and left us to our Dickens.

Andile and I hunched over the single yellow-paged paperback, our desks pushed together, immediate outcasts under suspicion of sucking up to the teacher, and also of being weird. I was keenly aware of the group of alpha girls giggling. I heard the whispered "dorks" move like a ripple through the rows around us.

When we'd first arrived at the school, I'd noticed them immediately, these shiny girls with matching hair bands, the ones who got their parents to pack them identical food in their identical pink lunchboxes: Ceres juices and dried mango and dainty, triangular, crust-less white bread sandwiches.

I would never fit in with those girls. I was too gritty, never clean enough, with too few items of clothing. In high school I found the extroverted, brash girls in my hostel who didn't mind me hanging around with them, girls like Di and Leah and that girl whose name I can't remember whose little brother fell out of the back of a bakkie and died when we were in Matric.

Lola cried her heart out at that boy's funeral, deep gulping sobs that embarrassed me. She told me afterwards that she'd been crying for all the boys she'd known who were dead. She said it was the first time she'd allowed herself to grieve for them, and I understood that she was talking about the liberation struggle but her sadness made me uncomfortable and I got away as quickly as I could. I'd give anything to be back with her at the kitchen table that day, asking her more about her life and what she went through before she came to The Pines, before she became my other mother.

Malcolm starts reading in his deep voice, and within four lines I can tell it's a standard Shakespearean sonnet with the typical iambic soft-hard rhythm, nothing experimental that I can pick up, unless he's experimenting with the hideousness of comparing his penis to a snail.

"Curling from its shell, leaving a long trail –"

Before he can finish, Andile is on his feet. His mouth is a slash across his face, and he doesn't look at me as he heads to the door. A moment later the bakkie's headlights fill the room with light as he reverses down the driveway.

Heather closes her eyes and takes a deep breath. When she opens them, she's composed herself. "Keep going, Malcs," she says.

When I hear the word "slime", I tune him out, and picture Lola's long fingers and her strong arms and the radius of warmth she kept around herself and how it felt to be in that circle of sunshine and sureness, and I realise the truth of what she was trying to tell me after the boy's funeral. Grief has its own timeline. You can be numb for years until something small sparks off a flare inside, and then it's off on its own trajectory.

My calves are ribbed with welts from mosquito bites. I press my thumbnail into each welt, marking them all with a cross. We did this as kids to stop the itching. Tshidi holds something out to me, a little pot of yellow goo, labelled in my mother's handwriting, "buchu and beeswax: insect bites". I twist it open and it smells like home, and by the time I've finished dabbing a fingertipfull onto each "x", Malcolm has finished, it's finally over, and Heather's talking about the striking rhythm change in the final lines.

"Thank you," I whisper, handing the pot back to Tshidi.

"Keep it," she replies.

Sullivan volunteers to go next, and Heather bows her head to him.

I try not to watch his mouth as he tells the story of a man with a terrible limp and a lisp who's in love with a girl who works at a train station. Every day, he watches her, and every day, he thinks he's going to talk to her, but he can't. Until one day, an aggressive woman with a briefcase starts yelling at the girl in her kiosk and the unnamed man is about to jump to her defence, but the train that was late has arrived, and as he's about to get on it, his and the girl's eyes meet, and Sullivan stops reading.

"That's as far as I've got."

"I think this is the sweetest one you've written so far," Megs says. "My mother's going to love it."

"My detractors call them stalker-romances," he says to me. "The feminists denounce me, obviously. But I've got a loyal readership in English-speaking elderly women."

"I think your female characters are empowered in their own way," Heather says. "They're obviously victims of the patriarchy, and your narrators are always men. But it's the women in your stories who decide the ending."

Tshidi shrugs on the other side of me. "I can't agree with you, Heather. Have you noticed that his female characters are always *literally* in tight little boxes? The train kiosk, that one with the commuters where the woman was stuck in her tiny car every day, the waitress in the café. They're stuck, waiting for a man to come and set them free."

"A café's not a box."

She holds up her hands. "Hey, I'm giving feedback. This is a space for sharing."

"Thank you, Sullivan. You've made good progress," Heather intervenes before he can reply.

Tshidi's arms are looped round her knees and I can finally read the tattoo on the inside of her right arm. It's four words, all lower case, stretching from the crook of her elbow down to her wrist: *we are the moon*.

She catches me looking at it and shows me her left arm: *nothing measured, small nor petty* says the simple italics font in the same pattern.

Poetry? Obscure song lyrics? Seeing the blank look on my face, she whispers, "Olive Schreiner". She traces the words on the inside of her left arm. "This is what she said about South Africa."

Then it's her turn to read. I listen to her describe a wasteland where Ndileka picks her way across an empty playground to the oasis that is the abandoned gymnasium, and I feel Sullivan watching me on my other side.

I turn to meet his yellow eyes, clear, unblinking.

My face is burning, the fire rages inside. I am paralysed, fused to the cushion. I listen to Megs reading about a pathologist who discovers half-digested meat which may or may not be of human origin in the stomachs of her murder victims. When the reading is over and after Heather has led us in a brief meditation, Sullivan squeezes my hand. Tshidi glances over before she stands up, looks like she's about to say something, but seems to think better of it and leaves with the others.

Once they're all gone, my mother looks me full in the face, the spotlight I grew up in, and says, "Well?"

"Well, what?"

She gestures to the empty cushions. "What do you think?"

I hear Malcolm filling the kettle in the kitchen and turning the stove on.

"I think you should have kept the furniture. My bum's completely numb."

She runs her hand through her hair, ruffles it up at the back. "I mean about the writers. Their work. Good? Bad? Atrocious? Transcendental? Don't you think Tshidi's such a maverick? She's only twenty-six."

I nod, listening to Malcolm rattling around in the kitchen.

"Roo, I wanted to ask you a favour."

Oh, god.

"Megs needs help in the kitchen. I'm wondering if you could give her some lessons. She said on her application that she could cook but she either lied or she harbours certain delusions. Her total incompetence around food is odd because her pathologist character is a keen cook, and she writes about it fairly convincingly, so of course I assumed she'd be up to the task."

The kettle whistles, and a moment later Malcolm appears carrying a mug in each hand. He cocks his head in the direction of the passage.

"Bedtime," he says to Heather, as if they've been together for decades. My skin crawls watching him looking at her.

"That's fine, Heather. I'll help Megs." When I stand up, pins and needles shoot heat up my calves.

Heather surprises me by coming over and putting her hand on my shoulder. "Thank you," she says.

I grab her hand before she turns around. "Who's Adrienne?"

She blinks, and Malcolm says, "My agent, that's who."

I don't take my eyes off my mother's face.

"She was ... someone very dear to me. My first girlfriend. At Rhodes."

"And she sends the writers to you?"

Heather nods. "She found me on Facebook."

"I'm going to bed. Your tea's getting cold," Malcolm says crossly, and leaves the room. The light seems too bright, my mother's face looks too old.

"Facebook? But you don't have the internet!"

"Oh, I do. Well, Di does. I got myself a cell phone about six months ago. Kolobe needed it for security, and I cancelled the old landline, what, five years ago? Di lets me use her Wi-Fi. Adrienne made me her friend through the Rhodes Alumni group, and we got talking. She asked if I was still on the farm because she was looking for somewhere to send her writers who were 'blocked'."

"She's paying you out of her own pocket?"

"I don't ask how it works, Roo. It's none of my business where payment comes from. I jumped at the chance to get guests here who weren't entitled yuppies, for a change."

"And Malcolm?"

The corner of her mouth lifts. "You know he was published in the *New Yorker*?"

"Apparently. Did you know that before he came?"

Her eyes move over my face, and she nods once.

"You've had a long day. Let me know if you need anything in the night. I'll leave my door open."

"Please don't," I say, as I watch her move down the long, dark passage towards the warm yellow glow framing her bedroom door.

I collapse into bed and two things occur to me before sleep takes me: that I forgot to ask Heather about the empty bank account, and that my pillow case smells freshly washed.

Four

I am showing Megs how to dice onions properly before lunch the next day when Di breezes in through the open kitchen door. She starts talking as if we're in the middle of a conversation.

"Skye, I know this is really rude, but would you mind catering for the party on Saturday? I'll buy the ingredients, if you can cook them? I was going to get Jacques to do some boerie on the braai but he's so useless, I thought I'd rope you in instead." She peers over my shoulder.

"She's such a pro," Megs says. "Look at those tiny little squares!"

"Once you know that French method, it's easy," I say, scraping the onions into the pan on the stove with the back of the knife.

"Geez-like, did that knife come over with Jan van Riebeeck?"

"I left my knives in Cape Town," I tell Di. "This one's fine. It's what I learned to cook with."

"No, man," she says, slapping me lightly with the back of her hand. "I got a nice set from my in-laws for Christmas. A not-so-subtle hint that I need to start cooking for my family like a good little housewife. I'll bring them round tomorrow."

"You know the story of Jan van Riebeeck was a major marketing exercise?" Tshidi looks up from her crocheting. She's using a different wool from yesterday's, which was thick and navy. The thread linking the ball of wool to her crochet hook today is a silky dove-grey.

Di rolls her eyes at me before turning around. "Sorry?"

Tshidi pushes her glasses back up to the bridge of her nose. "He's a myth. There may have been a settler by that name, but his big 'hero and father of the nation' identity was invented to mobilise Afrikaans people around a common hero in the nineteen-fifties."

"I dropped history in Standard Seven," Di says, placing six eggs in the tea towel on the counter.

"I have my Masters in history," Tshidi replies calmly, rolling her wool across the kitchen table so that it unfurls.

Di pulls a face at me, trying to draw me into her dismissiveness of Tshidi and her theories. I keep my eyes on the pan, stirring the onion and garlic. I hate that she assumes that I'm like her, that I'm one of her set. It's a familiar discomfort.

"I didn't think garlic needed to be stirred so much," Megs says.

"If you don't, it burns." I decide not to mention the smell in the kitchen yesterday.

"I have to run, I left Fallan in charge of Liam and the baby, amazing parenting, I know," Di laughs. "Skye, let me know what you want to cook for Saturday and I'll buy it when I go into town tomorrow."

"What's today?" I am totally unmoored, floating around somewhere between Misty Cliffs and The Pines. I'm here in body, but my mind hasn't caught up. I switched my phone on after waking up this morning in a moment of low will-power and there was nothing, from Cam or anyone else.

"Tuesday, December twenty-seventh, twenty-sixteen."

"Got it. I'll come around this afternoon."

"Come through the turnstile, I'll leave it unlocked."

I reach into the warm oven to remove the slow-roasted cherry tomatoes, which have been drying under a low heat since 10 a.m. When I straighten up, Sullivan is standing next to me in a new bandanna and a clinging vest that would look all kinds of wrong on someone with arms that weren't as neatly muscled and a chest that wasn't as smooth. He pops one of the dry red buttons into his mouth and chews slowly.

"I think I'm in love," he says, with his eyes on my face.

"Ga-doef" goes my ridiculous heart, before my brain can get it under control.

"Oh, for god's sake," Tshidi exclaims. "Is there something in the water here?"

"I'm serious, that was the best tomato I've eaten in my life. Try," Sullivan holds one out to her, and when she shakes her head, he shrugs and eats it himself.

Then Andile is at my elbow, steering me out of the kitchen and into the dirt outside. "What did she say?"

The whites of his eyes are shot with red and there are white flecks in the corners of his lips. He looks dehydrated, and as if he hasn't slept since I saw him last night.

"What did who say?" I am stalling. Megs leans out the kitchen door and asks what to do next, but retreats immediately.

"Heather! About the money. I can't stay here much longer," he pants. "Last night, with Malcolm, it was –"

"You can't leave before me! I need you here." I put my hand on his arm, hoping it will calm him down. It doesn't.

"What's the deal with the empty bank account?"

I grimace.

"You didn't ask her, did you? Roo, you promised!"

"You didn't stay for the whole reading – we had a deal! And I was tired, I forgot."

He takes a step back and shakes his head. "You're going to have to try again. I swear to you, I'm leaving in the next couple of days, whether you've found out or not. Do it while I'm here so I can help you figure out what's next or wait till I'm gone and figure it out yourself."

"Wait!" I tell him what Heather said about Adrienne. I expect his expression to clear, but he keeps frowning.

"I don't care! If Heather doesn't start getting an income, she's going to have to sell the farm and she's going to be destitute, and that's it. I'm going into town. I'll see you later."

"Where in town?"

"A bar. The Keg. Anywhere, I don't know."

After he's left, I stare up at the leaves of the teak tree above my head, like fingers fluttering against the burning white sky, feel the sharp hum of the cicadas vibrating through my limbs, thinking nothing, empty, drifting, until Megs sticks her head out the kitchen door again and says, "What does it mean if the garlic's gone all black?"

≈

When the shadows of the trees are so long that they stretch across the back lawn, and most of the heat has been sapped out of the day, I walk around the lake towards the avocado orchards on the border of Di's farm. Walking along the fence near the gate means wading through the warm fug of ripe bananas in the sun.

It's this rotting smell that has always put me off bananas. We only ever got the bruised ones growing up.

"But the brown's the best bit!" Another Lola memory, her long fingers twisting the top off the banana I'm holding.

My grandfather planted these trees because it fitted in with his ideas of living on a working farm, and the fruit gets bought wholesale by the co-op in town. Lola used to talk about the "banana money" paying for our school stationery at the beginning of every year.

Bunches of them as big as my torso are sweating in their blue plastic sheaths hanging off the trees. The bags protect the fruit from the cunning vervet monkeys chattering in the treetops.

The gate between Di's farm and ours has had an upgrade: it's now a tall turnstile operated by a scanner with a small flashing green light, unlocked, as Di promised.

My legs remember the way from the gate to the farmhouse, which is lucky because the orchards have changed since I was last here. The differences between Coucal Farm and The Pines are stark, especially since they're only separated by about an inch. Here, the avocado trees are universally painted white on one side, sunscreen to shield them from the midday heat, and there's no dead growth to be seen, no grass growing between the rows, no fallen fruit or leaves on the ground beneath the trees.

A tractor emerges from one of the rows in front of me. It's carrying two farmworkers in identical green overalls. The one in the passenger seat is holding a clipboard. They catch sight of me and wave, and I wonder what the protocol is for leaving access gates open. I can't imagine living on a farm that operates like a corporate machine.

Unlike The Pines, Coucal Farm's cottages are workers' housing. They've also had an upgrade. I count eight brightly painted houses as I walk past, with big windows and tied-back curtains, pansies in flowerbeds in front of each one, and through open kitchen doors, I see bright, white-tiled interiors. The last time I was on Coucal Farm was probably at the end of Matric, before I left for chef school, when the workers' homes still had outhouses.

The lawn that functioned as a cricket oval for all the years of our childhood is still there, now covered in children's paraphernalia: three bikes, rubber balls in varying states of deflation, naked plastic dolls, a wooden toy gun and an assortment of plastic buckets and spades strewn from one end to the next. The dam to the right of the house is not wide but looks deep, the water still and black in the shadows of the trees. There's a ramshackle DIY fence around it, made of chicken wire and wooden poles. A child half my size could step over it.

I'm about to ring the bell when the front door is wrenched open from inside. A girl with a mane of blonde hair looks me up and down.

"Are you a visitor?"

"Yes. Is your mom home?"

"Are you here to visit her or me?" She is wearing what looks like a sheet tied under her arms, and bright silver pumps.

"That depends. Who are you?"

"I'm Molly. I'm seven. Where's your car? Why aren't you wearing socks?"

The door is pulled open further and a smaller version of Molly but with shorter hair appears, wearing a skirt that's too long and has been rolled up at the waist.

"I'm Liam. We're playing queen-queen," he says.

"She's here to see Mom," Molly says to him, "and she doesn't have a car or socks."

"Skye! Please don't mind my children. Shoo," Di says, giving them each a nudge with her foot and gesturing me inside. She's holding a plump, bald baby that is sucking its fist. "We don't get many visitors here on foot. We don't get many visitors coming in the front door, come to think of it. I'm surprised it hasn't fused shut."

I can't find anywhere to put my feet that won't mean standing on a children's book or toy or blanket. My eyes start to water instantly, so I know there's at least one cat somewhere nearby, though the balls of fur in the corners could have told me that.

"Let's go to the sunroom, I've put some iced tea in there for us. I've spiked it with gin. It's after four, after all."

Liam and Molly careen off down the passage and slam one of the bedroom doors behind them. The interior walls have been knocked down, creating one big open-plan living space, which is probably lovely and airy when it's not filled with chaos.

There are shelves all the way up to the ceiling on either side of the flat-screen TV in the lounge area. All of them except the ones right at the top are bursting with everything from stuffed toys to DVDs to books piled haphazardly on top of one another. I can make out a coffee table under piles of newspapers, and there's a large wooden play-pen in the corner. Di lowers the baby into the pen and hands her a chew toy that looks as if it's been gnawed by a dog, and she yells, "Stellaaaaaa! Quinn's in the play-pen!"

"Like *A Streetcar Named Desire*."

Diana shoots me a questioning look.

"Marlon Brando? He's got a famous scene where he shouts out his wife's name, 'Stella!'?" Cam was a Brando fanatic. I was subjected to everything from *Streetcar* to *The Score* at least twice over.

"Stella's the maid. I think she's ironing in the laundry room. Let me go find her quick. The sunroom's the first door on the left. Go in, make yourself at home."

Di leaves through the kitchen door and I hear a chair scrape on the floor behind me. There's another blonde girl sitting at the round dining room table, colouring in. She lifts her eyes to me and smiles. Her features are finer than Molly's and Liam's, and she looks less like Diana than the other two, with a long face and a delicate nose dusted with freckles that I can see from across the room.

"Are you Fallan? I'm Skye. I'm Heather's daughter. Your mom and I went to school together."

She puts her pencil down and scratches the inside of her wrist. She's wearing a long-sleeved pink shirt with a sequinned fish on the front.

"Does that mean you're our next-door neighbour?"

"I suppose so. What are you colouring?"

"A mermaid," she says, turning the book around to show me.

"That's lovely," I say. "How old are you?"

"Five-and-two-thirds. On the fifteenth of January I'll be five-and-three-quarters."

"You know a lot of maths."

She scratches her other wrist and pulls the book closer to herself.

"Why aren't you playing dress-up with your brother and sister?"

"They always make me be the rooster," she replies. "They make me lie under Molly's bed and all I'm allowed to do is say cock-a-doodle-do when it's morning time in the game. Molly says there aren't enough dress-up clothes for three kids."

I watch her colour the mermaid's tail, shading purple into green.

"I wish I had sparkly pens. My friend Gabby's got sparkly pens with glitter in but Mom says I'm not old enough but Gabby's not even five-and-a-quarter yet and her mom let her get them."

"I've told you before, Fallan, different moms have different rules." Di's back inside, and a small woman in uniform follows her.

"Diana, you can't leave the child like this! She gets bored," Stella says, swooping down and scooping Quinn up out of the play-pen, tickling her under the chin. Quinn beams at her.

Diana looks at me and rolls her eyes and this time I'm not quick enough to avoid the look. "I can't believe the way this woman talks to me, honestly, but I inherited her, so what can I do?" I know she thinks she's talking quietly, but Stella – and Fallan – are both clearly in ear-shot.

I am intensely uncomfortable – can she not hear what she sounds like? – and cast around for something neutral to say to change the subject. "Fallan's got a good handle on fractions," I settle on.

"She's a little maths boff, this one. We don't know where she comes from!"

Fallan looks up and frowns at her mother. "Mom, if you have the rule that I'm not allowed sparkly pens why didn't Father Christmas bring me any? I asked him in three letters!"

"I am not getting into this with you again! He brought you a pedal bike, you should be pleased!"

"I didn't ask for a pedal bike and I even can't ride it because he forgot the fairy wheels."

"Father Christmas agrees with your father and me that you shouldn't need fairy wheels because you're already five and Liam's been riding his pedal bike without training wheels since he was two, for heaven's sake."

Fallan looks back down at her book and sighs wearily, as if she's the grown-up and her mother is the five-year-old. The five-and-two-thirds-year-old.

Two thirds of a year. Eight months.

"When's your birthday, Fallan? April?" Something has occurred to me, a whisper in the back of my mind.

"Yes. The fifteenth of April."

I remember the estimated due date slip from Dr Taylor, my gynae, that I kept for months before finally throwing it away, her scrawl spelling out: "EDD 15/04/2016."

"Hurry up, Skye, the ice in our gin is melting!"

When Di and I are settled on the wicker couches in the sun room, a cosy space filled with flourishing, fragrant orchids, a space obviously off-limits to her brood, I tell Di that I'm not drinking gin at the moment. She gets up to fetch me some white wine from the fridge.

"It's plonk," she warns as she leaves.

There is an undertone to the sweet smell of the orchids, a base note of ammonia, and I feel my pulse in my temples as my heart rate speeds up. It takes me right back to the *Fig & Brie* bathroom, which had just been cleaned when I went in there on the day I first met Tshidi.

It happened in the second week of October.

Five

Cam and I had only been together three months at that stage. I worked out that I'd got pregnant one of the first times we'd slept together, when I was on antibiotics for a sinus infection. Cam had loved the heat of my skin during my fevers. He'd found me irresistible, and we'd ended up having sex twice, three times a day in that week. I was woozy from the painkillers and high on what I suppose were love hormones. Feeling his cool, bare skin against the fevered burn of mine was a shot of pure oxytocin.

To be honest, I'd thought it was an urban legend that antibiotics could mess with the pill. But the third day of the inert pills came round without my usual PMS symptoms, without bloating and cramps, and, by the end of that week, I still hadn't got my period.

I did a test one evening when I wasn't due to see Cam. I was still living in the dive in Mowbray, and had told him I couldn't spend the night because I felt like I was coming down with something. I imagined blurting out "pregnancy!", and almost laughed, imagining his reaction.

The test line was so faint I could barely make it out. It's got to be negative, I thought. It's fine, I'm late, that's all.

A week later I still hadn't had my period. I was off the pill completely at that stage. One morning, I opened the digs fridge and was immediately repulsed by the smell, an odour I'd never noticed before. I closed the door, got my phone out my pocket and Googled "symptoms of early pregnancy". There it was: sensitivity to smell.

I did another test the next morning. I'd bought them on a two-for-one special, which seemed like a strange deal for the pharmacy to be running. Then again, I probably wasn't the only person who'd needed more than one test to be safe, to be sure.

The second line was clear as day, and impossible to ignore.

The first person I thought of was Heather. She'd be so disappointed. "If I'd finished my degree," she'd always say before launching into a monologue about all the things she'd missed out on because she got pregnant with me.

And here I was, faced with either giving up my dream of running my own restaurant because I'd decided to fuck my irresistible new boyfriend while I was on antibiotics, or making an appointment at a Marie Stopes clinic.

Knowing that Heather had faced the same choice with me, and that Lola had too, with Andile, stopped me from making the appointment. I did consider it. I looked up the location of the nearest clinic on the maps app on my phone. I planned how I'd get there, where I'd park my car. But I knew I'd never be able to go through with it. The cluster of cells inside me would turn into a whole person, like Andile and I had, and that mattered to me.

I'd phoned Dr Taylor's office and told the receptionist I needed a check-up because I was pregnant. She'd sent me for blood tests. When Cam asked why I had a plaster stuck in the vein in the crook of my elbow I told him I'd donated blood and he'd accepted it without missing a beat. When the test results were in, the receptionist booked me in for a scan when I would be nine weeks, an interminable three weeks later.

That was when I heard the heartbeat, at the last appointment of the day on a chilly evening at the end of September. The mugging happened when I was walking from Dr Taylor's rooms to Cam's flat through the heart of the City Bowl, with the glossy scan pictures of the little bean with the head and tiny gecko hands burning a hole in my handbag.

It was later than I realised, almost 7 p.m. I should have been more alert. Having grown up on the farm, I'd never been comfortable walking around in town alone. But there I was, caught somewhere between elation and hysteria on a deserted side road with dark falling quickly. I didn't see the men until they were all around me.

"Here," Diana says, shoving a wine glass at me so hard that the ice crashes against the side and the wine almost slops out. "Like I said, it's terrible, but my mother-in-law left it behind on Christmas Eve and she didn't get around to opening it, which was a big surprise for me. Usually when she has to spend time here, she can't get the wine down quickly enough. Medicinal purposes, she says."

She settles back against the cushions on the couch opposite me and tucks her legs underneath herself. I force myself to concentrate on her, to pull myself away from the precipice of the flashback, breathing through my mouth so that I can't detect the whiff of ammonia.

"She's taking the older kids to Durban with her in January. I'm going to get a blissful ten days all on my own, well, with Quinn, but still. You won't believe what a rigmarole it was to get all the documents they'll need to fly with her. Birth certificates, affidavits, what have you. I had to go to Home Affairs, like, four times."

Her face is thinner than I remember, her eyes bigger.

"Before I forget, those are the knives she gave me." She gestures with her glass of orange liquid, poured from a big clear jug brimming with ice and mint leaves. I look down and see a leather sheath with five silver stippled handles tucked into it.

"There's about five grand's worth of knives in this sheath," I tell her. Even straight after the mugging, I wasn't jittery around big knives like these. The only blades that make me nervous now are small ones that are sharper than they look and can be easily hidden in the palm of a hand.

"Please, take them. Lord knows I won't use them. Stella does all our cooking, the same way she cooked for Jacques and them when they were kids. Rys, vleis en aartappels, forever and ever amen."

"I could go for some meat, quite honestly. Heather's gone full-on vegan. Except for the honey, which she bottles and gives away, but doesn't eat, which, you know, makes me wonder about the ethics of the whole thing."

"She's been vegan for years. Since Andile's mother died, I think. She told me once it was because she felt guilty about all the toxins Lola had eaten, that that's why she got stomach cancer. I don't know, hey, I'm not sure life's worth living without meat. Or cheese."

I murmur acknowledgement and try not to show my bewilderment. That's why Heather's become so strict about food? Because of Lola? I'm the one who did the cooking for years before I left. Am I to blame, on some level?

I can't bear the thought, and push it out of my mind. "What should I make for Saturday night?"

"Can you do something with lamb? We've got half a sheep in the deep freeze. Jacques won it at the Lowveld

Show and we've been waiting to use it for something. A spit, maybe?"

"I don't know the first thing about spit braaing."

"Jacques and his bladdy useless mates can do the spit. But will you do the salads, the breads and stuff? Some sauces, and maybe starters? Puddings?"

"Puddings, plural?"

She looks at me out the corner of her eye as she takes a gulp of iced tea.

"You sound so prim and proper hey, Skye, it's hard to believe you grew up here like the rest of us!" She leans forward and her breasts threaten to spill out over the top of her sundress. "Look, Jacques asked me not to say anything, but I'm going to tell you why I'm so pushy with the catering and stuff. It's because we want to open a restaurant here, on Coucal Farm. We want to convert the old storehouse and offer something very unique, but we haven't found a chef, so Jacques thought we could ask you to do the food for your party, and we could see how you cook and if it's good, maybe hire you for the restaurant."

She sits back, never taking her eyes off me, gauging my reaction. I make sure to keep my face neutral.

"I don't know what my plans are, how long I'm going to be staying. Salads and sauces and puddings – plural – for the party, though, that's no problem. How many people?"

"Around fifteen, I think? I thought of inviting the writers. I'm sure they're going crazy at Heather's with no meat or smoking. Jacques's brother Ben will be home from the bush. He's arriving this afternoon." She checks her watch. "He should be here by now. Jacques went to pick him up in town and they probably went to The Keg."

"I'd better get going," I say, putting down the wine glass. My first sip has given me an instant headache.

"Let me call Jacques. I'll get him to take you home when he gets back." She pulls her phone out her pocket and has started tapping the screen when a car door slams at the back of the house.

"Good timing!" Di starts pulling me from the sunroom by the hand. "Take your knives, and I'll ask him to quickly drop you at The Pines."

There are three men's voices, and I hear a guffaw that I'd recognise anywhere.

"My sister's here! Jacques, you remember Roo?" Andile says, grinning. His eyes have the shrunken, far-away look they get when he is extremely drunk.

Jacques is short, stocky, no neck. Deeply tanned, and with a cap of fine blonde hair. He leans in for a hug and it's like putting my arms around a baobab trunk.

"Hi, liefie," he says to Di.

"Oh, it's 'liefie', is it?" She tries to lean away from his kiss, but he plants one loudly on her cheek.

The third guy is a stretched-out version of Jacques. He's in a safari suit and slops, and he's so deeply brown that I can't tell if he's covered in a fine layer of dirt or a very thorough suntan.

"Ben," he says to me. "I don't think you remember me."

"Not really," I admit. "There were a lot of you little brothers running around."

"Ben is on a few days' leave from Kruger. He's a ranger at one of the private lodges," Di says. "Where's all your stuff? By 'stuff', I mean laundry."

"In the bakkie. It's okay, I'll do it at the laundromat tomorrow."

"Stop showing off for Skye! 'Laundromat'. Please."

Ben smiles shyly. "Where's Fallan?"

"You don't ask about your other nieces and your nephew, do you?" Jacques is opening and closing kitchen cupboards loudly. Stella shuts one of the bedroom doors in the passage and comes into the kitchen, shushing Jacques. He asks her something in Afrikaans. She goes to the scullery at the back of the kitchen and comes back with three tumblers, puts them on the counter crossly, and admonishes Jacques by holding a finger up at him before sweeping out of the kitchen door.

Andile grabs one of the tumblers. "I've got whisky in the car."

"I'll get it. I need to bring Ben's laundry in in any case," Di says, following Stella out the kitchen door.

"Di, it's fine!" Ben calls out after her. He turns to me. "I was sixteen when my parents left, and Jacques looked after me till I went to college. Him and Di think I'm their son or something. Like Stella. She still thinks I'm five years old."

"Are you stealing my knife's wives? I mean, my wives' knifes?" Jacques asks me, squinting at the pouch in my hand.

"She said she wouldn't ever use them."

Jacques clicks his tongue. "My poor mother. Every year she spends more and more money on Christmas presents for Princess Diana and it's never good enough."

Andile is digging in his back pocket. He pulls out his wallet and scratches around inside it, pulling out a two-rand coin.

"Here, Roo, give this to Di. It's bad luck to give knives as a present."

One of Lola's rules. Never put shoes on a table. If you do, you have to put them on the ground and jump over them three times. Never open an umbrella inside the house. Peacock feathers are bad luck. Andile's eyes meet mine as I take the coin and I can tell that he's remembering too.

"Let's go home, Andile. It's been a long day. I'm supposed to help Megs make dinner."

"No, stay. One more. Look, here's Di with the whisky," Jacques sits down hard on one of the dining room table chairs, in front of Fallan's colouring book.

"Is Fallan asleep?" I ask Di when she comes in the door, lugging a bag of laundry in one hand and the fingers of her other hand clutched around the neck of a bottle.

"I hope not. It's only six o'clock. I don't think she's had her supper yet."

"I want to say goodbye to her quickly. I'll drive us back in two minutes, Andile, okay?"

He nods, his eyelids drooping.

"Pour me a whisky, Jacques," Ben says. "I'm going to say hi to Fallan."

"I do have other children, you know!" Jacques calls after us.

"Yes, but the others are bloody hooligans," Ben whispers to me, and I can't help but grin.

Inside the girls' bedroom, Molly is on the top bunk, with two Barbie dolls, one with short-cropped hair.

"Uncle Ben!" she says.

Fallan's in the bottom bunk, lying on her back, singing under her breath. She sits up and throws her arms open for Ben to hug her.

"Will you read to me tonight?"

"To *us*," Molly corrects her.

"Since when do you two share a room?"

"Since Mom needed to make mine into a spare room. For visitors. Maybe like that one?" Molly points at me.

"I came to say goodbye."

"She doesn't have socks," Molly says to Ben conspiratorially. He looks at me and grins.

"Me neither," he says, wiggling his toes in his slops.

"Bye, Skye," Fallan says to me. "Ben is going to read us *The Very Scary Crocodile* before bed tonight."

"No, he's not, you're too little for it," Molly says.

"Bye, Fallan," I say. Ben winks at me, and I give him a wave. I wonder how old he is. Probably too young for me to be wondering.

By the time I get back to the living area, Andile is sleeping with his head on his arms on the dining room table.

"He's not a happy camper," Jacques says to me. "He said something about Heather and money?"

I don't want Jacques involved, but Di jumps in quickly. "Is Heather worried about money?"

"No. That's the problem," I reply. "She hasn't said anything to you about it?"

She straightens up from the washing machine where she's been loading Ben's clothes and shakes her head. "She doesn't talk about herself at all. She's the most selfless person I've ever met. Seriously, Skye, if it wasn't for your mother, I'd go mad here all day by myself. She's a godsend."

"Oh, come on, liefie, you've got friends. Your mom comes to visit all the time." Jacques takes a sip of his whisky.

"My mother comes to visit the kids, not me. My friends all work, they don't come round in the middle of the day. School holidays are a freaking nightmare."

"What, so you want to go back to work? She's a lawyer," Jacques directs the last bit at me.

"Not a practising one. I've never got my articles."

"Used to work for the World Bank," Jacques says, "before I convinced her to be my housewife."

Andile stirs and I say my goodbyes, pressing the two-rand coin into Di's hands before we leave, steering Andile into the car by the elbow.

I drop him off outside Fever Tree Cottage, watch him stumble inside and close the door behind him. I resolve to have a straight conversation with Heather as soon as I can, for the sake of Andile's liver. He'll kill himself if he keeps drinking like this.

≈

There's a bag of pearl barley in the pantry cupboard, so I decide to show Megs how to make a risotto for dinner. By "bag", I mean a 10-kilo hessian sack.

"Heather, where do you get these massive bags of stuff?" I heave it off the shelf and put it down in front of Megs. "We need half a cup of barley per person," I tell her.

"Richard, the protea farmer down the road? His sister has a contact."

"It's like the black market for organic dried grains and pulses," Malcolm says. He and Heather are sitting at the kitchen table reading his hand-written sheets of poetry. Heather's got a pen tucked behind her ear. Every now and again she takes it out and makes a note in the margins.

"But where do they come from?"

Heather looks up. "His sister knows a farmer in the Western Cape who's cultivating heirloom varieties of barley and lentils and chickpeas. Drought-resistant. Very important for that region at the moment, as I'm sure you know. How have you been coping with the water restrictions down there?"

It's the first time she's asked about my life away from here. My real life, I should say. I shrug. "We – Cam – I – the biggest thing is not watering gardens or filling swimming pools. I lived – we live – in a flat, so that's obviously not an issue."

"I see," she says. She crosses something out on the page in front of her. "You've added a syllable here," she says to Malcolm. He looks over and grunts.

"Let's go see what's growing in the veggie garden," I say to Megs. "We want some squash, something starchy, some beans or aubergines."

"There are a lot of peas at the moment," Heather says. "Lots of herbs, too."

She points at the shears hanging up next to the kitchen door, and I grab a pair before Megs and I leave. I kick my shoes off at the door, expecting mud. It's getting dark outside, pale sky deepening into a dark purple.

Round the back of the house and behind the tractor shed – which hasn't housed a tractor since I've been alive – is Heather's vegetable garden. It's doubled, maybe tripled, in size since I lived here, with stakes neatly planted in freshly aerated and recently watered soil. There are little chalkboards at the top of each stake with the names of plants on them. The cool wet dirt rises up between my toes as I march down the rows.

Megs holds forth about her dieting friends using spaghetti squash as a substitute for the real thing until we find the marrow plants. The skins are already hardened, and they're the size of French loaves. I need to tell Heather to harvest them and hang them up: any bigger and they'll be too watery. Next to the marrow plants are watermelon vines, spreading leggily across the ground to take up about a third of the patch. I hand three marrows to Megs to carry and think about making a watermelon sorbet for the party.

The patty pans are next to the marrows. Each compact, bushy vine holds five or six bright yellow clam-like squashes, and they're smooth and cool in my palm. I drop 10 of them into my apron pocket and move on to the pea plants in the next row. Somewhere in the back of my mind I remember Heather's lessons on companion planting, of summer squash and peas and beans being best friends.

I pull handfuls of plump sugar-snap pods off the staked plants. They won't grow anymore in this heat, so we may as well harvest them all. Soon Megs's apron pocket is bulging with our glut of peas, and before we head back to the house, I snap off a few sprigs of coriander. I inhale the leaves' stink-bug smell, which always makes me feel simultaneously queasy and nostalgic. When we were 10 or 11, Andile went through a phase of trapping the bugs in his hands long enough for them to release their smell, and rubbing his hands against my nose. I got him back once and for all by sneaking one into his popcorn when we went to Coucal Farm for an outdoor movie night. I remember my giddy satisfaction as I watched him crunch right through it. He's hated coriander ever since.

I hose off my feet before we go back into the kitchen, and that's where Sullivan finds me, holding a posy of coriander in one hand and the hose pipe in the other.

"What's in your apron?" he asks softly, sidling up to me.

"Peas. No, patty pans." I am like one of those cartoons with the shape of a heart hammering out of my chest. I can smell his soap and feel the heat his body's giving off.

"Let me see."

I pull open the apron pocket. He looks down and puts his hand inside, brushing the tops of my thighs. He cups one of the patty pans in his fingers, rubbing his thumb slowly over the bumps. My knees turn to melted wax.

He drops the patty pan back into the pocket and brings his eyes up to mine. "You're flushed," he says.

"It's hot," I say, or mean to say. His eyes are a gleaming, burnished gold in the twilight.

"I'm so glad you came home," he says in a low voice. The word "home" brings me back to myself. I hadn't felt a rush of blood to the head like that since Cam and I first got together.

"That's because it means you don't have to eat Megs's food anymore."

"Hey! My cooking's not *that* bad!" Megs calls from inside the kitchen.

I wonder how much she's seen and heard. Nothing's happened, nothing overt, but I can't imagine that what I want isn't written all over my face. I take a step away from Sullivan, drop the hosepipe, and rearrange my features.

I leave Sullivan standing next to the puddle outside. After a moment, he comes inside and starts running water into the sink, piling teacups and teaspoons into it. He plunges his hands into the steaming water and starts rinsing the cutlery. I have to force myself to tear my eyes away from his wet, blunt fingers.

I hand the new paring knife to Megs. "Start chopping the patty pans. All in the same sized pieces. Watch your fingers."

Six

I wake up early the next morning, the air still cool and light, the sun not yet filtering into my bedroom through the teak trees. For the first time in days, I'm craving the solitude of a run. The solid seven kilometres from the house, past the lake, up the hill, around the bluegum bend, to the gate and back again is exactly what I need.

I find a pair of my school socks, marked for hostel, with "K-S Moore" sewn into the toe. The last socks I ran in were Cam's Falkes. It's only been 10 days since I borrowed them, and already the idea of that kind of intimacy with him seems impossible. I rummage to find my dark green school shorts, an old running bra in one of my drawers and another school golf shirt. They're all fresh-smelling, un-creased, as if I'd come back home for the weekend from hostel. The shoes squeak over the wooden floor but my mother and Malcolm don't stir. It's barely 6 a.m. and I'm reminded of the last time I snuck out of a house at dawn.

I start along the driveway and see a figure running up ahead of me, approaching the hairpin bend. Tshidi. Her hair's in a big bun at the nape of her neck and she's wearing spandex shorts, a breathable shirt and trail-running shoes with little rubber cleats on the sole. The way her muscles move in her calves tells me that she does this a lot.

I'm going to catch up to her soon. I can't keep running a few paces behind her and I don't want to run with her, but I also don't want to turn around and go back.

She hears my footfalls and turns around, stopping, her hands on her hips, her chest rising and falling. She's smiling. Her skin is dewy and her arms are willowy. If it weren't for her tattoos – *we are the moon* – she'd be an image straight out of a wholesome sports apparel ad.

"Your mother told me you liked running," she says when I'm next to her. "This altitude is killing me."

I wipe the streaming sweat off my forehead with the back of my wrist. Cam said I sweated less than any human he'd ever met in his life. If only he could see me now, perspiration pouring off my face after barely a kilometre.

"How do you feel about running with people?" Tshidi asks. She takes one look at my face and laughs. "You go ahead, I need to catch my breath."

I'm thinking I'm not too keen on her watching me shuffle all the way up the hill, when she says, "Wait, before you go. I don't want to interfere with your life or whatever. But Sullivan – I mean, it's completely obvious that he's hitting on you with, like, some serious intention. Which is, you know, whatever, each to their own, but you have to get that he doesn't respect women. Like, at all. His books have a feminist backlash for a reason."

My eyes are burning from the sweat leaking into them. "What do you want me to say?"

She holds her hands up. "I thought I'd warn you that he's got a rep. He's with Adrienne because his previous agent dropped him after a scandal at a big book-fest in the States. He was caught messing around with another author's daughter, who was like fifteen. He's thirty-eight. There's a reason he writes creepy protagonists so well."

"I'm only here another few days. I don't think any-thing's going to happen."

She bends down to tie her shoelace. "You're married, right?"

"In theory."

I'm anticipating a question about what happened the day we first met, so I indicate to her that I'm about to start jogging again. I feel her eyes on my back as I head off. I push myself up that hill so hard that my burning hamstrings distract me from the fist squeezing around my heart.

≈

I stop at the gate, my back itching from the sweat beading down my spine. I turn to look down at The Pines, past the glimmer of the surface of the lake, over the canopy of fir trees to the glint of the slate roof of the main house, cottage chimneys poking through here and there.

Heather is making her way to the washing line with a round basket. I watch her move, so tiny, so purposeful. I take deep gulps of soupy air, trying to breathe into the stitch, as Heather bends down, straightens up, bends down, straightens up, rhythmically, like she's doing yoga or tai-chi. Hanging the laundry used to be my job, as soon I was tall enough to reach the washing line. I loved the coolness of the damp sheets when they blew against me, and the faint, delicate scent of the eco-friendly liquid detergent Heather uses.

That smell, like a hint of jasmine, like the yesterday-today-and-tomorrow bushes in the garden, doesn't last long on clothing or linen. It's not as persistently fragrant as factory-made washing powder.

That's what the pillowcase in my old bedroom smells like, I realise. It must have been washed a matter of days before I arrived. It's what this school shirt smelled like before I sweated into it. The school shirt that wasn't folded up in the trunk between layers of tissue paper, as all my old clothes usually are. The school shirt that had recently been washed and ironed and hung up in my cupboard in anticipation of my arrival.

We didn't surprise Heather at all, Andile and me, when we arrived at The Pines. She was waiting for us. She knew we were coming.

I freewheel down the hill, passing Tshidi with barely a wave. She stops when she sees me, but I race past her, trying not to pound my feet, watching my step so I don't stumble and twist an ankle. My thighs are burning, my arms are pumping, I'm cutting through the moisture in the air like I'm swimming for shore.

I turn left off the dirt road onto the path made by 4x4s on the grass between the avocado trees, weaving and ducking under branches, my feet landing on squelchy, sucking patches of rank fallen leaves. By the time I get to the doorstep of Fever Tree Cottage, I'm ready to collapse onto the cool stone. I knock three times, hard, and push the door open to find Andile listlessly stirring a coffee cup at the kitchen counter. He rears his head and blinks at me blearily.

"Heather knew. She was expecting us. My bed was made when I arrived, my linen had been washed, my clothes were clean and hanging up."

Andile snorts into his cup, takes a glug.

"I'm serious! What are you drinking? Coffee? As in, not chicory? She doesn't keep coffee in the cottages for guests. Was there milk in the fridge? Proper cows' milk? Not nut milk or some shit?"

He lowers his cup and looks into it as if he's going to read the truth in the grinds settled in the bottom. "She knows I hate nut milk."

"Exactly!" I hold the bottom of my shirt and fan it to get some air moving between the cotton and my body.

"So she was expecting us," Andile says, slamming his mug down on the glass coffee table in front of him. "And?"

"The money! It means she made sure there was nothing coming into her account on purpose, so she could get us here. It means she does have money, somewhere, but not in the account you expected."

"Heather's never been into a bank in her life. How's she going to open a whole new account?"

It's what I've been wondering myself, the only hole in my hypothesis.

"She got onto Facebook, who's to say she hasn't also started internet banking?"

He groans. "I don't think I'm in the right frame of mind for wild conspiracy theories."

"If she wanted us to come here, both of us, at the same time, for the first time in almost ten years? She's got a reason, and it's a good one." Something occurs to me, and I gasp. "What if she wants to tell us she's decided to marry Malcolm?"

Andile grabs his phone off the counter and leaves the cottage with me, pulling the door closed behind him.

"If this is bogus, I'm going to be pissed," he says. "Though if it's true, I'll be more pissed. This is a lose-lose for us, you realise."

I squeeze his arm. I've got to the bottom of it, I've cracked it, we're going to find out that Heather's got loads of money, piles of it tucked away somewhere, and we don't have to worry about her, she won't be destitute, the farm's fine. There's a simple explanation waiting for us that will make everything fall into place. We'll go to the party on Saturday and both leave on Monday and we'll have had a whole week together for the first time in almost 10 years, an unexpected treat, like a holiday. Cam will have left me a million messages on my phone, Rory will have come back for Maya, the storm in a teacup around Zhou and Bushy Bun will have blown over and Cam will want me to come back and we'll carry on with the restaurant and Deacon will have forgiven me. We'll go to Japan in July and I'll look back at this time as a blip in our long, happy marriage.

It will be funny: "Remember that time I left you without telling you why, ha ha". I'll introduce him to Andile and bring him to The Pines sometime. He'll be so grateful I've come back to him, he won't care about how odd my mother is or how little money we had when I was growing up.

I am a chef, a married chef, I remind myself, with a successful restaurant and a very good-looking, wealthy husband who adores me. All I have to do to get back to my real life is have this conversation with Heather.

It's all I can do not to sprint to the house when we get to the driveway. Andile is panting, but I've got so much energy I can almost feel it shooting out of the tips of my fingers. I'm practically skipping.

He grabs my wrist. "I don't know what you're so happy about. There's no way that this plays out well for us."

"Maybe she wanted to see her children! To have us here for the holiday! Maybe she missed us."

"This is the endorphins speaking," Andile mutters.

There's a crested barbet trilling out its high-pitched drilling call in the trees, a kwêvoël a little further away, sending its gruff "kweeeehs" up into the atmosphere. It's a good day, a beautiful day.

"It's all going to be okay," I tell Andile. He looks at me sceptically and finally, finally starts walking again. In approximately five seconds we'll be in the house, we'll be with Heather, and we'll know.

Seven

"Well, of course I didn't *know* you'd both come home, but I was hoping you would," Heather says.

We're sitting on the small veranda, a cold breeze that smells like rain swirling around us. Andile is gaping at Heather, who keeps picking up her kombucha glass and putting it down again precisely in the circle of moisture it's left on the linoleum of the rickety table.

"But how did you open a new account?"

"I went to the bank."

"Physically into the actual, physical bank?" I can't picture it, my mother in one of her innumerable pairs of khaki slacks and the pleather sandals she's had since the 80s, pushing open the glass door of the bank on the main road, like any normal person.

She laughs. "Yes, Roo. I'd never wanted to go before. Never needed to."

There's a low rumble of thunder way off in the hills on the horizon. I can't stop my knee from bouncing.

"I'm sure you're wondering why I went to these lengths to lure you back."

"Yes, but I also think you should know that we were seriously worried about you. I thought you were going to end up destitute. I thought you'd gone off the deep end. I thought you were going to have to sell The Pines," Andile says.

Heather reaches over and squeezes his arm. I expect him to snatch it away, but he doesn't. "You worry too much, love. I won't be destitute. I'm not crazy – not yet, anyway. But there is something I wanted to talk to you about."

"Why didn't you phone us? Send a text? We'd have come."

Heather licks her lips and digs in her pocket for the tiny tub of coconut oil she's always got on her. She pulls her lips over her teeth and applies the opaque liquid with her pinkie finger. She doesn't answer until she's screwed the lid back on and put the tub back in her pocket.

"I didn't want to beg. Neither of you have been here in years. It's been five years for you, Andile, and almost nine for Roo. I was scared. I didn't want to ask you to come and have to listen to your excuses."

I look down, a flush crawling up my neck. I *would* have made excuses. I'd have said I was too busy with Cam's family or the restaurant.

"I'm trying to decide if I'm pissed off with you for manipulating us. It's pretty extreme, Heather. Don't take this the wrong way, but it's extreme even for you." Andile looks at her out of the corner of his eyes, not wanting to face her straight on.

The way the table's set up lends itself to Andile not looking her in the eye. We sit in the same formation as always, Heather at the head, me at the foot, Andile on the bench against the wall, and Lola's chair empty on the other side. She always sat with her back to the garden, the worst seat at the table, and I never once wondered why.

"I realise it's not the best decision I've ever made, but I had to get your attention somehow. We've all fallen out of touch, and I know as the mother it's mostly my fault, but – I've been struggling, guys. I've been very lonely."

I've got goosebumps, but not because of the cool gusts of wind. I've never heard Heather admitting to not coping. I wish she hadn't. I don't want to hear this. I don't want to pity her.

"The years since losing Lola have been the darkest of my life. I decided that it's time I choose to do something for myself."

I'm hanging onto her words, both knees bouncing uncontrollably, my hands shaking.

"I've decided that I'm going to move to Texas." Heather sits back, her smile spreading relief across her face.

"Texas?" Andile and I say at the same time.

"Yes. I'm moving in with Adrienne."

"But you don't have a passport!"

"I do. A British one, remember, because of my parents."

"What are you going to do for money?"

"I'm going to start off as a reader for Adrienne's agency. At least I won't have to worry about rent."

"What about The Pines?"

Heather holds up a finger. "That's why I needed you both to be here. I've got a lawyer –"

"How?"

"For god's sake, Roo, I'm a fully grown adult. I know how to take up legal counsel."

Heather spends so little time off the farm that I can't imagine her anywhere else: not the bank, not the airport, and absolutely not halfway across the world.

"I've created a trust over which you two have signing power, and I've put the ownership of The Pines into the name of the trust. My lawyer's drawn up all the paperwork, I've got the contract in my desk drawer in the library. If you sign it, you will own The Pines together as sole beneficiaries of the trust."

Andile slowly turns to look at me with wide eyes.

"Also, you should know that the company that owns Coucal Farm is interested in buying the land. They want to plant bananas on it. Most agri-businesses are looking to Mozambique these days but the company thinks Moz is too unstable. They'd rather plant here."

I half-pity, half-envy the me from 10 minutes ago who had no idea about any of this.

"Di's going to be here any minute. I'd better go get the washing off the line before the rain comes. I'll leave the two of you to discuss things. You're about to become business partners."

She's halfway through the heavy metal door leading to her bedroom when I find my voice. "What about Malcolm?"

"What about him?"

"Does he know you're going to be moving in with, um, with Adrienne?"

She looks up at the thunderclouds. "He's a fling. Nothing serious. A bit of fun." She looks at me and laughs. "He was published in the *New Yorker*, Roo! The *New Yorker*!"

The sky lights up for a second, and almost instantly we hear the first crack of thunder directly above our heads.

"Shit, the washing!"

Andile and I watch Heather rushing through her bedroom, look at each other and start laughing, softly at first, until we're both full-blown howling with disbelief. When the tears come, I'm helpless to stop them. He's wiping his eyes, too, and I don't think we've done this since our stoned hammock afternoons in high school.

"What's going on?" I ask once we've recovered.

He shakes his head slowly. "I have absolutely no idea."

≈

I've decided on the watermelon sorbet. Also, a salsa verde, pickled radishes, an Asian-style slaw, a sweet potato gratin, and chapattis. And to make sure I bring puddings-plural, I'm going to do a couple of dozen mince pies. It's after Christmas and they're more pastry than pudding, but they'll have to do.

Heather's offered some of the orange blossom water she puts in her bath to flavour the pastry. When she hands it over, I uncap the bottle immediately and breathe in the sweet citrus fragrance. My memories of Heather are arranged in my mind by smell. Anaïs Anaïs. Jasmine. Orange blossom. I slot this latest entry into the mental catalogue.

Once the rain has stopped, I go out to the garden to harvest a watermelon or two.

Malcolm is staking the tomato bushes.

"I have an allotment at home, but these African plants are something else entirely," he says, wrestling with a rain-spattered vine that keeps springing out of his spindly arms.

The two biggest watermelons are each half a metre across: dark green, mottled torpedoes sunk into the ground.

I start trying to squeeze one of the stems between the blades of the shears, but it's too thick, with a layer of fine white hairs coating it that I don't want to touch. I use the blade as a saw instead, wishing I'd brought gardening gloves. Malcolm ambles over.

"Your mother says she's told you about this mad plan of hers to relocate to Texas."

I don't look up. I crouch on my haunches so I'm not bending over and keep sawing.

"I can't fathom why anyone would give this up," he says, his arm sweeping over the farmhouse and the plantation and the garden.

"She's lived here practically her whole life, and she always wanted to travel."

Why am I defending her? I don't want her to go either. I need something solid underneath me and The Pines's soil has never shifted. It's about to, though. If we sell it, what will Andile and I have in common, other than our childhood? But another part of me is saying, take the money and run. There's no guarantee I'll get anything from my half of Bushy Bun, and then where will I be?

"Travel is one thing. Giving up your entire legacy, the land that makes up your whole estate, is not what I'd call advisable."

"I think she wants shot of the place. It doesn't hold the happiest memories for her."

"My dear, it holds *all* her memories."

This man who has known her for two weeks thinks he can tell me more about Heather than I know from having been raised by her straight-backed moral code. Other children had the Bible or the Quran to teach them how to be good, to spell out the rules for them, but we never did. We had Heather, and the foil of Lola's kindness and warmth.

I feel like saying, "Look, I don't want her to go either, let's hatch a plan to keep her here", but I know it won't work. Heather's an unwavering presence. She doesn't change her mind. She never has a change of heart. She brought us here to tell us that she was leaving, and to give us a gift. She doesn't care what we do with it, or how we feel. Either way, at the end of this retreat, she's going to get on a plane and she's going to leave.

I pocket the shears and lift the watermelon. It's heavier than I expected, the weight of a small child.

Malcolm smiles at me. "I would offer to give you a hand, but any iota of chivalry gets one in trouble these days."

I try not to glower and start to pick my way across the garden, hoping I'm not squashing any vegetables, hoping I don't trip. I can't see my feet.

"She's very opaque, your mother," Malcolm says to my back. I stop walking but don't turn around. "She thinks you're nothing like her, but she's wrong. You've an excellent poker face, just like hers. Impossible to know what's going on in your head. It's difficult to be intimate with people who don't open up."

I whirl around, the watermelon cupped in my arms, slippery with rainwater.

"I'm aware you don't want or need my advice." He smiles infuriatingly again and uses a black cable tie to secure the vine that he's finally tamed. "But take it from an old man who's had perhaps more than his fair share of love affairs. If you don't show some vulnerability sometimes, if you don't open up a little, Karoo, you might end up alienating the people who love you."

"Nobody calls me Karoo," I say, shifting the watermelon in my arms. It's so big it'll make mountains of sorbet. I don't need to come back out to harvest the other one. It can rot on the ground for all I care.

Eight

The party is two days away and I haven't started any prep. The less I do, the less I feel capable of doing. The thought of pulling up carrots, harvesting parsley, picking and pickling radishes, making mayonnaise, rolling out and chilling pastry, shopping for black sesame seeds and the ingredients for fruit mince is enough to exhaust me. I'm still in bed at 10 a.m., wondering how I managed to go for a run yesterday when today I can barely lift my head.

There's a soft knock on my door. Megs comes in and stands next to my bed, her arms folded and resting on her stomach. With her apron and white button-down dress, neat hair and kind eyes, she looks like an old-fashioned nurse. Her appearance is impossible to reconcile with the books she writes. There was another reading last night, and I had to sit on my hands to prevent myself from covering my ears as she described the way a young boy's arm popped out of its socket as the killer dismembered him.

"Do you have plans for the watermelon? On the kitchen counter? I was wondering if I could cut it up but couldn't find the right knife."

"I was going to make sorbet with it for the party on Saturday."

"Oh yes, that's Saturday. I've been dying for a drink." She slaps her thighs. "Let's make the sorbet, then! It'll need time to set."

I can tell I'm not going to get rid of her, so I reluctantly swing my legs down on the side of my bed and peer through the curtains. It's still overcast after yesterday's rain, but the clouds are higher, and the leaves of the clivias planted along the border of the lawn are nodding slightly in the breeze.

I'm still in my pyjamas, an old pair of pink checked cotton shorts and a black vest. I can't summon up the energy to get dressed, but compromise by brushing my teeth before joining Megs in the kitchen.

"The others are all busy working but we usually have a tea break at ten-thirty," she tells me, "so they'll be here shortly."

I pull the cleaver out of the set of knives Di gave me on Tuesday. It's lighter than it looks. Megs gives it an appraising eye.

"Stop it," I say. "You're thinking of disgusting ways to kill someone with this."

She shrugs. "I don't think I've done one with a cleaver before. Though I suppose it's a small version of an axe, isn't it."

I loop my apron over my head and sink the cleaver into the end of the watermelon, again and again, rolling it round until the top is lopped off.

I do it six more times, cutting perfectly even, round slices, deep pink enclosed in layers of white and green, tear-drop shaped pips nestled in the juicy flesh. The liquid spills over the counter and drips onto my feet.

"There," I say when I'm finished. "I'm going to look for a big enough container to put the sorbet in, and I'm going to ask you to slice these pieces into smaller ones."

"I suppose it's going to be up to me to mop the floor," Sullivan's voice says behind me. He's early for tea.

I'm rummaging in the cupboard under the sink, looking for a couple of old ice cream tubs (fruitlessly, of course – Heather hasn't eaten ice cream in nearly a decade) or one of my grandmother's big round plastic containers, when I hear Megs starting to cut the watermelon. Something sounds off. She's banging it too loudly, she shouldn't be swinging the knife down so hard. I look up and see she's using the cleaver instead of the chef's knife.

"Megs!"

She looks over to me and brings her other hand down with a muffled bang. Her eyes widen almost imperceptibly. Then Sullivan says in a high-pitched voice, "Oh my god, she's cut her finger off."

Blood spurts from the direction of Megs's left hand onto the white splash-back above the counter. Megs is staring down at it, still holding the cleaver in her other hand. I am too scared to look down at the watermelon.

Tshidi comes in the kitchen door and the blood keeps spurting, and Heather comes running down the passage with Malcolm behind her and it feels like my head is floating above my body. Sullivan's retching and Tshidi grabs him firmly by both shoulders and moves him out of the way. I expect her to go to Megs but instead she wraps me in her arms and turns my face away from the blood, and for one second everything is completely quiet and still except for the quick skipping of her heart underneath my ear.

Megs slowly lowers the cleaver and says in a clear voice, "I need some clean cloths. Wet, please. Also, a plastic bag, and something to make a tourniquet with, and I need to go to the hospital."

Her calmness gives me the courage to look down at the bloody mess under her left hand. Sure enough, the tip of her index finger is lying in between the chunks of watermelon on the chopping board. She took it clean off at the knuckle. I once saw a sous chef take off half his nail, in a diagonal swipe, but Megs's nail is whole on the severed fingertip. It looks tiny, like one of those pink musk-flavoured sweets we used to get in lucky packets.

Tshidi springs to the sink, leaving me in the middle of the kitchen, shivering, and unwraps new white-and-blue dishwashing cloths and runs them under the tap. Megs is holding her hand over the sink. Malcolm comes up behind her and gently lifts her arm up until it's above her head. "I was a medic in the army," he says quietly. Her blood is running in rivulets down her arm, snaking onto her pristine white dress.

Heather disappears and comes back with a pillowcase that she tears efficiently into strips. Malcolm binds it around Megs's hand and the base of her finger.

"What are these wet cloths for?" Tshidi asks.

"To put my finger in. The bit I cut off. They'll be able to sew it back if we keep it wet. And I need ice in the packet. Finger in the wet cloths, wet cloths in the packet of ice. It's very important that the amputated part doesn't touch the ice. It'll burn."

Sullivan is pale, motionless in the doorway. Tshidi hands him the cloths and he holds them stiffly. I help her put two handfuls of ice into a clear plastic bag – we first have to tip out Heather's sewing kit onto the table – and Tshidi grabs the cloths back from Sullivan's automaton grip and carefully wraps them around the tip of Megs's finger. She places the bundle gently into the packet of ice and seals it.

"I'll drive," she says, trying to hand the packet to Sullivan, who shakes his head and backs away. She hands it to Malcolm and says, "Let's go."

Malcolm and Megs leave through the kitchen door with an awkward three-legged-race gait, his left arm holding hers, his right hand holding the bag containing her fingertip. Sullivan gestures toward his cottage – his skin is literally green – and stumbles out the house. The only sound in the kitchen is the drip-drip-drip of the bloody watermelon juice onto the kitchen tiles.

Heather looks at me and exhales once, hard. "We don't need to try to salvage the watermelon, do we?"

"I'm never eating watermelon again."

We set to work tidying up. I've always considered myself to have a strong stomach, but I feel it heaving every time I pick up a piece of watermelon to throw into the bin of compostable kitchen scraps. Heather's got a bucket of water with earth-friendly soap in it, swiping the blood away with one lemongrass-scented swish after another. Lemongrass. Another scent to catalogue.

"How did she know what to do with her finger?"

"I imagine she's had to research something about amputations for a book at some stage. She knows the tricks of the trade," Heather replies as she pours the soap and water down the kitchen sink and then washes her hands.

I am perched on the side of a chair. I have the urge to bite my nails, something I've never done.

"I'd better get hold of Adrienne," she says. "I'm not sure what my liability is when it comes to accidents like this."

"It's my fault."

"No, Roo. It absolutely isn't."

"I didn't tell her which knife to use."

"She's a grown woman."

"I wasn't paying attention." My voice wavers.

Heather sits next to me. She doesn't touch me, because it's not something she does, but her voice is warmer than usual. "Why don't you have a bath. Use some of my Epsom salts."

"I feel so guilty."

"It was an accident. That means it wasn't anybody's fault. She'll be fine, the doctors in town are very good. Come on. I'll run it for you. You'll feel so much better."

I follow Heather to the bathroom and sit on the closed lid of the toilet as she runs the bath, shaking in flakes of Epsom salts from a small clay jar. The room is full of steam when she switches the taps off. It's deeper than any bath I've ever seen her run. She's wasting water to show she's worried about me.

I wait for her to leave before taking off my pyjamas, but she stays where she is. "Go on," she says, gesturing to the water. "It's nothing I haven't seen before."

I hesitate until she says, "There's something I want to tell you, and I don't want you to run away from it. Get in the bath and relax, and listen, okay?"

I lift my vest over my head and as I sink into the warm water, she says, "It's about your father."

≈

"You never asked about him and I never felt the need to tell you because it obviously didn't matter to you, and I always thought I'd do it another time. But now that I'm going away, and I don't know how long you're going to be here, and after Lola, I'm realising that 'one day' might be too late. I want you to know where you come from.

"It all started with going to Rhodes. I didn't know I liked girls, you know, like that, until I went to varsity. I

177

got to Grahamstown in the year nineteen-seventy-nine and it was an amazing place to be. There was so much to absorb, so much to learn. On my first day, when we were registering for our classes, I met Adrienne in the queue for English One, and she started talking to me out of the blue. I liked her mouth, and she smelled good, like Johnson's baby shampoo, this pure, innocent smell.

"A few nights later we were out at the Vic. I was there with my res buddies and she was with hers, and she bought me a glass of Cinzano. Revolting stuff, but I drank the whole thing and then she kissed me. Right there, in the middle of this crowded bar, where anyone could see. I knew I should have been shocked, but wasn't at all. Something inside me clicked into place in that moment. I finally understood myself.

"We started spending every possible moment together. We shared our tiny, single beds. In second year, we moved into digs together. We did all the same subjects. I didn't have any other friends. I brought her here to meet my parents a few times. I was convinced they had no idea who she was, but looking back, I'm sure they did. My mother, especially. They were tolerant in their own very old-fashioned British way, my parents.

"But by our fourth year, when we were both doing our honours, I was starting to feel claustrophobic. I hadn't had my own room since the end of first year. We shared hairbrushes and clothes and underwear – we were exactly the same size.

"I saw a guy from my Journ class handing out flyers for NUSAS in the quad one afternoon when I was walking back from a tut. It was nineteen-eighty-two, five years since Biko was killed, four years since Rick Turner was assassinated. I wasn't politically active *at all* but I'd started to feel things heating up around Grahamstown. There'd been talk at one of our tuts about trouble in the township near Cradock.

"I was desperate for a night out of the digs. There would be cheese and wine afterwards, the guy said, which I knew meant cheap box wine and no cheese whatsoever, but once I had the flyer in my hand it felt like a done deal, like after that I was compelled to attend.

"One of my Journ lecturers was there. Robert. He was doing his Masters and was only a couple of years older than we were, but he was married, with a baby. He was obviously a big deal to the others there. He made a speech about us as young white men and women creating cracks in the regime. He was very charismatic.

"He noticed me there and spoke to me afterwards. He asked where I was from, he seemed very interested, and I got a vibe from him. It had been so long since I'd been seen as anything other than Adrienne's girlfriend. People kept coming up to Robert while we were talking, calling him 'comrade', desperate for his attention. I was flattered that he wanted to talk to me, I suppose.

"He asked me to help with making more flyers and signs for an upcoming march, and I agreed immediately. We were the last people left in the student newspaper offices later that night, and he leaned over the tins of black paint we were using for the posters, and kissed me, and that was the beginning of what I suppose was our 'affair'."

I am struck dumb, unable to interrupt. I've never heard Heather say so much at once.

"There was nowhere we could go to be together, so we'd have sex in his car, parked in dark side-streets, or up at the toposcope. I started going to all the NUSAS

179

meetings. I missed one period, and then another one, and Adrienne kept getting more and more suspicious the more time I spent away from the digs. She supported the movement, she said, but couldn't afford the time away from her studies, and said that I couldn't either. I should have told her or broken it off with her, but I was a coward. I had this crazy idea that if she knew, she'd tell Robert's wife about me.

"Then Robert got arrested. A whole bunch of them did, they were ambushed at a meeting with one of the teachers from Rhini who was leading the movement in the township schools. I was at home that night, feeling terrible, knowing deep down that I had morning sickness. I'd told the others I needed to work on my thesis. When I found out the next morning that they'd all been sent to Die Rooi Hel, the prison in Port Elizabeth, I decided to go see if I could bail him out, or at least give him some spare clothes or talk to him. When I eventually managed to borrow Adrienne's car and make my way there, his wife had beaten me to it. She was standing in the parking lot, with the baby, both of them crying, and I realised that I'd been completely deluded. That he'd never leave her. I didn't *want* him to leave her. He wasn't mine – he was theirs.

"I came home to The Pines on the bus the next day. My parents were worried sick about me, but I told them to go ahead to the country club, that I needed to finish my thesis and had come home for some peace and quiet. My dad, as usual, had too much to drink at the club, and, well, you know the rest. Their car rolled off the road outside of White River. I'd been home for less than twenty-four hours.

"After the funeral, I sort-of drifted around, in this totally devastated daze. If it wasn't for Francina, our helper,

I wouldn't have eaten. Or I'd have killed myself. I thought about it, how I'd do it, and decided I'd use my razor blade in the bath, but the one thing that stopped me was the thought of Francina having to clean up.

"Also, there was you, moving inside me. It reminded me, bizarrely, of Adrienne, who I'd betrayed. That got me thinking about Robert and the rest of the NUSAS guys I'd abandoned. Of the cause I was too scared to carry on fighting for, that the country was going to hell and I'd run away from it all. But the one thing I couldn't run away from was you.

"About a week after the funeral, I got a phone call. Robert. He'd been released without charges. He had found out from Adrienne that I'd gone home. They thought they had a mole at NUSAS, he said. Things were going wrong, people were going missing. He needed somewhere to send the most vulnerable, somewhere they would never be found. He asked about The Pines. What he said sounded hopelessly romantic, 'it's our best hope', or something like that. I meant to tell him about you, but something stopped me. I think it was the image of his wife with their baby, both of them shaking with sobs. I couldn't do it.

"I agreed to let him send someone here – one person, a student who'd been a year behind me and who'd been living with the teacher from Rhini who was still detained. Robert said the guy had a target on his back.

"The student arrived in the boot of a car a few days later. He didn't speak to me. I hadn't been accepting any guests since my parents died so the cottages were empty, and he took one of them. If he recognised me, he didn't say. About a month later, another two guys came, and it was the same story.

"I had to let our workers go, then, even Francina, for their own safety, you know. I cashed out almost the entire pay-out from my parents' life insurance to give to her to make it up to her, and thinking back, I have no idea how the lawyer didn't know something was up while I sat in his office waiting for him to give me the forms to sign. I was shaking so badly I could barely hold the pen. I had to let everyone go in case the police found out what was going on and tried to question them. The activists never told me anything about their movements or their strategies or operations. It was safer for them, and for me, that way."

Heather dips her fingers into the bath water, then turns the hot tap back on, swishing the water around my body with her hand.

"It was this utterly bizarre time. I was living something resembling a normal life – planting vegetables and cooking stews and boiling the kettle on the stove for tea – and meanwhile I was alone and pregnant and – I kept thinking this – *orphaned* and there were people 'of interest' living right under my nose. If the tiniest thing tipped anyone off, it would all be over. I'd have gone to jail. But we got away with it. For seven years, we got away with it.

"Other than their life insurance policy, my parents had left me some money they'd had in investments in England – quite a lot of it, to be honest. But I couldn't do anything with it except live off it, because I couldn't leave the farm. Once the attorneys had released it into my bank account, I used it to buy food in bulk to feed the activists. I'd buy enough to fill the back of the bakkie so I wouldn't have to go to town too often.

"Nobody ever came to visit. I think everyone thought I was mourning my parents. I was, but I was also starting to show with you, and I was terrified of their disapproval about the pregnancy, which is ridiculous considering everything else that was going on. I was ashamed. I didn't know anyone who'd got pregnant outside of marriage. I felt so alone. I didn't have Francina any more, and I'd cry into my tea for my mother.

"Robert phoned again, in the spring. I remember looking outside while I was talking to him and noticing blossoms on the syringa tree. He said he was phoning from a tickey box in Port Alfred because he was sure his home phone was bugged. He said he and his family were going into exile in England the following month, and that he was sending a student from Fort Hare, someone in the upper echelons. He didn't use that word, I think he said 'key figure' in AZASO, that was the black students' group, and that the people who'd drop her off would be collecting two of the MK operatives and smuggling them across the border to Swaziland.

"*Her*. I remembered that. Another woman. I hadn't spoken to Adrienne, I couldn't talk to her, I couldn't tell her about you, and she never tried to get hold of me, either. I knew she'd be too proud and too angry to break down and phone, much less try to visit. I hadn't spoken to another woman in three months."

Heather reaches over to turn the tap off. I've got my arms clutched round my knees, scared to move in case I distract her from her story, but her eyes are far away.

"Lola arrived shortly afterwards. Nolitha. She was magnificent. We were close, instantly. She took over all the cooking for the activists, so I didn't have to be on my feet. She was much more involved in the movement and started coordinating transport of the activists to and from the farm. There were MK operatives who were moved from here to Mozambique, there were lawyers, other students, always men.

"About a month after she'd arrived, she started getting involved with one of them. He was an MK guy, a soldier. As far as he was concerned, we were at war, which we were, I suppose. One morning, when Lola came to cook everyone's porridge, I noticed bruises on her neck, each one a shadow of a fingerprint. Her voice was rough, scratchy, and I could see she was trying very hard not to cry. She came to live in the main house that same day. Lola said she understood that these weren't normal times, that people were doing things they'd never usually do, but she didn't want to keep living with him, either. He left not long after, and we never heard what happened to him.

"When I was about eight months pregnant with you, she started showing.

"Falling in love – it happened slowly for Lola and me, but it was like I blinked and she was suddenly my entire world.

"She helped me deliver you, which was easy as pie. You practically slipped right out. But when I helped her with Andile I felt so useless. It took thirteen hours from when her water broke. I was in tears the whole time. We'd suspected he was going to be a big baby, but I was convinced that he was breach and that I'd have to rush Lola to hospital, that if I didn't she'd get an infection, that the cord was around his neck – every horror story you've ever heard about home births. All I could do was bring her ice chips to chew, and boil and boil and boil the sheets and towels. You were so good and quiet the whole time, as if you knew something important was happening, watching with your big, round eyes. When he finally decided to make his way into the world, he was perfect. Big, and perfect.

"We carried on running The Pines as a safe house, pretending Lola was the maid if anyone asked. We heard about the terror of the Cradock Four, teachers, young men, fathers, murdered by the cops. They cut one of their hands off, as some kind of sick souvenir. This was when you and Andile were running around like feral little two-year-olds, not aware of anything outside the farm, not aware how many people would have condemned our family if they knew the truth. It gave me so much hope, somehow, seeing the two of you together, being kids.

"But things got worse before they got better. Under the State of Emergency, we didn't know who to trust, we didn't think it would ever end. We started getting more hopeful when the one guy, who arrived from AZASO around the time you and Andile turned five, told us that reform was on the way, that comrades had been visited in exile to negotiate with the government. De Klerk came in, and finally, finally, right before you turned seven, we saw on the black and white TV set that they'd unbanned the ANC, and that they were going to release Mandela. Finally, we were free."

Heather starts scrubbing my back, the sure strokes I remember from childhood. Lola used to run the sponge over me in soft, gentle circles, but Heather was all brisk-ness and efficiency.

"I heard through Jeanette, the NUSAS secretary who organised a reunion, when was it, it must have been two-thousand-and-four, yes, for the ten-year anniversary of democracy, that Robert and his family had moved back to Grahamstown, that he was lecturing Journ again, that his discharge papers from Die Rooi Hel were framed in his office, but I had no interest in seeing him or talking to him. I didn't hear from Adrienne until she found me on Facebook earlier this year. Maybe I should have cared more, maybe I should have made more of an effort, but everything else felt so far away, like it hadn't ever happened. Just after that, Lola started getting sick, and I had my hands full and couldn't think about anything else."

I realise I've been holding my breath.

"Does Andile know this? About his father?"

Heather reaches for my towel and holds it up for me, wraps it around me when I step out the bath. "Yes," she says.

Nine

I am avoiding Andile. I should be able to tell him that I know, but I can't get my head around it. Andile, the most harmless, easy-going person I've ever known, fathered by someone who was violent, someone who hurt Lola, affectionate, soft-spoken Lola. It doesn't add up, my mind's going around and around and around, but keeps getting stuck on the image of Lola with the man's fingerprints on her throat.

I'm lying in the hammock in the avos, the place I feel closest to Andile. The cotton is ripe with mould, sun-bleached and worn through in places, but it still swings like it used to. The sun flashes through my closed eyelids in bursts, interspersed with shadows of the trees above me. I think about Lola telling us about where babies come from. Now I know why she and Heather always tried to make sure we knew that fathers were necessary for conception but not for parenting, that nurture was what mattered, not biology or DNA or blood.

I need to get a hold of myself. Heather lived through hell and came out the other side. I can, too.

I need to talk to Andile, maybe not about this, but at least about what we're going to do with the farm. And, I think, as I hoist myself upright, I need to start cooking and prepping for the fucking party tomorrow night.

I make my way back up to the house and decide to go see Andile as soon as I've julienned the carrots and cabbage for the slaw. After Malcolm and Tshidi brought Megs home yesterday afternoon, with her hand in a splint and her fingertip successfully stitched back on, Heather took the bakkie to the shops with my list and my bank card. She wrote the PIN on her hand and I didn't have the heart to tell her that that wasn't the safest place to keep it. I made everyone a Spanish tortilla with thyme from the garden and potatoes I found in a brown paper bag in the pantry – they were stippled with eyes and possibly poisonous, but I went ahead anyway, needing to feel useful – and laughed with the others when Megs offered to help me slice the potatoes.

Malcolm asked what I needed from the garden when I was on my way to the hammock earlier today, and there are glistening wet, smooth carrots in the colander on the kitchen counter, and two tightly curled heads of purple cabbage on the draining board. Since Megs's accident, when I watched him bending his head and talking to her quietly, my feelings about Malcolm have turned a corner. I'm not repulsed by him anymore, which feels like progress.

I'm hacking through the cabbage with the cleaver when Di breezes in through the kitchen door. She wastes no time. "I saw Tshidi and the others speeding up the road here yesterday and caught them before they got to the gate. Is Megs okay?"

I nod. "I haven't seen her today, but apparently her finger's fine. Heather was worried that it would slow down her writing. She's quite far behind, apparently."

"Was there loads of blood? I bet I'd have fainted."

"Sullivan almost did. It was messy. I've seen worse in a kitchen. I'd take an amputation over a burn any day. The smell, you know."

I start peeling the carrots into ribbons. They're beautiful, not like the knobbly squat ones we used to grow. Di peers into the bowl and says, "I can't remember the last time I ate coleslaw. With Jacques and his family it's always sweet stuff. Carrots, butternut, gem squash, sweet potato – all with sugar. The kids like it though, don't you?"

I turn around to see Fallan hovering in the doorway, wearing a pair of denim shorts with little palm trees printed on them and a T-shirt with the picture of a mermaid on a rock on the front. I put down the carrot and the peeler. "Would you like a milkshake, Fallan? Heather got some paw-paws from the co-op this morning, I can steal some milk from Andile and blend them up for you?"

She nods quickly, and I start peeling the thin skin off the warm paw-paws.

"Yes *please*, Fallan. Honestly, the manners. Three weeks off from school and the kids turn into pumpkins."

I smile at Fallan, who gives me a shy grin back. She comes into the kitchen and sits down at the table, her ankles tucked neatly underneath her chair. She's very composed for a five-year-old. I was nowhere near this neat at her age.

"Don't get comfortable," Di says to her. "I'm here to drop off the eggs, and some bougainvillea sprigs, and then we'll be on our way. Heather loves the bougainvillea flowers, but pulled all hers out because they're invaders." She lays three branches covered with papery mauve flowers on the table.

"You'd think she'd get rid of the pines," I say. "Thanks for the eggs. I need the yolks to make mayonnaise."

"Speaking of things she needs to get rid of: do you think Malcolm will come along tomorrow night? Him and Heather?"

"Doubtful. I don't think he does parties."

"I love Heather, but between you and me, that man is the pits."

I shrug, remembering the gentleness on his face while he was tending to Megs yesterday.

When Diana tells Fallan that it's time to leave, she says, "But I haven't had my milkshake yet and I'm bored at home."

"You need to practise riding that pedal bike of yours or your dad's going to complain that it was a waste of money."

"Father Christmas gave that to me. Not Daddy."

"What I meant was –"

"It's okay. I know he's not real. Molly told me."

"She's a little shit, your sister."

"I know that too."

Diana grabs her basket off the counter and asks me if it's alright if she leaves Fallan with me. "I'm going nuts over there with all four of them by myself. Stella's sick or her child's sick or her mother's sick or something, I can't remember what she said, so I've got my hands full."

I say that of course I don't mind, and that I'll walk her back home later once I've finished prepping the other side dishes. "I'll bring them up to you when I drop Fallan off. We don't have much fridge space here."

"Come at five-ish and we can have a sundowner."

I have no intention of sitting in Di's sunroom with the smell of ammonia in the air and the vile wine in my glass, but I agree and wave her off.

190

I show Fallan how to make mayonnaise. She pours the avocado oil into the mixing bowl with the egg yolks and apple cider vinegar so that the mayonnaise emulsifies while I use the hand blender. When we're finished and the sauce is a thick, glossy yellow, she looks up at me and asks, "Is it milkshake time yet?"

≈

Andile is lying on his bed texting when Fallan and I walk into Fever Tree Cottage. He jumps when he sees us.

"You should knock!"

"Sorry. Habit. You've met Fallan?"

He puts down his phone. "I met her at Christmas. How's the bike?"

She wrinkles her nose. "I don't like it. It's too hard to ride."

"Andile taught me to ride my bike when we were little. Maybe he can teach you too."

"I don't like things that are difficult."

Andile laughs. "What are you guys up to?"

"We're here for some milk."

"Please," Fallan adds.

He heaves himself off the bed and follows us out the bedroom into the kitchen. As he hands me the milk, I say, "Can we talk?"

He takes one look at my face and says, "Heather told you about your father, didn't she. About mine."

I hesitate before nodding. "Will you come with me to walk Fallan home at five, and we can talk on the way back? I need your help to process everything. It sounds like I have a – sister? Brother? A half one, I mean. My father had a baby when – I obviously already have a brother, but I mean there was another baby when –"

"I know what you mean," he says, smiling softly.

I exhale, and change the subject. "Who were you texting? Virika?"

He grins, a flash of light. "Maybe."

"Does she want to come visit yet?"

"Not quite. But I'm getting there, I think. Wearing her down."

"Ah, romance."

"Says the person who's separated from her husband and flirting with some weird writer she's known for two minutes."

I shoot him a look but find it hard to be irritated with him, especially with Fallan looking so happy she might bounce right out of her skin. My steps are lighter going back up to the house, and Fallan and I have a race from the driveway to the kitchen door. I have to hold the glass bottle of milk with both hands so that I don't drop it.

The rest of the afternoon passes in a whirl of ingredients – flour, eggs and orange blossom water for the mince pie pastry; raisins, currants and citrus peel for the filling, which Fallan can't stop picking at on the sly; toasted black sesame seeds for the slaw, parsley and basil from the garden and avocado oil and lemon juice for the salsa verde; flour, oil and sea salt for the dough for 30 chapattis; finely sliced sweet potatoes and cashew cream for the gratin; and, finally, paper-thin wisps of radish in apple cider vinegar, sugar and salt.

Fallan and I are both sweating by the time we hang up our aprons. She's wearing my old one from when I was a teenager, with the recipe for roast pheasant printed on the front, the one my grandmother brought over from England, tied in a big knot at her neck so it doesn't hang on the ground.

It's 5 o'clock on the dot when we amble up the driveway. Andile carries a tray of bowls full of our afternoon's work to Coucal Farm, all with white beaded nets covering them to keep the flies away, leaving me to carry only the dish of slaw. Fallan and I hold hands all the way, my palm sweating onto hers.

"It seems to be getting hotter," I say to Di when she opens the door for us.

"It's going to be a wet-sheet night for us," she says.

"Tell me that doesn't mean what I think it does," Andile says, wiping his feet on the rubber mat on the back doorstep.

Di kisses Fallan on top of her head as she pushes past. "You and your filthy mind. It means that we'll need to soak the kids' sheets in water and cover them before they go to sleep. It's the only way to keep cool on nights like this."

"Mom, I'm going to put my swimming costume on!" Fallan calls from down the passage.

"Okay!" Diana shouts, before turning to us and offering us a drink. I shake my head in case she remembers the wine, and Andile's about to, too, but she says, "You've got to be kidding me. This is the only thing that's got me through the day, the thought of having a drink and some grown-up conversation. One drink, that's it."

"I'm fine," I say. "Where are Molly and Liam?"

"Watching the iPad in our room, under the aircon," Di replies. "Come, let's go sit in the sunroom."

There's a stand-up fan blowing warm air round the room, and I sit down directly opposite it. Thankfully, there's no smell of ammonia in the air today. A moment later, I hear swift footsteps padding along the passage and turn to see Fallan running past the sunroom door in a streak of pink, pulling a towel along the floor behind her. Then I hear the screen door in the kitchen slam shut.

Di and Andile are talking about the party. Something pulls me up, like a string attached to the top of my head, and I walk out the sunroom and down the passage, and by the time I've got to the kitchen door, the soles of my feet are prickling like they do when I'm confronted with heights or a near-miss in a car.

Fallan's towel is on the grass and her body is in the dam. All I can see of her is her forehead and the top of her head, her nose and mouth and the rest of her underwater. She's directly upright, her arms flailing up and down, barely making a splash, but she's not managing to get her nose or mouth out of the water, and her eyes scream at me, enormous, and I hear the single thought in my head as if from outside of myself: *Don't lose her.*

I vault over the fence and run into the water. It's a sheer drop from the edge and I sink instantly. I see Fallan's arms and legs moving frantically, sending a blur of tiny bubbles upwards in the murky, lukewarm water. I fight my way to her in slow motion. The time it takes me to reach her are the longest five seconds of my life.

I grab her under her arms from behind and lift her face out the water and lay her head on my shoulder with her back against my stomach and start kicking us back to the edge. She doesn't take a breath until we're almost there. Above our heads, a go-away-bird fans out its fringed wings as it launches from a tree, the halfway-risen moon waits for nightfall, we are the moon, we are the moon, we are the moon, I recite in my head with each kick, and Fallan cries out for her mother.

Part 3

Coucal Farm

One

It's the day of the party. I haven't gone home since yesterday evening and am wearing one of Di's dresses that keeps falling open across the chest. Andile's promised to bring my red dress from home when he comes back, which is a mixed blessing. I spent the night on the floor in Fallan and Molly's room, watching Fallan's chest rising and falling, listening for every breath. I'd count to a hundred and then back to one and start again, all night, until the rooster crowed huskily at dawn.

I am watching Jacques and Ben unload the rented spit from the back of the bakkie, shading my eyes from the sun. The fact that the party is going ahead is surreal to me, but I realised as soon as I pulled Fallan out of the water that what had happened didn't mean to anyone else what it did to me.

It didn't seem to have affected Fallan, who was popped straight into a warm bubble bath, given sugary rooibos tea and within half an hour was playing with Molly on the iPad as if it was a normal evening. I've been cold since it happened, shivering whenever I stand still for too long.

But for the first time since coming to The Pines, since leaving Misty Cliffs, I have clarity. In the morning, I help with the kids, making mouse-shaped flapjacks, brushing their teeth, or, in Liam's case, swiping the toothbrush in the vicinity of his mouth and hoping it connects with a tooth at some point. While I'm busy, I decide that I'll go along with whatever Andile wants to do with The Pines. It doesn't matter to me anymore. My vision has narrowed to the size of a pin-hole. To the size of a self-possessed five-year-old with freckles and hazel eyes.

"Right. The sheep should be defrosted," Jacques says, wiping the grease off his hands with a grubby cloth he's pulled from his back pocket.

"Why do farmers always have those cloths in their back pockets? Is it part of the uniform?"

He looks down at it, and then back up at me, frowning. "Are you sure you're alright? Your skin's very white."

Ben looks over from where he's closing the canopy of the bakkie. He's been shooting me concerned looks all morning.

"I'm fine. I was worried about secondary drowning, but I think we're in the clear."

"You know what I thought last night? I told Di and we nearly peed our pants we laughed so hard. I said, her name was a bit of a clue, wasn't it? Fallan. Fell in. We should have been expecting something like this!"

Ben doesn't laugh, and nor do I. He has very dark eyebrows for a blonde person, I think. His lashes are dark, too, and very long.

"I'm going to start rolling out the chapattis. What time are people coming?"

"I don't know," Jacques says. "Five? Six? It's Slowveld time, people rock up whenever."

"I'll come with you," Ben says, jogging to catch up with me. "I can't stop thinking about what would have happened if you weren't there," he says once we're out of earshot.

"Di and Jacques think she can swim. She can't, she obviously can't. She wasn't swimming."

"I'll tell you what, before I leave tomorrow I'll put up a proper fence, a high one, with a gate."

"You're leaving tomorrow?"

"I'm back on duty at the lodge from Monday. You should come out for a visit sometime. I think maybe you need a break."

"That's what I'm supposed to be doing here, at home. Taking a break."

"Is it working? Are you relaxing?"

His eyes are a molten chocolate brown. I feel my ears starting to go warm. I try not to smile back at him. "Not exactly."

After shooting me a knowing grin, he goes back outside to supervise the loading of half of an animal onto a spike that will turn its body around over a fire and slowly cook its flesh. Dammit, I think to myself, I'm starting to think like a vegetarian.

Andile arrives while I'm up to my elbows in flour. He drops a gym bag on the floor at my feet. "I told Heather what happened. I brought you a change of clothes. She made me pack you all kinds of other shit as well. I told her you'd be going home tonight but she had a bee in her bonnet. Like, literally. She was spinning the combs for honey when I saw her."

Di's rolling pin is ribbed with sticky bits of old dough. I look around for a glass jar to use instead.

"Can we talk about what we're going to do with The Pines?"

"Now? I need to start on these chapattis. They aren't going to roll themselves."

"O, fok. Chapattis, is it? What's wrong with supermarket bread rolls?" Jacques heaves the cooler box full of ice and extra-tall beer cans into his arms, looks at Andile and jerks his head in the direction of the garden.

"I'll be there in a second. I have to talk to Roo about something."

"We should get her a lifesavers vest or something. Put her on duty tonight to make sure nobody jumps into the dam and drowns," he says, chuckling.

I shoot a dirty look at his back, and Andile squeezes my shoulder. "He's good people," he says.

"They keep joking about it. Joking about their daughter drowning. There's something wrong with them."

"They say she's gone swimming in that dam by herself a hundred times, Roo." He puts his hands up as if to ward off any argument from me. "I'm not saying last night wasn't different, I'm saying they didn't see what you saw. Give them a break."

I wrap a sheet of wax paper around an empty glass jar, twist the ends, and start rolling.

"She could have died."

"But she didn't. Thanks to you."

"That's not the point."

"I'm not here to argue with you about this. I'm here to argue with you about The Pines."

He waits for me to respond and when I don't, he pushes on. "You know how the house and cottages are all looking really good? Freshly painted, varnished, whatever?"

I shrug.

"Heather says she got it all cleaned and fixed up so that we'd get a better price for it if we sell."

"What do you want to do with it?" Roll, roll, roll. Pick up, spin around, plop down, roll, roll, roll.

"I want to sell," he says quietly. "I could use the money for the rest of my post-doc. Maybe buy a flat in Umdloti. If Heather's not here, what would we have to come back to?"

"That's fine with me," I say, picking up another fist-sized dough ball and flattening it with the heel of my hand before picking up the rolling jar.

Andile's shoulders sag. "Are you sure?"

I shrug again. "I am if you are."

"This is crazy. We can't make this kind of decision like this."

"Well, whenever you're ready. Would you mind moving? I need to cook these."

He steps away from the stove, his arms hanging at his sides.

"What's going on with you? Stop shrugging, you're making me crazy."

A burst of music comes from the bag at my feet. It's that early-90s song about a woman who is touch, sight, smell, taste and sound, the one Cam said reminded him of me. He had terribly cheesy taste in music, but I found it sweetly touching when he set it as the ringtone for his number on my phone.

"Is that nineteen-ninety-five calling?" Andile says.

"Funny." I rinse my hands under the tap, wipe them on the front of Di's dress and fish around in my bag, guided by the vibration of the phone. I lift it up slowly and turn it over, and there it is, on the screen, Cam's face, his Ben Affleck jaw, aviator sunglasses, two fingers held up in a peace sign, a photo I took of him on Penghu Island when we bunked our organised tour and found a tiny café operated from an old woman's home. It was the day of the snails.

Andile looks over my shoulder at the screen. "Is that him?"

I nod, numb. I want to push the green-phone icon, drag it to the right, put the phone to my ear and hear his voice, but I can't. I drop the phone back into the bag and, at a loss, pick up the plate of chapattis.

Andile cups one hand round the back of my neck, leans his forehead against mine. His breath smells like mint, like always, because he's got an old habit of chewing a few leaves of spearmint from the side of the driveway, where Heather grows it as a ground cover.

"I should be able to say something deep here, but I don't have anything," he says.

I squeeze out a laugh, and he lets me go.

"Leave this stuff, you can do it later. There's a great big beer out there with your name on it."

I let the plate clatter to the counter. "Let me go change into my ridiculous scrap of a dress. I'll be right there."

On my way to the bathroom, I peer into Fallan and Molly's room. Fallan's got a thick book open in her lap, and she's telling Molly something about dinosaurs, a meteor, volcanoes, a cloud of ash, the end of the world. Joy erupts in my chest. She's still here, and the world is still intact.

Two

"Hey, could you pick up some hamburger rolls? Two dozen? Thanks, boet."

Jacques hangs up the phone and winks at me. "See? Bread rolls sorted. Gary's bringing some, so you don't have to do those chapattis or whatever. Remember Gary Blake? He's on his way with his wife."

"He's a pro golfer, right?"

"Ja, and you should see his wife. He met her in London, her family moved there when she was little. They were in exile. She was Mrs South Africa a few years back."

Di is sitting on Jacques's lap next to the spit, which he and Ben have set up on the front lawn. I'm standing next to Andile watching the meat turn slowly round, about midway through my second can of beer. I'm facing the dam, too nervous to have my back to it, as if it will sneak up on me from behind.

"I keep hoping we can have a pool party sometime so I can see her in a swimming costume, but Di keeps pulling the handbrake."

Di swats his chest. "You're disgusting."

"I'm right, hey, guys? Ben?"

Ben swirls his can of beer and pours the last sip into his mouth. "Not my type."

"What, you mean female?"

Ben wrinkles his nose and squashes his beer can before lobbing it into the open bin. "Too fake," he says, darting a quick look at me.

"Admit it, Ben, you bat for the other team."

Di pinches Jacques through his shirt and tilts her head in my direction. "Don't be a homophobe. Not in front of these two."

"Or at all," Andile says under his breath so only I can hear.

We may as well still be teenagers, I think, looking round. Di's drinking a cooler, something neon pink. I tell Jacques I'm going to cook the chapattis anyway, in case there's not enough food. The writers arrive while I'm flipping them in the hot cast-iron griddle pan on the stove.

Tshidi gives me a little wave and flops down on the cat-hair covered couch with her crochet needle and a ball of wool the colour of Di's drink. Outside, Megs is telling the story of her amputated finger, with the occasional gasp and "oh my *god*" from Di drifting into the kitchen. Sullivan comes in last, holding a bunch of coriander tied with a piece of twine.

"I'd have brought flowers but there aren't any I could pick in your garden."

"This is great, I forgot to bring coriander for the slaw. Thank you."

"I heard what happened with the little girl. You're a hero."

I shake my head. "It was weird. I felt like something was pulling me towards her." There's a tense kind of awareness stretching between us like a taut elastic band.

"A sixth sense, maybe? Are you a secret psychic?" He's leaning across the breakfast nook, and as I smile at him, I feel the tension snap and disappear.

"I'd noticed that the dam didn't have a proper fence round it. Fallan came running past without arm-bands on. You wouldn't need a sixth sense to figure out what would happen." I put the chapattis in a roasting dish in the warming drawer of the oven, covered with foil. "I hope people eat these."

"I'll eat them all if I have to. What are you drinking?"

I lift my apron over my head. "I had a beer outside but two of those is about my limit. They're massive."

"Nice dress. Do you drink whisky?" He holds up a round white tube with green lettering on it, one of the bottles that lives behind the teller at bottle stores, and costs as much as I spent on my last pair of decent running shoes.

"I'll drink that kind."

"It's peaty as fuck but it's a special occasion."

"Is it?"

"New Year's Eve. Nearly twenty-seventeen. Seventeen's my lucky number."

He pours two fingers each into the tumblers I've put in front of him and clinks his glass against mine before threading our fingers together and pulling me towards him. His hand is so warm. Cam's were always cold, as if his body was too long for the circulation to reach all the way to his extremities. He never liked holding hands; he used to fidget after a few seconds before giving my hand a last squeeze and dropping it. But the way Sullivan has mine grasped in his as he leads me outside makes me realise he's not going to let it go anytime soon.

The blood-warm whisky rests on my tongue and lights me up inside as it slips down my throat. I feel another spurt of joy at the thought of Sullivan's long, blunt fingers holding mine, but as soon as we get to the fire, I come back down to earth.

Gary Blake is there with a bald head and the shiny smoothness that comes from having a lot of money – and regular facials. He's holding the hand of a woman in high-heeled boots that are sinking into the grass. She carries a handbag that I can tell is designer, and with her soft afro and cheekbones that could cut glass, she's clearly way out of Gary's league.

Di, Megs, Ben, Jacques and Andile all turn to look at Sullivan and me, holding hands and leaning into each other. When I see Ben's face fold in on itself and slam shut, my hand drops Sullivan's as if it's burned me.

Gary comes over for a hug – an unprecedented move on his part – and says in Sullivan's direction, "Andile told me at The Keg the other night that you're married! Is this the guy?"

I catch Andile's eye and he winces a sorry, but it's too late.

Gary's looking from me to Sullivan, perplexed, and Di bursts out laughing.

"Flip, this is awkward," she says.

Three

It's the ex-Mrs South Africa who saves us.

"Please forgive my husband, he's a social philistine. I'm Zama." She gives me her hand and for a second I think she's expecting me to kiss it, but she gives mine a little shake instead.

"You went to school with this lot?"

"Yes. Except for Andile. He's my brother."

Zama cocks her head to the side. "I think your mother's my client. I'm a lawyer."

"See, baby, if you went back to work, you'd be able to dress like Zama," Jacques says to Di.

"Baby, I'd have to lose about fifty kilos to dress like Zama."

"You're Heather's lawyer?" I ask.

"I do mostly estates, family law, that kind of thing."

"You know Andile went to the private school from Grade Ten on a rugby scholarship. He's not one of us," Jacques tells Zama.

"I was in it for the food. We used to get ice cream after lunch," Andile laughs.

I gulp down my whisky while they're discussing the worst meals we got served at hostel at the government school.

Sullivan watches me with one eyebrow raised. "Another?" he asks.

I nod, and he takes my glass back to the kitchen. He must have known all along that I was married. But when Ben breaks away from the group, something in the hunch of his shoulders as he stands over the spit tells me he had no idea.

"I suppose I failed to mention to you that I'm, you know. Married," I say when I'm standing next to him, watching the sheep's body turning over and over. "I think – I mean, I'm sure — my marriage is over anyway." Cam's smooth face, his long lashes, the tufts of hair that stick out over his ears when he wakes up, appear before my eyes, and I blink to burst the picture.

With a wobble in his voice, Ben says, "What about this writer? Sullivan? Are you guys together? Because I thought – you and me?"

I try to touch his arm and he turns a few degrees to the right, away from me. Not enough for it to be obvious to anyone else, but enough to give me the message that he wants to be left alone.

Di grabs my hand as I walk past her. She's grinning, as usual, but her smile doesn't quite reach her eyes. "Did you break my brother-in-law's heart?"

Ben is opening a beer, glugging down one, two, three mouthfuls without coming up for air.

"I hope not," I say, watching him across the lawn.

She lets go of my hand. "He's never had a girlfriend. His brothers tease him, but I think it's because he takes things seriously. Like, if he was into a girl, he'd be into her a hundred per cent."

"I think he's sweet."

She gives me a coldly assessing look.

"Do you want some advice?"

"I absolutely don't," I say, knowing she's going to carry on anyway.

"I'm not exactly a relationship expert, having been with that moron for basically my whole life," she says, gesturing to Jacques, who is starting a game of boule on the grass next to the house, "so I wouldn't blame you for not listening to me, but I think you need to stop leading Ben on."

I've never heard her sound so serious.

"I'm going to find Sullivan with my drink," I say, turning towards the house.

I find Tshidi and Sullivan glaring at each other across the kitchen. He hands my glass to me, a little fuller this time. "Going to the little boys' room," he says, heading out the kitchen door. "By which I mean, I'm going to piss against a bush outside."

Tshidi gathers up her wool and hugs it to herself. "Megs and I are going back to The Pines. She needs to rest. Do yourself a favour, Skye, and stay away from that guy. He's using you. He says he's started working on something new, and I'm worried that it's about you."

I smile against the rim of my glass. "What makes you think I'm not using him?"

"The way you look at him," she says. "Come to a reading sometime this week. He might bring out his new material, and you'll see."

The rest of the night moves quickly. People from school start to trickle in, people I haven't seen in a decade and a half and whose names pop into my head immediately. Somewhere between my third and fourth whisky I decide to try to talk to Zama about Heather, about the farm and what we should do with it, but she's never alone.

When it's time to eat, Ben helps me set the outside table with reed placemats, wooden salad servers and

20 tealight candles. People take their plates to Jacques carving at the spit and heap slaw and pickles and sweet potato and chapattis onto their plates. The bread rolls, I am gratified to see, remain untouched.

"Thank you, chef," Di says, raising her glass to me, and everyone touches their glass to mine. Ben smiles at me from across the table, and Sullivan, sitting next to me, puts his hand on the inside of my thigh, against my skin, sending goose bumps from the crown of my head right down into my heels.

I watch him eat. He fills chapattis with bits of everything and crams them into his mouth sideways, licking his fingers and flicking his tongue up to the sides of his lips to catch the sauce he's left behind. It's messy and taking up his full attention and makes me hungry. Cam would be using a knife and fork. I'm so relieved he's not here that I'm practically dizzy.

Later, when the others are counting down to the New Year, and we're the only two people inside except for the sleeping children, Sullivan pulls me into the dark guest room and rests his hands on my hips. He strokes his hands from my shoulders down my arms, once, firmly, and I'm convinced he's finally, finally going to kiss me, when he says the most devastating thing, the two most objectionable words in the English language.

"Good night."

I watch him leave the room, so turned on and frustrated I could scream. I want to tear my dress off and throw the lamp against the wall and fall on the floor and bang my heels against the wood until he comes back, but instead I curl up on the bed, forgetting who's been sleeping in it, and drift off to sleep with the room spinning around my head.

Four

I open one eye and the first thing I see is the ugly black digital watch on Ben's wrist. It's 6 a.m. He's facing away from me, his arm resting on the bed between us. Cam would never wear a watch like that.

I can hear the girls stirring in their room across the passage, and I start inching my way out from under the covers, wanting to check on Fallan immediately. I lift the duvet and see that I'm not naked, I've still got the ridiculous dress on, and Ben's wearing boxer shorts. Thank god.

As I put one foot on the floor next to the bed, Ben turns over to face me. He smiles sweetly, sleepily, and I swear his pupils dilate when he sees me.

"Morning. Sorry for crashing in your bed," I say.

He keeps his eyes on me and shifts closer, reaching around my waist, pulling me towards him.

"No, you're not," he says in a teasing voice.

I want to see Fallan and don't want him touching me.

"Seriously. I forgot you had this room."

"Oh, come on, Skye," he says, shifting his weight so that he's leaning over me, his body stretched on top of mine. "Enough messing around."

I don't want to be rude. "I'm going to go see if Fallan's okay."

"She's fine." His face comes towards mine, and I turn my head so his mouth brushes my cheek. I try to duck my head under his armpit, but he brings his elbow down and blocks my way with his arm.

He puts his full weight on me and I can feel his erection through his boxers. He's not very heavy and I could probably squeeze out from under him, but I don't want to move any part of my body that's touching his pants.

I'm not scared, but I get the prickling feeling in my skull that tells me I'm about to be.

He puts his mouth on top of my mine, and I can't move my head this time because his forearms are on either side of it, keeping it upright. I know that if I open my lips and go through the motions, he'll relax his body long enough for me to get out from under him, but I'm also trying to breathe and my jaw is clenched tight. His breath smells like dirty teeth, that whiff of rot you get at the dentist.

Ben draws his face away from mine and looks at me with something like disgust.

"You wanted this yesterday, didn't you?"

He moves off me and I roll away from him, and as I'm about to sit up, he grabs me by the waist, pulls me closer, pins me against himself, his erection against my tailbone. He grabs my vulva through my dress, hard, squeezing his fingers around it, squeezing, squeezing, and then he lets go and rolls away from me.

My eyes prick with sudden tears. I am in so much pain I can't breathe. My whole body is on fire.

"Fucking cocktease," he says, and sits up.

Seconds later, Fallan bounces into the room.

"Hi Skye, hi Uncle Ben," she says. She's wearing a tiny pair of cotton shorts and a pyjama T-shirt that says "Ain't nobody got time for that." I would never buy her T-shirts with slogans, my brain thinks. I'm burning, throbbing between my legs, I need to splash cold water on myself, but can't move in case it makes it worse.

"What are we going to do today, Skye?" Fallan asks.

I clear my throat. I can't let her see how upset I am. "We're going to make something greasy and wonderful for breakfast. Why don't you go get dressed?"

She bounds out the door.

Ben pulls his trousers on, not looking at me, stuffs the few items of clothes lying on the floor into his kit bag, and walks out the door.

"Uncle Ben, we're making greasy breakfast!" I hear Fallan calling to him from her room, and her joy forces me out of bed.

Andile, it turns out, passed out in a lawn chair at around three this morning, so he's sitting at the dining room table with Di, Jacques and Ben while I make egg and bacon with herb aioli on the bread rolls.

I am too scared to sit down, I can't bear the thought of putting any pressure on myself down there, and don't want to eat. Fallan whisks up the sauce while I fry each egg to order, and make sure Andile's is the runniest, with the albumen only barely cooked through. When he cuts into the roll and the sunny yolk oozes out, he groans, breaks off a piece of bread roll and dips it into the pool on his plate.

"Roo, I love you."

"She's good, hey," Jacques says to Di. "A very good cook."

"Baby, *I'm* a cook. Skye's a chef. They're very different."

"Liefie, I've never seen you cook once in your entire life."

Di jiggles Quinn, who's started grizzling, on her knee. "I think she's teething. Look at this rash on her chin. Molly! Liam! Breakfast!"

While she's handing them each half a bread roll in the kitchen and Fallan's out of earshot in the scullery – she insists on washing up – I ask Di if they're planning on doing breakfasts at their restaurant. I want to secure my place here, to make sure I can stay close to Fallan.

She roots around in the cupboard above the kettle among the boxes of medicine until she finds a bottle of paracetamol, and she pops the cap off, avoiding my eyes.

"I'm not sure. Jacques and I haven't spoken about it properly yet."

"You mean breakfast?"

"I mean the restaurant."

"I thought you said –"

"Can we please talk about this later? My head is killing me."

"Sure. I'll be around. I don't plan on going back to The Pines."

"Sorry?"

"I thought, I mean, if you don't mind, it would be easier for me to stay here than in the house with my mother and Malcolm. I can help with the kids while they're on school holiday. It's not like I have anything better to do."

Di blinks. "Okay. I suppose if the restaurant does happen –"

"If?"

"I mean, *when* the restaurant opens it would make sense for you to be here, wouldn't it? Heather's leaving The Pines soon and you can't stay there by yourself."

I have to fight to keep the smile off my face. Let Di think my moving in was her idea.

"Di, I'm off," Ben comes into the scullery with his hands in the pockets.

"I'll leave you two to say your goodbyes." Di shoots me a pointed look and backs out into the kitchen.

I force myself to look at Ben's face. His forehead is smooth, his eyes are bright, the face of a man with a clear conscience.

"I'll make that fence for the dam when I'm back in two weeks."

Two weeks. I hoped it would be longer.

He leans over and tries to hug me for a second, whispering, "Hopefully by then you'll have stopped with your bullshit."

I don't exhale until I hear him slam the door of Jacques's Land Rover and the car starting up outside.

At the sink, Fallan is scrubbing at the whisk with a brush that I am not a hundred per cent sure isn't used for the dogs or the phantom cat.

"Fallan, should we play dress-up? You and me?"

Her face lights up and she drops the whisk and the brush in the sudsy water. "Shotgun the light sabre!" she says.

Five

Andile and Heather come around the next evening to talk about The Pines. I put out a pot of tea, English Breakfast, in a shiny blue ceramic teapot on the table in the sun room.

"I can't remember the last time I had caffeine," Heather says, blowing into her teacup.

Andile cracks his knuckles one by one, a habit he was always scolded for, gently by Lola, stridently by Heather. He's nervous.

"I believe you'd be okay with selling The Pines?" Heather asks me as if we're discussing a piece of furniture or an old car.

"When Andile and I spoke about it, we agreed that if you're not there anymore, what's in it for us? We can't run it on our own, we both have other lives."

"I thought we should at least discuss it among ourselves before we get Zama in with the paperwork."

"We met her on Saturday night, she's lovely."

"Her parents were legends of the struggle. At the TRC it came out that there was a letter bomb with her father's name on it – literally – but that it was delivered the day after they went into exile. Their domestic worker opened it. They started an organisation in her name that funds domestic workers' education. Zama's head of the board."

"Well, I suppose that makes it okay then," Andile mutters.

Heather looks at him sharply. "Are you alright?"

"It's typical, isn't it. The domestic worker gets killed, her employers become legends."

"But this fund –"

"A fund, wonderful. They were the ones who had the capital, the connections, to emigrate. She's the one who ended up dying because of it."

Heather sets her teacup carefully back in the saucer and leans over to place it back on the coffee table. I hear a few loud thumps in the girls' bedroom and wonder if the kids are launching themselves off the top bunk again. Di is lying down with Quinn. She's been complaining of a two-day hangover.

"We're moving off-topic here, Andile. We can talk politics and history another time."

"No. There was something I wanted to say, and it's kind-of connected to all this. One of the reasons I would be okay with selling The Pines."

Heather sits back in her chair.

"I know you and my mom loved each other. But I don't think you were fair to her. It probably wasn't something you noticed, how … subjugated she was. Even though she was given way more than most black women were. You and her, you were never equals."

"What relationship is ever equal?" I say, hating the thought of outwardly cheerful Andile rubbing up against this grain of resentment for so many years, the idea of Lola having been downtrodden.

"Maybe no relationship is, I don't know – but lately I've

been thinking she'd have been much better off if she'd gone into exile. With other people who were real activists. She'd have been recognised, at least."

"You wouldn't have been born! If she hadn't come to The Pines she'd have never met your father –"

"We all know she'd have been better off without him in the first place." Andile is sweating in tiny beads along his hairline.

Heather raises her eyes to the ceiling. "Tell me why you think this. Why you think she was 'subjugated'. By me." She's wearing a skirt I don't recognise, and a beaded necklace. She's never worn any jewellery except for special occasions – my graduation from chef school, Andile's rugby prize-giving ceremonies.

"For one thing, we ended up speaking English, not isiXhosa."

"English made more sense here! Nobody here speaks isiXhosa. And you did speak it, both you and Roo grew up basically bilingual."

"Until we went to school. You know how much of it I speak now? None. I may as well have been adopted by a white family. There was no effort at all to teach us about Xhosa culture. Instead we read *Great Expectations* and Shakespearean sonnets and whatever the fuck else, always learning about your culture, your family, your past."

"Lola didn't want to contact her family when she first came, it was too dangerous. After that it seemed like it was too late to explain everything. They were conservative, she said. They wouldn't have understood, about us, about your father not being around."

"But that's the thing. She was always going to be the more vulnerable one. Because she was living in your house, on your land, with nobody to support her."

"It was as much her house as it was mine. She always knew that."

"It doesn't matter. It's done. I wanted to tell you that I'm okay with selling The Pines because it's not my legacy and it wasn't my mother's."

Heather reaches across the couch and takes both of Andile's restless hands in hers. "She was the love of my life, Andile. You and Roo were the love of ours, together. Land, property, language, it doesn't matter."

"It doesn't matter to you because you've always had it."

She keeps holding his hands. A door slams down the passage and I know I should go see what the children are getting up to, but I don't want to move.

"I'm giving you and Roo the farm because Lola taught me that nothing matters except spending time with the people you love. You know what would break Lola's heart?"

He meets her eyes for the first time.

"Knowing how far we've all drifted apart. I want you and Roo to find a way to see each other after I've left. I was hoping you'd keep the farm so you could have something in common, a home base, but I don't mind if you sell it, as long as you find some way to be close again. You were always so close."

Andile sniffs and wipes his nose with the back of his hand, nodding.

"For what it's worth, I'm going to be right here. On Coucal Farm. Don't tell anyone I told you, Di wasn't supposed to say anything to me." I tell them about the restaurant, about living here, so that I can be close to Fallan.

"What about your marriage?" Heather's got what Lola used to call her stress stripe, a vertical wrinkle directly between her eyebrows.

"He tried to call you yesterday," Andile adds. "I think he wants to make up."

"I'll call him back but first I need to see a lawyer. Zama, maybe. I own half the restaurant, I'm sure it's going to tank anyway, but if it's worth selling, I need my half of the profits. And I need to send him divorce papers, obviously."

"Roo, are you sure? You've only been here a week. People fight."

Another door slams, and Molly shouts out, "I'm going to tell Mommy!" and I stand up. "That's my cue. It's over, Heather. Me and Cam. I had a rush of blood to the head or something when I married him."

Heather and Andile exchange a look.

"Will you let me know when we need to meet with Zama and the company's lawyers? To finalise the sale?"

"Sure. I'll give you a call. It's strange knowing you're so close, but not in your own bedroom."

She drops a kiss on my cheek and says to Andile, "Let's go see what we can rustle up for the writers' dinner. I'm almost relieved Megs chopped her finger off. Even if it does mean we end up eating rice every day."

Mention of the writers reminds me of what Tshidi said before she left on Saturday night.

"I'll see you at the reading tomorrow night," I tell Heather, and turn to hug Andile before he leaves. I know it's not the last time I'll see him before he goes back to his normal life, but it feels like we're saying goodbye. Maybe because we really are doing it. We're selling our home.

Six

Di's given me the keys to her red-dust-coated 4x4 and asked me to take the girls to town, handing Quinn over. Jacques has taken Liam with him to the Malherbe Farm, the company's biggest, to play with the owners' boys.

Di is having what she calls "me time". I didn't say anything when she asked if I could take care of the girls this morning, but as I drive into White River, I'm thinking all kinds of uncharitable things.

So far, I have not seen Di do much actual parenting. Stella takes care of the fundamentals: the feeding, the cleaning, the brushing, the dressing. If the kids were horses, Stella would be their groom. From what I can see, Di's duties include yelling at them when they try to hurt one another, changing Quinn's nappies – unless it's a "code brown", when the baby gets handed promptly to Stella – and switching the TV on in the evenings.

The car's fully kitted out for the kids, with a DVD screen against each headrest. Quinn's strapped into her backward-facing cocoon of a car seat in the passenger seat next to me, which I am sure I will not be able to buckle her back into.

"So, guys, we're going to sign you up for swimming lessons and go to the library. How does that sound?"

"I don't like the library. It smells funny," Molly whines.

I stop at the robot at the intersection of main road and look down at Quinn, whose fuzzy head is wrapped in a peach-coloured headband, topped with a floppy flower. Fallan told me it's so people know she's a girl, as if the ruffled bloomers and coral top with little cap sleeves weren't enough. She meets my eyes with a slobbery grin and kicks her legs against the seat. Her eyes are startlingly blue.

The swimming school I looked up online is at the other end of town, on the Nelspruit road. They offer private lessons, or family ones, and I'm thinking it would be great to get the three older kids down there at least once a week. Whether or not Ben builds a new fence for the dam, they need to learn to swim.

I feel my frustration with Di and Jacques flare up again. They've got a child who's about to start crawling, and a laissez-faire attitude to open bodies of water. How can they not have fenced the dam off properly? They've been parents for seven years and I can't help but think that it's a miracle their kids have all survived till now.

After getting a fees schedule from one of the teachers at the school and waiting while Molly and Fallan stare at the otherworldly emus in the field next to the pool – the owner farms them for oil that gets used in cosmetics, an unpleasant nugget of info I don't share with the girls – we go back into town to the library.

Molly's right, it does smell funny, more like wet carpets than old books. We arrive as story-time is starting. Molly and Fallan join the circle of kids in front of the clunky shoes and thick calves of the woman reading a Julia Donaldson book. I find a child-sized chair in the kids' section and dig a bottle of warm water and the formula dispenser out the nappy bag. I'm inordinately pleased with myself when I manage to pour the powder into the water and pop the teat into Quinn's mouth without spilling. She sucks hard, playing with her earlobe, her eyelids hovering at half-mast.

I don't notice the woman beside me looking at her until she says, "I love her little outfit." She's about my age, also carrying a bulging nappy bag, also cradling a baby. "How old is she?"

"Uh, six months."

"George is four months, but he's massive. His older brother's huge too – he's over there." She points at the circle. "How many do you have?"

"Four."

"Girls? Boys?"

Are all mothers subjected to this line of questioning every time they meet a stranger, I wonder? It's like a blind date, but worse.

"Three girls. This one, and the blonde one over there, with the hair. Her sister's next to her, with the pigtails."

She sighs and shifts the baby to her other arm. "I always wanted a little girl. It must be so much fun going shopping for them."

I use the burp cloth from my shoulder to wipe the drool off Quinn's chin.

"I'm going to walk around with her for a bit. There's a book I'm looking for."

"An actual adult book, for yourself? To read? By yourself, in your own bed, not aloud? I've forgotten what that feels like."

"Haha, yes, totally," I bluff.

I heave the nappy bag onto my shoulder, hold Quinn upright, facing outwards, in one arm, and ask the librarian where the adult romance section is. She points me towards the shelves near the entrance. Before long I've found the "T"s, and on the lowest shelf I spot a paperback spine with the name Sullivan Troy on it.

I put Quinn on the carpet and hand her a rattle from the bag. I sit with my legs splayed on either side of her in case she falls over and turn the book in my hands. *So Close to Me*, it's called. The cover's not as corny as I'd imagined: no heaving bosoms, no ripped chest muscles. Just the silhouette of a girl, in a short, flared skirt, hovering in a doorway.

I flip it over to read the blurb and quickly check the publication page, scanning for a year. 2014. It's a recent one, but it's been thumbed through so many times it's worn at the corners, the cover not quite closing. Two years ago. My heartbeat quickens.

Story-time's over, and Molly and Fallan are fidgeting, ready to go home. I lift Quinn, who's rubbing her eyes with her fists like a cartoon of a tired baby, and sling the nappy bag over my shoulder, holding Fallan's hand as we cross the street to our car.

The other mother is leaning into hers, strapping the baby into his car seat, which looks similar to Quinn's. I peer through the window as we pass, watching her hold the top buckles and slide them into the holster at the bottom. She straightens up and looks at the four of us.

"Your girls are gorgeous," she says.

My heart sinks as Molly says, "She's not our mom, she's our neighbour. My mom's at home having me-time."

The mother's eyes meet mine. She's quizzical but there's something like pity in her face, too.

"Well, you're very lucky to have a neighbour like her. How much is their mother paying you?" she asks in a joking voice.

Fallan looks up at me. "Do you work for us? Like Stella?"

"No, honey. I do it because I love you."

"And me. And Quinn," Molly says accusingly.

"Of course." I give the other mother – the *only* mother – a small smile and steer the girls to the car. I can feel her eyes on my back.

I manage to get Fallan and Molly strapped in, and after a few tries with Quinn, who's fallen asleep on my shoulder, get her buckled in, too. The mother eases her car out into the road as I put the key in the ignition, and her fingers ripple in a little wave as she passes us.

I watch her car moving away and wonder what she must think of me, a woman her age, spending a Tuesday morning looking after her neighbour's kids, not because she's employed to, but because she *loves* them. I catch Fallan's eye in the rearview mirror. She sticks her tongue out at me and blows me a kiss.

We pull away from the curb, the DVD starting up again. As Fallan and Molly start to sing along to the theme tune, I think about Sullivan's book. The blurb says it's about an older man who falls for a teenaged girl, and all I can think about is what Tshidi said when I literally ran into her at the bluegum bend at The Pines. There's the sting of suspicion in my throat. If the new material Sullivan's working on is about me, my going to the reading isn't going to help – he won't read it for the group if I'm there. I need to find out if Tshidi's right, but how?

Seven

Once the kids are bathed and settled in front of a TV show about a team of vegetable superheroes, I give Di the fees schedule from the swimming school.

"Is this the cost *per lesson?*"

"Yes, but it's a private lesson, it'd only be the three of them. It's the quickest way to get them water-safe."

"There's no way we can afford this. Not with their school fees. Government schools were fine for Jacques and me, but no, our kids get only the best, so we're paying out our arses. I know you freaked out the other night, but they're fine. They don't need private swimming lessons."

She hands the printout back to me and leans over to pour her cooler into a glass.

"I'll pay. For Fallan. I'll take her to the lessons, too. They've got an opening on Wednesday afternoons. We can start tomorrow."

Di tosses the bottle in the bin and turns to me. "Why would you do that?"

"I think it's important."

"Well, Liam hates water anyway, and Molly's been having lessons at school. So I suppose it's most important for Fallan. I feel bad, though. You're not exactly earning money at the moment."

"I want to. It's fine."

She smiles over the rim of her glass at me. "I thought your mother was our saving grace, but you're on a whole other level, Skye."

I check the time and say I need to pop round to The Pines for the reading.

"Take my car, otherwise you'll have to walk back in the dark. Jacques's at the farm AGM till midnight so he can't come fetch you, either. Molly de Villiers, get your backside off the windowsill! Right! Now! You're going to fall through the window one day and nobody will feel sorry for you!"

It's not dark enough for headlights yet. As I'm easing the car down the hill at The Pines, I see a movement in the rows of trees to my left and stop the car. A female bushbuck stares directly at me, all fluffy-topped ears and twitching nose. She's the first one I've seen since coming home. She tosses her pretty head and picks her way delicately between the avocado trees, and a moment later, she's invisible.

As I pass the entrance to Ivy Cottage, which is Sullivan's, I hit the brakes. It's three minutes to eight by the car clock. I pull over on the side of the road, close to the cottage entrance. I can see through the avo trees that the lights are all out. Sullivan's gone up to the house already.

One of Heather's rules is that the cottages are never locked. When Andile moved into Fever Tree Cottage when we were 15, he asked for a key and Lola told him that when the activists stayed in the cottages, they didn't bother with locking the doors because if there was a raid the cops would get in one way or another. Not having to lock the doors made them feel safer at The Pines, somehow. So he'd have to live the same way they did, the same way the yuppie guests did, with nothing to hide and no need to keep other people out.

I open the flashlight app on my phone and see a little WhatsApp symbol in the notification bar. My first message since arriving from Misty Cliffs. There's no Wi-Fi here and I don't have data, so whoever sent it is going to have to wait.

I move slowly through the avo trees, dredging up mulchy leaves and trying not to hit my head on low branches. The flashlight on my phone casts a bright light on the ground ahead of me. My shoes are covered in damp clods of red earth, and I slip them off on the path so I don't leave tracks on the step.

In Sullivan's bedroom, there's a small desk, with three A5 notebooks on the left-hand side, and a row of five silver ballpoint pens lined up vertically on the right. There's a low stool on wheels pushed in under the desk. The train station story, the one Sullivan's busy on, has obviously been taken with him to the reading.

I'm expecting to have to riffle around to find his notes, but his new work is right there in the first notebook I open. As usual, the first-person narrator is nameless. The woman he's pursuing is called Zoe. She's a farmer's wife, he's a landscaper. She's young and fresh-looking and smells of damp soil. The first time he sees her, he reaches into the warmth of her apron pocket and watches her knees buckle. He looks into her eyes and sees them go "opaque with longing", and he has to force himself to step away from her. Her husband will be home any minute.

I expected his writing to be cheesy and ridiculous, but this is disturbingly true to life. He's turned that moment, and my desire, into something he can sell.

I put the book back so that its edge once again lines up precisely against the spine of the one underneath it. I check that the pens are perfectly straight, and turn to leave, but then I have an idea: a way to take something personal from him, something private, the way he took the apron-pocket moment from me.

The bedroom is neat and uncluttered, and it doesn't take me long to find his wallet. It's a soft, buttery suede, the same colour as his eyes. Inside is his South African drivers licence. He's 38, like Tshidi said, born in June. He used to have a goatee – horrendous – and his name is Sufjan Kamali. Now I know his name. His real name. I slot the licence back into his wallet and place it on the bedside table where I found it.

After closing the door behind me, I'm left alone with the quiet darkness and the shadows in the avo trees. Tshidi's cottage, Kwêvoël, is on the other side of this row of trees, and I start making my way there, shining my phone light ahead of me. I've missed the start of the reading, and Heather doesn't tolerate tardiness, so there's no point heading to the main house. I decide to wait for Tshidi to come back from the reading to tell her she was right.

I'm halfway down the row when I hear a deep grunt and the sound of a heavy body shifting on the leafy ground up ahead. I lift my phone to illuminate the space ahead of me. Four trees away is a low rump with a thin, flicking tail. The hippo bull. I can't see the cow anywhere, but she can't be far, and I back away as quietly as I can, cringing with every leaf-crunching footstep, praying he doesn't turn around.

I make it back to the car without the bull seeing me, and sit for a second in the driver's seat, my heart galloping, my breathing shallow. We were always told that hippos covered great distances at night, but I've never come across one this far from the lake. By the time I'm ready to turn the key, it's almost 9 o'clock, and I see the light of a torch bobbing along the path. It's Tshidi heading to her cottage. I lean on the hooter. The torch stops moving, and swings in my direction.

"Stay where you are," I call to her out of the window. "Hippo."

I hear her swear in the darkness, and I start the car.

"I'll drive you to your cottage," I say, reversing out the way I came and giving the bull a wide berth as I swing round onto the road.

"My hero," Tshidi says when she opens the door, and I can't help smiling.

Eight

Two-and-a-half hours later, I'm in Tshidi's cottage and bursting for the bathroom after four cups of black rooibos tea that I wish had been wine. We've been talking about Olive Schreiner, mostly, and I've made a commitment to go with Tshidi to visit the house in Cradock in the Eastern Cape where Schreiner lived as a teenager. Tshidi says it's perfectly preserved and wonderfully creepy.

"She wrote *The Story of an African Farm* under the pen name Ralph Iron. Like, could you *get* any more macho? She started writing it while she was a governess – basically an indentured servant. She had all these unpopular ideas, she was vocally anti-war, and a totally bad-ass feminist. For a woman to have these kinds of intellectual or abstract ideas, you know, at the end of the nineteenth century – it wasn't exactly encouraged. Her publishers insisted after the first print run of her book that she publish under her real name and wanted to promote the fact that she was from Africa, like she was some kind of exotic drawcard for them, and she hated it."

"What made you choose her? Of all the historical South African figures –"

"You mean, why choose a white person to do my thesis on? I ask myself that all the time. I got so much grief from my supervisor for not going with an influential black South African, someone no one knew about, something that would shed light on one of the forgotten figures who were written out of history, but, I don't know," she shrugs, and takes a sip of tea before continuing.

"My parents weren't thrilled either, believe me – my dad's an anthropology professor and my mom's in the history department at UCT. Apples, trees, I know. I suppose I've always felt this incredible attraction to Schreiner. She was sent off to work when she was fifteen. She was basically raised by her older brother, who ended up working on the diamond fields. So it's not like she was from a wealthy family of educated people. She was like the Brontë sisters of South Africa. Or Louisa May Alcott. All these women who wrote these absolutely seminal books while also earning a living for their families, working as teachers and governesses and basically grinding away against poverty but also being passionate political and social activists?"

I'm jiggling my leg to distract myself from how much I need to pee. I don't want to break her chain of thought. She's so enthusiastic that it would seem rude to interrupt her to fulfil a bodily function, but she notices my leg and bursts out laughing. "Do you need the bathroom, Skye?"

"*So* badly."

I come back into the kitchen to find Tshidi ready to pour boiling water into our cups. I pull mine away before she can lower the kettle over it.

"I'm going to be off soon."

She puts the kettle down. "You still haven't told me why you were parked outside Sullivan's cottage."

"I was checking something. After what you told me. You were right. He's a total creep."

She takes a sip from her mug and grimaces. "Hot!" She blows across the surface of the tea. "I didn't want to be right, you know."

"I'm glad you said something." My attraction to Sullivan – to Sufjan – has gone up in a puff of smoke. "I've been thinking about Cam, my husband. I don't know if we're done with each other yet – does that make sense? I don't think we can stay together, but we can't leave things like this."

"Did you have trauma counselling? After the baby?"

I drop down into a kitchen chair. "Not exactly. I was having counselling for a mugging at the time."

"So, you never spoke to anyone about the baby? Specifically about the baby?"

I lift one shoulder, and she puts both hands down flat on the table, gearing up to say something.

"I know!" I say, before she can get started. "At the time I didn't want to think about it. I definitely didn't want to talk about it. It felt like, like a bruise, but in my mind. I didn't want to press on it."

"I think everyone in South Africa needs counselling round the clock, quite honestly. We've all got some kind of PTSD, even when there's nothing specific that's happened to us, personally. And you had this specific thing. That you've never talked about."

"Until now, you, this, there's been no one I could tell. Cam didn't know about it, so how could I tell anyone else?"

She purses her lips. "Babe, okay, but my feeling is you've got to talk about it and talk about it and talk about it until it's healed. It's like this bruise that's right there, under the surface, and – at the risk of completely mutilating this metaphor – if you don't talk about it, the bruise stays fresh and painful, but if you talk about it, it starts to fade."

I'm tracing the wet ring my mug left on the table, round and round, and she changes tack. "Can I ask you something? I've been wondering what's going on with you and this Ben guy. I noticed a definite vibe between you at the party."

"Seriously?"

Tshidi laughs. "Look, all I have to distract me from starting my final chapter, which I am *dreading*, is crochet, and chatting to you, and I swear I'm getting early onset rheumatism because my knuckles are killing me and I can't face the thought of crocheting, so here we are."

"Okay. Well, firstly, there's absolutely nothing going on." My tone gives me away, and her eyebrows shoot up.

"Did something happen?"

"Sort of. It was weird. I don't know how to describe it."

"Try."

"You're very insistent, you know that?"

"I like to think of it as *persistent*. Determined."

"Pushy. Stubborn."

"Whatever. You have to tell me because I've trapped you in my lair and am not letting you go until you give me the information I demand. I can wait this out way longer than you can. I'll stare at you till you tell me everything."

I sigh, wanting to be exasperated but not managing to work myself up to it. Is it possible to fall in friendship, like you fall in love? This heady relief and joy at having an ally, falling mentally into step with someone in the space of a conversation, is the same kind of rush.

"I'm only telling you because I need to go to bed, like, immediately, because I am shattered." I go on to tell her about Ben grabbing me, and what he said afterwards.

233

"He called me a –" My breath has started coming in short, sharp bursts. "He called me a cocktease. When was the last time you heard that? It's the most old-fashioned sexist slur I've ever heard." It's almost funny, saying it like that, but I have to put my head between my knees.

Tshidi stands up and puffs out a breath. "I was expecting some kind of sweet star-crossed romance from when you were kids. Not this. It makes me so fucking livid! That even sweet-looking little boys with long eyelashes do this shit, the ones who seem like the good ones. Come here," she says, almost roughly, and pulls me up to hug her.

Of course, I'm crying now, but this time it feels good, cleansing. Like I'm safe. Tshidi's anger on my behalf makes me angry too, displacing the grubby smudge of shame. We pull apart and my breathing's back to normal. I notice with something close to wonder that my hands are steady and my palms are dry. No shakes, no clamminess.

"It's assault, you know that, right?" she says. "He assaulted you. It wasn't your fault."

"Well, cognitively, yes, I know that. When I think about it."

She puts a hand on my breastbone. "You need to know it here. Feel it in your bones. It's the truth. Whenever you think about it, just think 'It wasn't my fault'."

My head feels clear and still, like the smooth surface of a lake on a quiet night. I wonder if this is what peace feels like as I thank Tshidi and tell her good night before setting off on the bumpy road back to Coucal Farm.

Nine

I hear Jacques get in from the AGM while I'm lying in bed later that night, gearing up to open the WhatsApp notification I got earlier. It's close to midnight and I should go to sleep – Fallan will be up in six hours – but I have a bad feeling about the message and don't feel like I have the nerve to open it.

Jacques comes clomping into the house and kicks off his boots in his and Di's bedroom, which shares a wall with the guestroom. Di shushes him so he doesn't wake up Quinn, who's in a cot in their room. I hear him whisper something about The Pines but can't make out anything else. Maybe they're talking about the restaurant – maybe they decided about it at the AGM.

Oh, what the hell. I open the message.

It's from Cam. He's left a voice note. I put my earphones in, close my eyes, and brace myself.

"Hey. I wanted to tell you, we've let Zhou go. I bought him a flight back to Taipei, paid him a fat bonus, hoping he won't start talking about all of this. He left last night. So we have nothing to worry about there. But my dad's PR people think Bushy Bun's a lost cause, that we won't be able to come back from this without a complete overhaul and it doesn't seem worth it at this stage."

There's a rumble in the background, a smooth hum, and I realise Cam sent this voice note from a car. Who was driving him? Deacon? Is he listening to all of this?

"I was thinking we could shut down the business and make a tidy profit from the property. My dad knows of a buyer and is getting an offer put together, we should get it over email in the next few days. We'll split it down the middle, obviously, after we pay my dad back. He's calmed down a lot about it. He's taking it as one of those investments that didn't work out. But he's told me that that's it. He's not investing in anything else of ours again, not until we prove ourselves. One second, I'm pulling into a petrol station."

I scramble to sit up and switch on the bedside lamp, as if that will help me hear Cam better, to understand what he's trying to say. Anything of ours? He thinks we're going to keep our business partnership? And Deacon's not driving him – it sounds like – like he's driving himself? But he told me he couldn't drive, right at the beginning of our relationship. I'd driven him around for the 18 months we'd been together, and he could drive the whole time?

"More news: I've got Maya with me, and I'm taking her back to Rory, to Motherwell. I wanted to fly with her, right, because the drive is insanely long, but I don't have her birth certificate, if she even has one, and kids in South Africa aren't allowed to fly without one. Of course the fact that I'm not her parent or guardian means that ID or no ID, I wouldn't be able to fly anywhere with her anyway, not without a signed affidavit from Rory, so it's all a bit of a balls up, to be completely honest with you. At least she's slept for most of the way so far."

His voice breaks off and I hear him asking for the car to be filled up with unleaded.

"Anyway, I'm sorry I've not tried to get hold of you. I know you freaked out. I get it. You thought my dad and I were angry, and we were, but we're not anymore. I should have spoken to you about Maya. You didn't think it was a good idea to take her on, and you were a hundred per cent right. I'm sorry, Skye. I'm so, so sorry." He whispers the last part, and there's a pause before I hear the car starting again.

"Could you phone me, please? I was wrong, and I'm taking Maya back, and yes, maybe Bushy Bun's dead in the water, but we can start something else. I have a plan. Talk to me. Please. I'm staying over in Knysna. I'll be at the hotel in about an hour. I want to hear your voice. You don't have to forgive me. Just let me know if you're okay."

I'm the widest awake I've ever been. Cam thinks we're still together. Cam thinks we're having an argument. Cam thinks this is a tiff that will blow over. Before I can change my mind, I scroll through my contacts to his name, and hit the green phone.

I count eight rings before he picks up. "Skye?" He's whispering. "Can I call you back in the morning, I'm absolutely knackered, it took Maya like three hours of screaming to get to sleep and I've got a long drive in the morning."

"You're driving? Yourself?"

"I can explain that." He sounds like he's perking up a bit.

"Are you in the hybrid? How did you find it? I parked it at the airport and didn't tell you where it was."

"It's got a tracker, love. I looked it up online after I realised you were gone. Are you still pissed off? I wouldn't blame you."

237

I feel my shoulders sag. His bounce-back buoyancy is making me feel more deflated than I already was. "I'm not pissed off anymore, no."

"Oh, brilliant. I can't wait to see you. Can you meet me in Port Elizabeth? You're at your mom's in Mpumalanga, right? I'm sure there are flights from there. I'll be in Port Elizabeth tomorrow evening. I know you needed some time and space, and it's all fine. We've got a buyer for the property, we'll get some capital and I've got a good idea for –"

"Cameron! Listen to me." I don't bother trying to keep my voice down. "It's done. I'm done. You told me you couldn't drive and you're doing a cross-country trip with a sixteen-month-old by yourself? Plus, the whole Zhou thing is not at all my fault. Yes, I told Talia about it, and I shouldn't have, but he was all your idea. I had nothing to do with your arrangement with him. Whether or not we were married, I'd be insane to go anywhere near you as a business partner again. And as my husband – how could I ever trust you again?"

I hear him breathing heavily. He wasn't expecting this. Cam has never not got his own way, not in his entire adult life, and I imagine his bafflement at discovering that that's what's happening.

"I can't be married to you anymore. I can't be your business partner anymore."

He tries to speak, and a croak comes out. He clears his throat. "Skye. We love each other."

I want to reach through the phone and grab him by the throat and shake him. "Cam, it's late, I have to go. I'm going to go see a lawyer –"

"Don't say that," he says in a low voice.

"I can't do it anymore. There's too much between us that's wrong. Too much has happened."

"You're still angry about Bushy Bun. I know you got a fright, but we can make this better."

I need to hang up before I throw the phone across the room and wake up the whole family, if I haven't already.

"I'll keep an eye on my emails for the offer on the Bushy Bun property," I say as firmly as I can. I hit the red phone icon, and he's gone.

Ten

I didn't get much sleep after my call to Cam. My eyes feel sandy, my footsteps sluggish, and I feel very alone, until Fallan hugs me from behind while I'm waiting for the kettle to boil in the kitchen the next morning.

She plants a kiss on the small of my back, and I turn around and crouch down to hug her. She's still bed-warm. When she pulls away, I notice the eczema on her wrists for the first time, with thin scratch marks running down her forearm. She sees me looking and puts her hands behind her back.

Di comes in the kitchen door, and says, "I've just delivered the eggs to The Pines. Heather says to go over there tomorrow evening, Zama's coming around. She says you and Andile are prepared to sell!"

"I think we need to try something with Fallan's diet. For her eczema. We can try cutting out grains and dairy and sugar?"

Di bangs the empty basket down on the counter. Fallan has drifted to her colouring book on the dining room table. Molly and Liam are riding bikes outside, and Quinn is strapped to Stella's back while she mops the passage.

"She's five years old," Di says.

"Five-and-two-thirds!" Fallan counters, bent over her book.

"I think we should try." I lower my voice. "She's been scratching, it must be so uncomfortable for her."

"You think? I've been trying to fix it since she was a baby. Specialists all said she'd grow out of it. She hasn't. I've tried all the natural remedies, baking soda in the bath, no petrolatum products, soap-free washing powder, Heather's honey, and nothing works. The only thing that will work is if she stops scratching at it."

"It's not her fault. She probably does it in her sleep."

"The doctor said she should sleep in gloves. Molly teased her about them the first night we tried and I didn't have the heart to do it again."

Di moves to the couch and collapses on it, propping her feet on the coffee table when Stella comes around with the mop. I can't see her face, but her voice when she speaks again is small and tired.

"If you think it might work, go ahead, try. Just know that I've tried everything else. Give me some credit for that."

"Of course," I say. "Can I take some chicken out the freezer for lunch? May as well start immediately."

She waves her hand, acquiescing and dismissing me in one gesture. She picks up the remote and flicks to a cooking show.

Fallan wants to help with lunch, so I put a step-stool next to the kitchen counter and give her a butter knife and a bunch of chard from the fridge to chop while I look for sundried tomatoes and coconut milk in the pantry.

I zap the chicken in the microwave to quick-defrost and start slicing mushrooms. When Fallan's finished, I peel three cloves of garlic and hand her the garlic crusher. The head of it is square, not circular like the one at The Pines, which has been around at least as long as I've been alive.

This one's much lighter, flimsier, and the first fat, tear-drop-shaped garlic clove doesn't fit as snugly as it should. I put my hands over Fallan's to squeeze the arms of the crusher closed, and show her how to scrape off the mush that comes out through the holes on the other side with the back of her butter knife.

I start browning the defrosted chicken breasts in a pan with oil from the sachet of sundried tomatoes and leave Fallan to do the second clove herself. When I was her age, I was baking basic breads and making what became my signature dish for years, spinach off the stalk sautéed in frothy butter with slivers of garlic and a smattering of nutmeg. Andile and I never saw processed food until we started going to school, and the bright colours of the packets of chips and biscuits the other kids brought in their lunch-boxes mesmerised me. I coveted them for years. At boarding school I spent all my pocket money on crisps and chocolate bars from the vending machines in the hostel corridors.

"Like this?" Fallan asks, her fingers stretched between the arms of the garlic crusher. She's squeezing so hard her arms are shaking, so I place my hands over hers and apply pressure. I feel the crusher suddenly give way with a crunch, and Fallan shrieks with fright.

She drops the crusher and starts wailing, and I look for pieces of her fingers on the floor, examining her hands, her arms. When Di comes skidding in Fallan's got both hands held up to her left eye. When she can take a breath, she says shudderingly, "My eye! There's garlic in my eye!"

I'm so relieved I collapse back onto my heels on the kitchen floor. Molly and Liam come running in from the front garden, with fearful little faces. Di is folded around Fallan, her hand on her head, rocking her back and forth and saying "It's alright, it's alright," over and over.

I put my hand out to touch Fallan's knee, and Di slaps it away.

She says, through her teeth, "She's not your goddamn sous chef, Skye."

Fallan shifts closer to Di, her wails having given way to sniffles. Di picks her up and carries her down the passage, saying, "It's okay, Fell, Mommy's got you, Mommy's here."

I feel something cracking inside me, like the walls of my heart are caving in.

"Something smells nice," Molly says, taking my hand. "What's for lunch?"

≈

After we've eaten, I wash the lunch dishes by hand, carefully, meticulously, and when they're washed, I dry them slowly and hang up the dish towel. Molly and Liam are lying on a picnic blanket under the trees in the garden. I've told them to count the go-away-birds and to call me when they get to 100.

I knock lightly on the door of Di and Jacques's bedroom and push it ajar. Fallan's asleep on the bed, and Di is sitting at the bedside table plucking her eyebrows in the mirror.

"Sorry. It's half past two. The swimming class is at three. Can I wake her up?"

Di looks at me in the mirror. Her mouth is set in a straight line, and she nods.

I touch Fallan on the shoulder and her eyes fly open. She hugs me round the neck. Her left eye is red, and her face is tear-streaked.

"I'm sorry about the garlic," I say.

"It wasn't your fault." She sounds 10 years older than she is.

Di's back straightens almost imperceptibly.

"Can you go get ready for your swimming lesson?"

She bounces out the room to fetch her swimming costume, and I ask Di if I can take her car.

"Sure. The keys are in my bag in the lounge. Look. I've been wanting to talk about your living arrangements. I wanted all this to work out: you staying with us, working at the restaurant, all of us moving into the main house at The Pines eventually."

She turns back to the mirror and starts plucking the other eyebrow.

"But I just got a call from Jacques. He's with management. I told him you guys were ready to sign the offer to purchase, so he can get a head start on the paperwork from the company's side. It turns out they want him to manage The Pines as well, once the sale's gone through."

I shift my weight, wanting to leave with Fallan immediately, but she keeps talking, looking at my reflection in the mirror.

"It doesn't look like the restaurant's going to happen. There's no way Jacques will be able to manage a separate farm plus this one plus start a new venture. I'm sorry. You're going to have to find somewhere else to stay, if you're wanting to stick around. We don't have enough space as it is. I'm sure you'll be going back to Cape Town soon anyway."

Her words fall on my ears like stones, each one sinking me lower and lower. If I'm not here, who will keep Fallan safe?

"I have to tell you something. About Ben," I blurt out. "I'm worried about him with Fallan."

"Ben?" She turns around to face me.

"The other morning. After the party. He, he assaulted me. In bed. I need to tell you because Fallan –"

"I don't want to hear about you and Ben!" She puts her tweezers down on the dressing table and puts her head in her hands. "I'd like you to start packing your stuff, please."

I shove my clothes into the gym bag Andile gave me. I go into the girls' room and throw a few pieces of Fallan's clothes from the chest of drawers into the bag on top of my things. The fish shirt, the mermaid shirt, some shorts, three pairs of pastel-coloured Barbie panties.

There's a filing cabinet in the passage where Di keeps the things the kids aren't allowed to touch. It's the only place I can think of where Di might keep official documents. I try to still my racing thoughts for long enough to concentrate, try to remember what Cam said about flying with a child if you weren't the parent, what Di told me she'd had to do to get the paperwork for the kids to fly with her in-laws.

I pull the top drawer out as slowly as I can so that no one hears the metal screeching, and flip through the files until I find a stack of four envelopes. I open them until I find the one holding Fallan's birth certificate. I slip it into the side pocket of the gym bag. In the next drawer are photocopies of Di and Jacques's ID documents, certified two-and-a-half months ago, plus the affidavits signed by Di and Jacques. I remove a copy of each of their IDs, and one copy of the affidavit. They've left the line for Di's mother-in-law's signature blank, and I swoop a few indeterminate loops on it. I put the ID copies and the affidavit in the side pocket of the bag with Fallan's birth certificate.

On my way out of the house, I grab her toothbrush from the bathroom.

Fallan is waiting for me next to the car, her swimming costume and pink swimming towel in her arms. I dig the keys out of Di's handbag, throw the gym bag in the boot and strap Fallan into her car seat. I start the car and it's only as we're driving past the lawn and I see Molly and Liam lying under the trees, pointing up into the branches, that I remember they're there. Oh well, I think, without slowing down, not my problem anymore.

We drive through town, up the main road, and I keep telling myself we're going to the swimming school, until we drive past the turn-off and keep going. I tell myself we're just going for a little drive until I put my flicker on as we approach the airport turn-off. We take the turn and I tell myself we've still got time to make it to the lesson, and that I'll do a U-turn as soon as there's somewhere to turn around.

It's not until we're pulling up to the airport and I look in the rear-view mirror at Fallan staring out the window with a little smile on her face, her swimming costume and towel balled up in her lap, looking so trusting and so happy, that I realise what I've done. What I'm about to do.

I stop the car in the middle of the parking lot and try to force myself to breathe. My hands are shaking so hard it takes me three tries to work the button to get my window down. I'm sucking in the humid air and telling myself I need to start the car again and at least pull into a parking bay before I attract attention. I'm trying to figure out if the ringing in my ears is from my own panic or the noise of cicadas outside when I see Siyabonga Khumalo, driver to the stars, standing outside his car on the other side of the parking lot.

I practically fall out of the car, hoping Fallan can't see my face. On my journey across the parking lot, I keep my vision trained on the figure of Siya as if he's the horizon and I'm bobbing, seasick, on a boat.

He catches sight of me when I'm a few feet away. I look back to Di's car, the front door wide open, Fallan strapped into her seat in the back, stranded in the middle of the parking lot where anything could happen to her.

Siya looks at me with a deep quizzical crease in a horizontal line on his forehead.

"It's you," he says mildly. "With the gate. And the mother."

I nod and feel tears streaking down my cheeks.

"Jesus. What's the matter?"

Through a shuddering breath I manage to gasp out, "Please help me. There's a girl in the car. I need you to take her home. And me. I need you to take me home. Please."

Siya looks at me for a beat without saying anything, and then turns around to lock his Corolla. He sweeps me with him to Di's car without touching or looking at me, but it's not displeasure coming off him. It's concern.

When Fallan sees me through the window, she looks at me with something I've not seen in her eyes before. Suspicion. As if I'm a stranger. Which, I realise, I am. She's not mine, and I'm not hers.

"Come," Siya says to me. "Park the car under the cover. I'll take you home in mine."

"What about her car seat? We can't take her without it."

"You think I've never installed a car seat before?"

It's true, he's a pro, and Fallan's seat is in Siya's Corolla within minutes. He settles her in, and she never once asks what's happening or where we're going. I move the gym bag and her towel and costume into Siya's car.

There's a pine-shaped air freshener hanging from the rear-view mirror, swinging in the warm air blowing from the fan. The clock on the dashboard says it's 15:35. Twenty minutes since I last checked the time. Months and years.

"Put your seatbelt on, please," he says.

I comply, and he asks if there's anyone at home. "My mother."

"Phone her. Tell her whatever you need to tell her. I think it will be bad if you surprise her like this."

I don't fall asleep this time. I follow every curve of the road through verdant streets and over tree-lined hills. I dial Heather's mobile and she picks up after the first ring. At the sound of her voice, my throat closes.

"Roo? What's the matter?"

"I'm on my way home. With Fallan. I need you to take her back to Di."

"How far away are you?"

One thing to be said for Heather is that she keeps her composure, no matter what. She is exactly the kind of person you want on your side in an emergency, like when you lose your mind and almost kidnap your neighbour's daughter.

"We'll be there in ten minutes."

"Okay, see you then."

"Mom?" The word is sweet and strange in my mouth. A pause. "Yes?"

"Will you wait at home for me?"

"I'll be right here," she says.

Eleven

Siya refuses to accept any money. He seems insulted that I'm trying to give it to him. His kindness undoes me, and I fight to hold it together. Heather manages to push a jar of honey onto him.

Before Heather takes Fallan home, I hold Fallan's small frame to me.

"Are you coming back to my house?"

"I don't think so."

She seems to accept this, and takes Heather's hand to walk across to Coucal Farm. Heather's got Fallan's car seat in the crook of her other arm. What on earth is she going to tell Di?

Malcolm's in the vegetable garden, and I have the house to myself. I lie down on my bed and fall immediately, miraculously, into a deep sleep, like my mind's shutting down so it doesn't have to deal with what I've done.

I wake up with Heather placing an ice-cold facecloth that smells of lavender on my forehead. "Lavender", I catalogue. This has been Heather's remedy for sickness of the body and the heart for as long as I can remember. The smell reminds me of lying in this same bed in this same position with the curtains drawn against the bright sun, the weight of Heather sitting at the foot of my bed, the day I got my first period.

I count my breaths – in, hold, out; in, hold, out – until the cloth has gone warm from the heat of my face. I hold it out to Heather, who takes it to the bathroom. I hear her rinsing it under the tap, and then she comes back, lies down next to me, close enough that neither of us falls off the bed, both of our heads on the pillowcase that first gave me a hint of Heather's love for me, of her faith that I would come home.

It helps that I can't see her face. We're both staring up at the ceiling, at the 12 squares that divide it neatly, at the blades of the fan turning in circles and the cord swinging back and forth like a quietly ticking metronome.

"The baby would have been born on the same day as Fallan. Not the same year, but they'd have had the same birthday, the fifteenth of April. It would be eight months old."

That's how I start. I tell her about the sleepless nights spent worrying about money, about where to live, about not wanting to tell Cam, to keep it a secret until I was sure, and after I *was* sure, about not knowing how to tell him while I was traumatised after the mugging.

I tell her about walking back from Dr Taylor after hearing the heartbeat. ("They can hear it that early? That's amazing. I never had a single scan with you," she says.) Walking through the darkening streets in Tamboerskloof, and looking up suddenly and seeing a group of men in front of me, boys, really, they couldn't have been more than 20 years old. There were five of them, and they fanned out around me.

Only one of them spoke. I can't see his face in my head. I couldn't remember what he looked like minutes after it happened. He asked for money, and I said, sorry, not today, as if they were beggars, and tried to step aside, away, but they were all around me. My bag was ripped off my shoulder from behind and the one who spoke moved in very close to me and held something to my stomach.

"Don't make me do something I don't want to do. Don't make me do something bad to you," he said. I looked down. There was the pointed blade of a flick knife resting below my belly button, where the baby was curled behind layers of muscle and the walls of my womb.

He jerked the tip of the knife, narrow and sharp, through the thin cotton of my shirt and I felt it nick into my skin, stinging like a paper cut. He could have plunged it right inside me, if he wanted to. Instead, he flicked it back towards himself, wiped it quickly against his trousers and used it to pull up the sleeve on his left arm, showing me tattoos on the inside of his wrist that I assume were gang signs. I couldn't read them and can only remember their colour, a faded blue-black.

I felt my bag thrown at my back, and heard footsteps running down the hill behind me, the laughter of the other men ringing out down the road. The one who spoke tucked the blade back into the handle of the knife, smiled at me, said, "You're the lucky one," and followed the others down the hill.

The street was empty. The tall blocks of flats with their blind, shuttered windows rose up over me. The cut in my stomach was pulsing in time with my racing heart. I bent down shakily to pick up my bag. My wallet was gone, of course, my phone, too, but the slip from Dr Taylor was still there, with "EDD 15/04/2016" scrawled across the top.

I held my stomach all the way home. Cam was cooking when I arrived. I fell into his arms and showed him the cut, watching his face drain of colour before he turned to the kitchen cabinet to scrabble for disinfectant wipes and gauze. I didn't tell him about the scan pictures in my bag, or about the heartbeat that I couldn't stop hearing, like the crashing of waves on the inside of a seashell pressed against my ear.

Once he'd swabbed the blood off the cut and covered it with gauze and a bandage, and I'd assured him that I'd got worse injuries while working at Mon Petit and that it barely hurt at all, and had convinced him I absolutely did not need to be rushed to the emergency room, he found me the number for a telephonic counselling service that was compatible with my medical aid. He insisted that I call immediately. I couldn't stop crying, and he sat with me while I sobbed into the phone and slowly relayed the details to the husky-voiced woman on the other end. He rubbed my back for hours. He phoned his parents and told them about it. He called in to *Fig & Brie* and left a message for my boss to say I wouldn't be in the next day, and he cancelled his meetings for the next day, too, so he could be with me.

Two weeks later, I still hadn't got around to telling him about the baby. I started bleeding while I was at work. I stuck a pantyliner in, we were on deadline, and I'd read that spotting was normal in early pregnancy, and that's obviously what was happening. But then I felt something drop in my lower abdomen, a heavy tugging. I went back to the bathroom, and found my underwear soaked through with blood.

I staggered out of the stall and there was Tshidi, whose name I didn't know at the time. I'd seen her around, with her competent bearing and perfect posture. She took a look at my face, the face of a stranger clearly in distress. I told her about the blood, and she swung into action.

She got Dr Taylor's number from my phone, called her, and managed to get through the secretary to speak to the doctor herself – a minor miracle – who told me to meet her at the hospital where her rooms were. Tshidi walked me down to the lobby and waited while Ashwin called the company driver ("Trust me, babe, everyone uses the car for non-work things, I've done it loads of times," Tshidi had said when I tried to protest), and gently closed the door of the car once I'd got in.

In the emergency room, after I'd been examined, Dr Taylor, in her uniform of brightly coloured blouse and red lipstick, used her level voice and her neat hand gestures to explain that I could choose to let my body take care of things naturally, which shouldn't take long, judging by the volume of blood, or I could have a D and C right away, which would mean going under general anaesthetic and having the "contents of my uterus" scraped away.

I couldn't bear the thought of watching my baby leak out of me and craved the oblivion of anesthetic. I wondered at which exact moment in the past two weeks that tiny heart had stopped beating. Before I went under, I asked Dr Taylor if there was anything I could have done to keep it and the last thing I remember is her squeezing the hand that didn't have the port in it, and shaking her head.

I woke up less than an hour after I'd been wheeled into theatre. Two hours after that, I was discharged. I walked back to the office to fetch my car, marvelling at the fact that it was late afternoon, the usual time I'd be heading home from work on any ordinary day. When I got back to Cam's flat, I told him I was feeling queasy. I got into bed, drank the honey-lemon tea he made me and fell dead asleep.

Since I'd never told him about the baby, I couldn't tell him about losing it. Two months later, he suggested that we open a restaurant together, and within weeks Bushy Bun was registered, and the property on Bree Street had been bought, and Cam was taking me to Taiwan, and our lives were unfolding the way he wanted them to. I could never tell him about the baby. Our baby. At the time I thought, well, I couldn't keep the baby, but at least I can keep Cam. I wish it had been the other way around.

When I've stopped talking, Heather lays her hand on my cheek and pulls my face to hers.

"Listen to me."

I feel tears leaking out the side of both my eyes, and she says, "Roo, you've been so brave."

I close my eyes. "I loved it. Her. It felt like a her."

I feel the mattress shifting underneath me and when Heather starts talking again, I can tell that she's lying on her side, watching me.

"That's the thing, isn't it, about parenting? How quickly you fall in love? Now you can imagine how you would have loved that child if it had worked out. It means you can imagine how much, for example, I love you."

My tongue feels thick in my mouth. Heather has never said those words to me.

"I know we've never warmed up with each other, not properly. It's why I wanted you and Andile to come out here before I left."

My instinct is to say that I don't know what she means, to dial down the intimacy, but her body is tense next to mine and I know she needs me to hear this.

"Your bond with Lola, it was immediate, from day one. The two of you were so in sync. I know she was more of a natural mother than I was, to you and to Andile, and I

254

would say sorry for that, but I was being the only mother I knew how to be, and apologising would be disingenuous.

"I want you to know, Roo, that I've loved you every day of your life, even when I first found out, even when all I had was the idea of you. Even though you were never planned. The way you loved your baby. My love for you – it's grown bigger and bigger every day you've been alive."

The fan whirs. My eyes are dry and clear. "I know," I say. I find that I do. That I've always known.

"Good."

Outside, there's a single piercing "kweeeeeeeeeeeeeeeh", and I see the mohawk of a go-away-bird in the palm tree through the window. Another crowned head pops up next to it, and as one, they spring off the palm tree leaves into the blue air.

Twelve

The next day, I'm getting ready to go fetch Di's car from the airport. Heather told her it had broken down on the way to the swimming lesson, and that we were getting a mechanic out to check on it. I've left it as long as I possibly can before she starts getting suspicious, and I'm on my way to Fever Tree Cottage to ask Andile to drive me out to the airport in the bakkie.

I haven't seen him since coming back to The Pines yesterday, but he has to be around somewhere. If he's not in his cottage, I'll try the hammocks in the avos, I'm thinking, when I see a familiar car coming down the road, turning on the bend in the bluegums, heading toward the house.

It can't be, and yet it is. It's the hybrid. Cam's hybrid. He's here. At The Pines. In the car I chose when we first got together a year and a half ago, when I thought he didn't know how to drive. Cam has driven all the way to the north-eastern corner of the country from the southern-most tip of the continent. To see me.

When I spoke to him the night before last, he was in Knysna. That's at least a day's drive from here. How would he manage it with Maya, by himself? The car is about to pass me, and I duck behind the trunk of a tree, not ready to see him yet. Then I realise that he's not alone, that it's not him who is driving. Andile is in the driver's seat, Cam in the passenger seat, and Maya, in her car seat, is in the back. I watch the car pull up in front of the house, and Cam's unmistakable silhouette, his sharp shoulders and the outline of his messy, too-long hair, steps out of the car.

I move out into the driveway from the trees and he seems to sense me behind him, because he turns around immediately to face me. He lifts a hand. It's not quite a wave. I start walking on wobbly legs.

When I'm standing right in front of him, I see that his eyes are swollen, his face is grey, and his hair is greasy. He looks worse than I've ever seen him. He looks small.

Something like warmth spurts behind my sternum. I want to smooth his shirt across his chest, but when he looks down at me, he's not the Cam I know. His eyes are dark and shuttered. His eyebrows are drawn down, unusually static, giving nothing away.

I've almost forgotten about Andile, who gets out of the car and says cheerily, "Hey, sis."

"What's going on?" Trying to make sense of him and Cam together is making my head hurt.

"Tell her," Andile says to Cam, opening the back door to lift Maya out of her car seat. She's fast asleep.

Cam picks up a sports bag from the floor of the passenger seat, keeping his eyes on me.

"Remember how you told me *over the phone* that you wanted to split up? When you implied that you wanted *a divorce*?"

Andile is moving towards the house, Maya's head resting on his shoulder. When did I last see him? In Di's sunroom, when we spoke to Heather about selling the farm. Three days ago. He's been with Cam?

"I'm sorry." It's all I can think to say to Cam.

"After you hung up on me, I looked Andile up on Facebook and messaged him. He replied immediately and we chatted. I needed to get to you, but couldn't have managed the drive all the way up here from Knysna with Maya. He volunteered to meet me in George. He flew in yesterday, and we've taken it in turns driving. We spent last night at my folks' place in Joburg."

"That's insane."

"He's a good dude."

I'm caught between feeling touched that Andile would travel all the way to the other side of the country to bring my husband to me, and irritated that he's allowed me to be ambushed like this.

Cam is looking at the house. "Are you going to invite me in? I'm starving."

It's almost lunchtime for the writers. Everyone will be here soon. Everyone will meet Cam.

I pull a chair out at the kitchen table and gesture for him to sit down. "Give me one second," I say.

I walk down the passage, looking for my traitor-slash-hero of a brother. He emerges from my bedroom and pulls the door quietly closed.

When he catches my eye, he doesn't have the decency to look shame-faced.

"What the fuck, Andile?" I hiss, hoping Cam can't hear me from the kitchen.

"Roo, I love you, but you have been absolutely batshit fucking crazy since you came back. He's your *husband*. You told him over the phone that you wanted to break up? And expected him to – what? Accept it?"

"You don't know what happened. We don't have a normal relationship."

"Oh, get a grip. There's no such thing as a normal relationship."

"He can't be here. I don't want him here." My voice is verging on a whine, but I can't help it. I'd throw a tantrum if I thought it would help me get my own way.

"It's time you start acting like a proper adult human being. I can't help you anymore than I already have. It's up to you now."

"We've broken up!"

"What, because you've decided not to try to save your marriage? You're losing your damn mind, and here's a guy who cares enough about you to drive all the way here from fucking *Knysna* to make things right with you and you think it's fine to cut and run? He deserves for you to at least talk to him and not hide out here in the passage like a goddamn child, Roo. Honestly. What is the *matter* with you?"

Andile's never spoken to me like this. I see the look of disappointment in his eyes, and my heart quivers. "I don't know," I whisper.

"I get that you've been going through some heavy stuff but guess what? So. Have. We. All." He punctuates the words with chopping motions on the wall of the passage with the side of his hand. "None of us can help you with this stuff, Roo. You need to dig yourself out."

I push the heels of my hands into my eye sockets. What have I done? I've pulled out all the stabilising blocks in the Jenga of my life and the whole thing has come tumbling down, and I can't blame anyone but myself.

I follow Andile back into the kitchen. He claps Cam on the shoulder, and Cam looks up into his face.

"Thanks for everything, man," Cam says to him earnestly. "I wouldn't have made it here without you." He's got such an easy, genuine charm about him, and I realise for the first time that he's the way he is because of Rory. He's probably had to be well-liked and uncomplicated since they were little, he's had to force himself to be the sun, forever trying to eclipse Rory's dark moods.

A wail comes from the direction of my bedroom, and Cam stands up. Andile motions to him to sit down again and says, "I'll go to her."

After he's left, Cam pulls me down into a chair, and keeps hold of my hand. His fingers are cold, but he keeps holding on. We sit like that in silence for so long that soon the ticking of the clock fills the space between us, and the quiet has its own texture – soft, comfortable, warm. I am feeling so settled inside the silence that I almost jump when Andile appears in the kitchen with Maya in his arms.

"She doesn't want to go back to sleep. I'll take her outside for some fresh air," Andile says, looking for all the world as if he's cared for Maya her whole life.

We watch Andile stepping out into the sunshine with her in his arms, and Cam turns to me.

"What's going on, Skye?"

"I have to tell you something," I say.

Thirteen

To Cam's credit, he doesn't drop my hand or shift away from me when I tell him what happened with Fallan yesterday, when I found myself at the airport with her, equipped with her birth certificate and a forged affidavit. His eyes widen, his eyebrows shoot up, but he doesn't stop listening.

I tell him about what happened after the mugging. About our baby. As it turns out, Tshidi was right. The bruise is a little less tender than when I told Heather about it. The only time I falter is when I see the pain in Cam's eyes and realise that I've had 15 months to grieve, in my own roundabout way, but that for him, the worst moment of it, the moment he'll never be able to forget, is unfolding right now.

"I probably shouldn't have told you. You wouldn't have known and it's made you sad for no reason," I say. "There's nothing you can do about it and it's this horrible thing that you have to live with."

"It's *our* horrible thing," he says, after a beat.

"Cam, I've been so selfish." I take my hand away from his and cover my eyes with my palms. "I don't know what's been wrong with me."

I feel Cam's hand on the back of my head, cradling it like the delicate skull of a newborn.

"You've gone through this all alone. But now we're going to help each other."

"I don't think we're going to make it. After everything – keeping this a secret from you, and everything with Bushy Bun, and leaving you? We've fucked so many things up."

He takes my hands off my eyes and makes me look at him.

"We can't end this, Skye, right when we're finally being real with each other."

"You've always been real with me." When he doesn't answer, I follow it up with, "Haven't you?"

He shifts his eyes back down to the table. "The truth is, I felt you pulling away from me ages ago, probably around the time of the mugging. I was terrified you were about to break up with me, and so I rushed ahead with Bushy Bun, making it something you couldn't refuse, and proposed to you, and by then you couldn't very well say no, could you, because of the restaurant? I was so terrified of losing you. It was so weak and selfish and manipulative and so, so shameful."

I search his agonised face, the edges of it that I love, the luxurious curl of his eyelashes, the strong cut of his jaw that now seems incongruous on this soft-centred man. It's a superhero jaw. His face makes him seem infallible, but he's a mess inside, too, like me, like any other person.

He meets my eyes from his place next to me at my mothers' kitchen table, and it's like I'm seeing those dark blue, almost navy irises for the first time.

"It *was* manipulative," I say. "But you were reacting to me, to my behaviour, and you didn't have all the informa-tion. Plus, it's not as if I said no. I went along with things.

262

You didn't force me. It's not as if I didn't – as if I didn't want you, or, or love you."

He closes his eyes, and when he opens them, I expect to see something like relief, or hope, but, if anything, they're more clouded than before. "There's something I need to tell you, too."

I look down at our linked hands. This is it, I think. This is the thing that's going to make it impossible to stay together.

What he says is, "I have a phobia of driving."

"Sorry?"

"Driving a car. I have a paralysing, big-deal phobia of it with a capital P."

"Are you serious?"

"Completely. I've been going to therapy for it. Intensive therapy, since before we met. Lately I felt like I was getting over the worst of it. I was hoping to surprise you by driving us home from Misty Cliffs."

"You must be over it. You drove right across the country to get here."

"Andile did a lot of the driving from George. But I'd have done it by myself if it meant it would keep us together." He grimaces, and my hands reflexively squeeze his. "It was such an embarrassing thing about me, and when we met it was easier to tell you I didn't know how. I didn't want you to know how weak I was. Or how scared. You were so confident and you're such a good driver and never seemed scared of anything."

A laugh surprises me by rumbling out of my chest. "I'm a complete disaster, clearly."

He pulls me towards him and cradles the back of my head again. "*My* disaster," he says, and hesitates for a moment, his eyes scanning my face, before pressing his mouth gently to mine. His lips curve against mine in a practised, familiar fit, and then there it is, the flavour of Cam, a delicate umami I've tasted nowhere else.

I push myself closer to him as endorphins flood my body, leaving my fingers tingling and my limbs heavy.

Andile's voice drifts in from the driveway and I pull away reluctantly.

"I suppose you're going to have to meet my mother," I say. "She's going to be thrilled you're here. She's out in the garden with this guy she's dating. He's *much* older. Ancient."

Cam looks puzzled. "I thought she was gay?"

"So did we," Andile says from the doorway. "But it's a spectrum, you know." He's holding Maya up to watch the go-away-birds in the trees above their heads.

Cam gives my hand a final squeeze before dropping it to take Maya from Andile.

As I watch him scoop her up with a graceful ease, I am thinking that there's plenty of time to tell him all about my childhood and Lola and the truth about my father and what The Pines used to be and what it's going to be and where I come from and who I am. We have so much time.

Fourteen

Andile goes absolutely apoplectic when I tell him about what almost happened with Fallan, and especially when he hears that I need him to somehow get Fallan's birth certificate, which is still in the gym bag, back to Coucal Farm.

He leaves the kitchen for a few minutes to stop himself from throttling me, taking a series of calming breaths so deep I can hear the air whistling in and out through his nose from where I am sitting at the table. When he comes back inside, he agrees to sneak the birth certificate back into the filing cabinet the next time he goes to Coucal Farm. We're going to have to destroy the forged affidavit.

"What about this, Roo?" He holds up Fallan's purple toothbrush, which looks sinisterly out of place in the bright sunlight of the kitchen.

Cam snatches the toothbrush from Andile's hands before dropping it into the dustbin without a word. He peers into the bag and rifles quickly through the bundle of clothes I threw in.

"The rest is fine. You packed her clothes for after her swimming lesson. It's fine."

"You're telling her this is fine?"

"She knows, Andile," Cam says so quietly I almost miss it. Andile's eyes slide to me and back to Cam. He nods once and squares his shoulders.

"Tell me where you found her birth certificate."

I draw a diagram of where the filing cabinet is. I write the words "top drawer" on the piece of paper. It's the back of one of Malcolm's drafts, with Heather's neat red notes in the margin. Andile takes the note and the bag, and says he'll be the one to collect the eggs from Coucal later to give him a reason to visit.

"I'm not making any promises, Roo," he says as he leaves the kitchen. "I'll be as sneaky as I can. You know I'm not built for subterfuge."

Then it's me and Cam alone at the table. Maya is keeping herself occupied with my old metal mixing bowls and wooden spoons in the corner of the kitchen.

"If that girl's parents ever find out," Cam says tentatively, as if he doesn't want to startle me, "you'll probably be facing charges of attempted abduction."

Those two words give me a stomach-dropping vertigo, and the edges of my eyes prick with tears.

This is the moment I know I'm going to be spending the rest of my life with my husband. When he should back away and hold his hands up and away from me, when he should leave me, he folds one of my hands into both of his, and says, "You going to prison would put a bit of a damper on the rest of our marriage."

I snort and brush off the tears about to spill from my eyes. He says, quietly, that we will find a really good therapist and I will have years and years to talk about what I nearly did. To process it and accept it, he says.

He's speaking as someone who knows the power of putting experiences into words. He's been doing it for years. Maybe there *is* hope for me.

Later that afternoon, after Heather and the writers have all met Cam – it was all so much more civilised and affable than I ever expected, handshakes and hugs – we leave Maya with Heather so that Cam can drive me back to the airport to fetch Di's car.

He never moves above third gear, going a good 20 kilometres below the speed limit, his eyes flicking up to the rear-view mirror every few seconds in a nervous tic. Di's keys are jingling in the centre consol, and I can't stop my leg from bouncing with nervousness.

"So, tell me your plan," I say, hoping to distract myself. "You said something about having an idea for another business."

He bites his lip and says, "I don't know if I can drive while talking."

"It's good practice. And the straight bit of the road's coming up."

He shifts in his seat. "This is what I was thinking. We drop Maya off with Rory in Motherwell –"

"She's expecting this?"

He nods. "She broke down and phoned us at Misty Cliffs. She misses Maya. She wants her back. She said she was going nuts away from Em-Zee, but that he's told his advisors they're going to have to find some way to spin the love-child angle because he doesn't want to be away from Rory or Maya again. I told her we'd drop Maya off with them in a few days."

"That's wonderful," I say, meaning it. I've had enough of Rory to last me the rest of my life, but I find myself wanting some kind of happy ending, or maybe beginning, for her.

Cam has managed to lift his foot further off the gas and the hybrid is crawling along in the left lane.

"After we've dropped Maya off, I thought we could go check out this place my dad's heard about in Port Elizabeth. It's in an old part of town that's apparently on the brink of gentrifying quite seriously. Imagine the City Bowl, fifteen years ago. It's an old café set-up, but if we like the space, we could use the money from the sale of the Bushy Bun property – I've mailed you the offer for you to sign, by the way – and we could renovate it however we wanted. The property's going for a steal so we'd have enough left over for kitting it out."

"I'm going to have some money, too. We're selling The Pines. Andile and I are splitting the profit. I'll get about two, two-and-a-half million."

I hadn't meant to tell him, but the thought of keeping a secret from him sits like a shard of bone in my throat.

"You should keep that," he says, as if it's obvious. "That's your inheritance. Don't put it in the restaurant business, that would be madness."

"What if I donated it? Like to a scholarship for teens who want to get into the hospitality industry or become chefs or open their own restaurant."

I can tell from the tension in his shoulders that he doesn't want to take his eyes off the road, but he grins broadly and quickly swipes his gaze to me. "I can see that."

"If we open another restaurant, or a café or whatever, I want it to be vegan, or at least vegetarian."

"That makes sense," Cam says. "You were raised that way. It's very trendy, too."

"I want to train up a few women in the kitchen so they can go on to start their own things if they want to. Women who wouldn't have the opportunity otherwise. Give them a share in the place once they've been in the kitchen for, say, six months? I'd have to work on the business model, but maybe you and Deacon can help with that."

Cam nods and I can see that he's concentrating on my words. "How long have you been thinking about this?"

"Consciously? I think I came up with it right now. But it's probably something I've always wanted to do. Oh, and while we're in the Eastern Cape there's someone I want to go see, in Grahamstown. He's my – father? I may have a half-sister or brother, too."

We're pulling into the airport parking lot, and Di's car is right where I left it, eons ago. I scoop up the keys and before I hop out of the hybrid, I tell Cam not to worry, and, once I've got the car started, to follow me back home.

"Always," he says, winking at me.

≈

Cam collapses into my bed when we get back to The Pines, after making sure Heather doesn't mind keeping an eye on Maya for a little longer. When I set off to deliver Di's car back to Coucal Farm, I see Heather and Malcolm walking down the rows of vegetables in the garden with Maya on Heather's hip. They're both pointing out plants to her.

I leave the car next to the little dam at Coucal Farm and place the keys softly on the doorstep without catching sight of anyone. I walk back home through the bananas, knowing it's the last time my feet will tread that familiar red-dust path, missing Lola more sharply than usual.

I set to work preparing a feast from comfortingly humble ingredients, legumes and grains and a small block of goat's cheese. Heather and Malcolm come back in from the garden, and Heather settles Maya on her lap, snapping fat peas out of their shells for her to pick at.

Andile got the goat's milk feta from Coucal Farm when he collected the eggs earlier. He tells me that he felt like an international super-spy, "not in a good way", when he slipped Fallan's birth certificate back into the filing cabinet. I add it to a salad with Malcolm's soft butter lettuce and some toasted pumpkin seeds – making a separate bowl without the cheese for Heather – and slide the wholegrain bread, which I've known how to make since I was old enough to read, into the oven. There's a celebratory hum in the air, probably thanks to the beers Andile's brought to share with dinner. Heather hasn't said anything about the contravention of one of her rules. She's been too busy playing with Maya.

I join Tshidi on the kitchen floor, where she's resting her chin on her knees and taking the occasional sip from the glass of beer next to her.

Sullivan and Megs are both still writing in their cottages – dinnertime's officially an hour away – and this room holds all the people at The Pines who matter to me, other than Cam, and I know that we won't be in this kitchen together like this ever again.

"It looks like I'm going to the Eastern Cape in a couple of days," I tell Tshidi. "Maybe we can meet up at Schreiner House in Cradock when you're done here?"

"Deal," she says, smiling. "You're going with Cam?"

I nod. "Things are still weird. But I'm hoping they'll get better. We can't pick up where we left off."

"How are you feeling about it?"

I've never had the kind of friend I could talk to about the soft, bruised places inside me. Now I've got Tshidi, and the tentative promise of a future with Cam. Something new. I remember the bone-deep pleasure from our kiss earlier, and I feel wings beating in my chest.

I take a sip of her beer and say, "I feel hopeful."

"Have you told him about the farm? That you're selling it?"

I hand the beer glass back to her. "Yes. I was going to invest it in our next restaurant, but he said that would be crazy. I've decided to use it to set up a scholarship for underprivileged kids who want to become chefs."

"You're donating your fuck-you money? In the spirit of redress and reparations?" The lift of her eyebrows shows she's teasing, but her level gaze is serious, appraising.

"I don't think I could keep it, quite honestly. I don't feel like it belongs to me."

"Speaking of things that belong to you. I've finally finished my crochet project – which means I have to start the final chapter of my manuscript, no more excuses," Tshidi says. "I didn't know what I was making until I'd finished it and sewn on the eyes."

She reaches into her cloth bag and pulls out a navy blue and dark pink go-away-bird, with a grey mohawk of wool, and round, shiny button eyes, dark and reflective. She hands it to me. "It's yours."

"You know, if dystopian African fiction doesn't work out for you, you should sell these. Get an Etsy shop, you'd make a fortune."

Tshidi snorts and picks up her beer glass again. "My mother would *love* that."

I stroke the go-away-bird's pom-pom mohawk, set at a jaunty angle. "It's exquisite."

I sense a pair of eyes on me and look up to see Maya reaching for the bird. I scoot towards her and put it in her hands. She points the bird's beak at me and says, "Kweeeeh", clear as a bell.

Andile snaps his fingers triumphantly. "I showed her the go-away-birds when I was with her earlier. She remembers!"

"What a clever girl you are," Heather coos into Maya's ear. I remember exactly how that felt, to be small and safe, balanced on her sturdy lap, her arms around my middle, her voice in my ear. It took me forever to realise it, but the man with the knife was right. I am the lucky one.

Acknowledgements

To the person reading this, thank you for taking a chance on a debut South African novel by an independent publisher. The fact that you chose my book to read among all the many first-rate novels in the world is an immense privilege.

Go Away Birds started as a messy, long-ago NaNoWriMo draft, and I have so many people to thank for getting it to where it is today.

Firstly, I am endlessly grateful for the invaluable insights and warm enthusiasm of my creative writing mentors, Claire Strombeck and Mike Nicol, on the first draft of the manuscript.

I'm also thankful to my first reader and longest-serving ally, Nikki Stuart-Thompson, whose vast knowledge of important things like the names of avocado varietals and how to be a truly excellent friend were instrumental in *Go Away Birds*. She's also the only person I've ever met who is a faster reader than I am, which I really appreciated when I sent her one of the first drafts.

Effusive thanks also to Vicki and Lauren Edwards, whom I'm lucky to call friends as well as family, for so supportively reading and talking to me about various drafts of the manuscript.

Some of the subjects that came up in the story required additional research for me to do them justice. For her consultation on the Pinyin names of the dishes Skye serves at Bushy Bun, I have long-time resident of Taiwan, Rae, to thank. I'm also indebted to the rich detail about the tragedies and triumphs of the resistance movement in the Eastern Cape in the 1980s provided by Bridget Hilton-Barber in her memoir, *Student Comrade Prisoner Spy*, which I used as a resource to inform Heather's background.

Naturally, any errors, inaccuracies and artistic licence on these points are mine alone.

Speaking of errors and inaccuracies, I think it's important for me to include a note here about the names of cities and towns in this story. After serious deliberation, I decided to use the former names for Qqeberha and Makhanda, because in late

2016 and early 2017, when this story is set, they were still going by their previous names of Port Elizabeth and Grahamstown. The same principle goes for the mention of Rhodes University. Nelspruit, however, was officially renamed to Mbombela in 2009, and the characters in this story still use the old name, which I chose to use based on my own observations of the way people speak about the city.

I owe a debt of gratitude to my brilliant editor, Emily Buchanan, slayer of "ye olde diluting adverbs" and purveyor of bolstering words like "courage!", which I needed in spades as I went through the editing process. Emily, thank you so much for your clarity of vision, your kindness and your dedication to this story.

To Jesse Breytenbach, thank you for creating such a beautiful cover for this book – it's lovelier than I could've imagined.

I will forever be grateful to the inimitable Colleen Higgs for her faith in the potential she saw in the manuscript, and for all her gentleness and wisdom in her dealings with me, a massively inexperienced first-time novelist.

And to Dylan, my sage, my touchstone, my beloved: nothing in my life (writing this book; raising children; making tea or G and Ts for two) would be as much fun, or matter as much, without you.

Printed in the United States
by Baker & Taylor Publisher Services